A Visi

WinGS

by

Sue Whitehead

A Magical 'Flight' of the Imagination

With Illustrations by the Author

Note for Librarians: A cataloguing record for this book is available from Library and Archives Canada at www.collectionscanada.ca/amicus/index-e.html
ISBN 1-4120-9950-1

Printed in Victoria, BC, Canada. Printed on paper with minimum 30% recycled fibre.
Trafford's print shop runs on "green energy" from solar, wind and other environmentally-friendly power sources.

TRAFFORD
PUBLISHING™
Offices in Canada, USA, Ireland and UK

Book sales for North America and international:
Trafford Publishing, 6E–2333 Government St.,
Victoria, BC V8T 4P4 CANADA
phone 250 383 6864 (toll-free 1 888 232 4444)
fax 250 383 6804; email to orders@trafford.com
Book sales in Europe:
Trafford Publishing (UK) Limited, 9 Park End Street, 2nd Floor
Oxford, UK OX1 1HH UNITED KINGDOM
phone +44 (0)1865 722 113 (local rate 0845 230 9601)
facsimile +44 (0)1865 722 868; info.uk@trafford.com
Order online at:
trafford.com/06-1707

10 9 8 7 6 5 4 3 2

ACKNOWLEDGEMENTS

The main inspiration for this book came from the work that my husband, Roger and I did caring for sick and injured birds in the Mid Wales Hospital. So I owe the greatest debt to my father, Ken Whitehead, who started me on the path when I was a teenager by bringing home an injured kestrel. Sadly he died three years ago, but his support in the writing of the first draft of this novel was invaluable and it is, therefore, dedicated to his memory.

So many people have inspired and helped me, from Colonel Nick Faithful who first taught me how to care for the birds, the writing group I attended for many years and the love and support I received from all my wonderful family and friends.

And then, of course there were the birds, especially the peregrines whose breathtaking skill and beauty captivated me; Lady, our first peregrine, then Flicker and the most important of all Magic, the little tiercel whom we kept from death for a year.

Thank you everyone and may your inspiration through me bring a little light to people's lives.

A VISION OF WINGS

It wasn't that unusual to find a cardboard box left on the doorstep. It usually contained an injured buzzard or kestrel for me to treat in the Bird Hospital I ran. What was unusual on this occasion was the bird it contained – and the unexpected effect it was to have on my life.

I'd been running the Wild Bird Hospital on my own for over two years now, ever since Gabriel left to go to Australia, taking part of me with him. The warning signs had all been there, but I'd been so involved in the exhausting work of caring for the birds, I hadn't noticed. So I was left to struggle on emotionally as well as physically – trying to force feed an injured buzzard, kestrel or owl with small bits of meat or day-old chick, is a job better done with two, one to keep a good grip on the legs while the other opens the sharp beak and gently pushes small pieces of meat down the reluctant throat.

There was a marked increase in the number of scars I had since Gabriel left – on my arms and wrists and even one on my thigh, from the talons of those birds of prey who didn't altogether appreciate that I was trying to save their lives. Once gripped they were very reluctant to let go of their piece of flesh

– my flesh – and all I could do was to wait for them to relax and withdraw and then hurriedly check for pierced arteries.

Sometimes I felt very alone, particularly when I was most tired. Just to have someone around to make a cup of tea would have been nice and sharing the day's experiences and stresses with Bran, the dog, was not quite as rewarding as with a responsive human being. It wasn't that I didn't have offers – some men seemed to find my combination of auburn hair and green eyes attractive, but they tended to be put off when they found that I sometimes had to dash off to chase a buzzard round a muddy field rather than have a quiet evening in with them.

So I was left with only Bran for company. He was, though, a useful early warning system of visitors and had a good deep bark to keep away intruders, which was useful when I had rare birds in of interest to collectors. He also did his best to cheer me up when I was at my lowest which seemed to be more often of late, I realised. What with the stress of never knowing how many birds I'd have in that day and trying to earn all our livings by making jewellery and doing some secretarial work – and no Gabriel to help. ... well I needed a holiday.

The birds were very little company, being wild, and very much preferred me to keep my distance. That was until a bird arrived in that cardboard box and turned my life completely upside down.

It could only have been a moment of carelessness that had brought her to me. She was dazed by a blow to her skull and the uselessness of her legs indicated an injury to her back as well, which was forcing her to sit on her tail. All her magnificent strength seemed to have left her and I wondered how such an agile creature could have so injured herself. From the moment I peered into the box, expecting a buzzard, and met the huge, dark brown eye, ringed with pale yellow that stared steadily out at me, I knew that this bird was going to be different.

The streak of creamy white which descended from the eye leaving a black head and moustache before plunging down to the broad, cream coloured chest, told me she was that most beautiful and powerful of all raptors, a female peregrine falcon, the fastest creature alive. The blue-black of her back, faintly barred with grey, still shone with health, disguising the injury beneath. Looking at that steady eye, I could not believe – nor wished to believe – that the back was broken.

I took her to Nigel Mantle, the vet I used for most of the birds needing treatment because I liked his quiet way with them. We also both shared a special love for peregrines. I didn't know what I would do when he retired in a few years time.

Nigel examined her carefully while she remained calm and quiet. "Well, Sara, she doesn't seem to have any broken bones, but there is obviously some severe damage to her back which is preventing her standing. Try massaging the muscles in her leg and see if you can encourage some movement. I'll give her a dose of steroids just to get things going."

"Thanks, Nigel." I put her back in the cardboard box. "It's odd that she's so easy to handle and yet there doesn't seem to be any concussion to account for it does there, despite the bump?"

"No – her eye is bright and steady. Nor does she have any sign of rings to indicate she might be a falconry bird." He sighed. "I don't like seeing such a beauty brought low, though. It's up to you now, Sara – only time will tell how much damage has been done. Bring her back if you're worried."

"Thanks, – I will."

"Isn't it about time you found someone to help, Sara? You're looking very tired."

"I manage. It's not that easy trying to find someone who's willing to lead my sort of life."

"Just make sure life doesn't pass you by, Sara."

"You mean kids and things don't you, Nigel?" I teased him. "There's plenty of time for that – I'm not thirty yet."

"Still you need to look after yourself more, take some time off."

"Yes, Nigel." I replied dutifully.

It took only a few days of gentle massage and the manipulation of her legs before she began to show the signs of recovery that confirmed that her back wasn't broken. During this time she displayed a definite attitude problem, but not the one I was used to – no tearing beak or piercing talons to add to my scars for her, just a quiet acceptance of me and what I did to her. So pleasant was this that I found myself spending more time with her than the other birds in my care, the ones only too willing to use beak and claw.

So that I could monitor her progress, I kept her in the studio with me and she would watch me as often as she could, seeming to try and catch my eye, but I was adept at avoiding a bird's eye as it disconcerted them to be stared at. Once, though, as I held her on my knee to feed her, she turned her head unexpectedly towards me and I saw myself reflected in the lustrous brown of her eye and felt a strange feeling of being drawn into the depths of her soul.

Something weird happened then – I was aware of a profound feeling of warmth deep in my heart, the warmth of love and mutual dependence beyond anything I'd ever experienced. I had never felt such love for a bird before. Shaking my head in an attempt to clear the sensation failed to remove the warmth, and as I held her, feeling every feather of her, my fingertips tingled with the contact. Her calm acceptance of the situation was a lesson to me and I have no doubt her very calmness sped the process of her healing and that she knew this and many more of the secrets of the universe.

Then one morning, only six days later, there she was standing on her own and I knew we'd won – between us we'd successfully woven the threads of healing. Soon she'd be out in the winds cutting her way through the thermals with the speed and mastery that is the hallmark of a peregrine. So I named her Mistral after the winds that blow, not knowing then where these winds would sweep us, nor that her need of me went beyond the physical. The threads that wove us together would plunge me into a world both precious and fearful.

Flying in aeroplanes, particularly small ones, gives that strange but exhilarating sensation of being cushioned on the invisible gossamers of air as you soar above the clouds. You feel alone, miles from anywhere, just the air around you and the limitless horizon – well, the first dream began like that.

Weightless and free, I soared above the clouds, unfettered by my body, as I mastered the air. So many times I'd dreamt I was able to fly, but this felt different, somehow more real and I wasn't suddenly going to be jolted awake, shaking, with that awful feeling of plunging to the hard earth. This was more gentle, more natural – even when I turned to glide silently through the clouds to the air underneath, I was in control and it felt good – I really could fly.

Spread out below me was the forest – every track running from it, every hill, every stream. I'd never seen it from this angle before but it felt right, it looked right. I focused on my stone cottage nestled under the hill, cocooned by the trees sheltering it from the wind and rain – and then I was flying down towards it fast. At the last minute, with a rush of wings, I was up skywards again, exhilarated beyond belief.

Then the dream broke and I woke up – not with a jolt – but a terrible feeling of loss at being once more earthbound. I wanted to be airborne again.

For many nights the dreams continued and I had my wish. Each time I flew it was more controlled, the sense of freedom beyond anything I'd ever known. But it was a while before I was able to pinpoint the source of these dreams, and a further time before I'd believe it.

The bond between Mistral and I continued to strengthen as I exercised her in the training aviary throughout the day ready to return her to the wild. I learnt to value the quiet way she went about becoming such an important part of my life, but I feared it might cloud my judgment – that I might hold onto her longer than I should – not give her the freedom she needed. Strangely, I felt complete when she was around, happier, calmed by her serenity, and I didn't want to lose the companionship which lightened my days.

Usually releasing a bird is a task full of joy, providing, of course, they're ready to go – otherwise it is more a task of retrieval! There is nothing like watching a bird you have cared for taking again to the freedom of the air, stretching wings long confined in the welcoming thermals, eager to fly again. With Misty, though it was so different, this was a friend – no – more special than a friend, more of a soul mate – and I didn't want to lose her. I'd no idea then that she had no intention of letting me go.

Normally I take the birds to be released as near as possible to where they were found and launch them into the air. I couldn't bring myself to do this with Misty, partly because I'd no idea where she had been found before appearing on my doorstep – but also dreading the finality of it. So, ten days after she'd arrived with me, I left her aviary door open, leaving the decision to her.

Next morning it was empty – she'd taken her freedom. I can't describe the sense of loss I felt – a light had gone from my world leaving a hungry void. Yet the warmth was still there deep in my heart, as though I only had to turn my head and she'd be there.

Going out into the cold sunlight of the April day, I shivered as a slight breeze tugged at me. Automatically I looked upward, scanning the sky for any bird that might be up. And there she was.

I watched spellbound as she called out and then closed her wings and hurtled breathtakingly fast down towards me. At the last minute, before I could chicken out and duck – no more than five feet above my head – she twisted and soared up again, powering her way back into the thermals. She repeated it several times as though tempting me into aerial games with her – what was I still doing on the ground – I should be up there with her. My heart was so filled with the joy of her trust I almost did feel airborne.

Several days went by with her visiting me like this, not just for food but to sit by my side while I talked to her, even coming into the house while I worked at my jewellery bench. This was just such unusual behaviour. Thoughts of her filled my days and at night I dreamt my dreams of flying. I was content – then.

She went missing for two days and I feared for her safety. She was well able to care for herself, I knew that, but I could not protect her from those unscrupulous people who will shoot peregrines despite the laws of protection. But I needn't have worried – on the third day she was there in the sky above the house, waiting to lead Bran, and me on a two-mile walk.

She led us on, impatient with our slow speed, until we skirted round the side of the forest and headed downhill for a bit before turning the corner which led to a waterfall and the deep, rocky gorge through which it dropped, ideal peregrine nesting site. The slopes which led from the gorge to the valley below were bare, waiting for the first fresh growth of the bracken which would carpet their sides with green before turning a glorious golden brown in the autumn.

Suddenly there was a sound above me – the echoing call of a peregrine – not Misty but another. Both birds landed on the top of the cliffs which head down the valley from the waterfall. The grey of the stone disguised them well but I was able to make out the other bird – a bird as big as Mistral. Now female falcons are a third larger than the male, the tiercel, so at first this confused me – it was the time of year for pairing, but not with another female!

Peering through my binoculars I could see that the back of the bird was a slightly different hue to Mistral's and I wondered if it was an old bird hence its size. Whatever – I was left in no doubt that this was Mistral's chosen mate as they rose from the cliff together and flew joyously side by side before tumbling through the air together, twisting and mock grabbing as they turned this way and that at tremendous speed. I could feel the elation in her wings and my heart rose with her and wished them well.

She'd taken her independence – and I knew that this was right – but couldn't help wondering what difference it would make to our relationship. Suddenly I smiled – that quiet, warm place was still there, deep inside. I only had to reach for it (or walk two miles) for reassurance. The exercise would do me good.

So it proved as I visited her most days watching the progress of mating, egg laying and brooding. As with everything she did, she treated this task with solemn responsibility and only allowed the male a few minutes of brooding time while she stretched her wings. This she also did wholeheartedly and I could feel the joy that flying brought her as though the air was vibrating through my own body, so that, if I closed my eyes, I was there with her.

Whether it was the warm spring sunshine, or the peace emanating from a dozing Misty, I don't know, but, one afternoon, I fell asleep propped against the rocks opposite the nest site. Immediately the flying dream began, only this time the sensation was so strong that I was frightened awake crying "Misty". My eyes were drawn instantly towards her, fearing something was wrong, but I could see that she too had been startled awake. She turned her head to stare at me from the ledge and I stared back, my heart still pounding. I stood up, shaking off the sensation that ran through me, telling myself to be sensible, and hurried home.

Mistral had been brooding her eggs long enough either to produce a brood of young peregrines or prove that the large bird she'd chosen as a mate was the same size as her for other reasons than being a large male. But the day the first egg should be hatching, the weather changed to a storm that knocked down branches and flooded the path to Mistral's cliff, preventing me visiting her that day and the next. With the eggs so near to hatching – I hoped – I was worried that the storm may have prevented her from finding enough food.

So it was probably that worry which caused me to dream that night of flying into Mistral's aviary and hunting around for food. Finding a small scrap of meat I hurried away with it towards the nest ledge, only to drop it before getting there and it just disappeared. The flood of disappointment woke me up and I lay there aware of a sharp hunger.

Up until now I'd avoided taking food for Misty, considering it would be interfering now she had a mate to provide for her, but the dream and the storm had me concerned. So, putting some meat in a bag I set off for the cliff along the paths made muddy by the storm.

Before I'd even rounded the corner of the forest, Misty was aware of me. Calling her mate to take up nursery duties, she flew like a rocket to me calling as she came. I had the food ready and she landed beside me, looked me straight in the eye flooding me with gratitude, and then she was off with the meat back to the ledge. I realised that it wasn't only the storm and her own hunger that'd worried her.

Arriving at the nest she tore the meat carefully into tiny pieces and offered them with the greatest delicacy one by one to her first-born chick, a little bundle of white down with huge eyes and gaping mouth. For a bird with such a large, strong beak it was an act of such gentleness and I felt a soft, satisfied glow and a pride as great as if it had been my own young. As that sensation flooded me I caught Mistral's eye and even from that distance, something passed between us. Far from pushing me away during this special time for her, she had some need of me and I knew I would do everything possible to protect her offspring.

But then the wish isn't always father, or mother, to the deed. I wasn't there when the nest was attacked, but knew about it that night. The chicks, three of them, were about five weeks old, nearing fledging. As they exercised their strengthening wings, great clouds of down would erupt from the ledge, gusted by the violent activity of their exercise. The oldest, a male, was ready to leave the safety of the nest, a full-grown juvenile peregrine. Their backs were grey brown, each feather trimmed with russet from which little tufts of down stuck out like blossom against the dark bark of a tree. Those large liquid eyes that I loved so much in Misty, stared down at me from the ledge while they sunned themselves, and the oldest tried to summon up the courage to launch himself from it and trust to the power of his wings.

I wasn't there when he took his first faltering flight, could only guess at the fear, quickly replaced by the elation of discovering this new substance which supported his wings and kept him way up from the hard ground; could only guess at the pride in Mistral's eyes, so quickly replaced by a shout of anger as, unaware of any danger, the youngster continued to circle on new confident wings, never seeing the raised gun. Before her eyes she saw her child blasted from the skies in an exploding mass of feathers, dead before his little body hit the ground.

In my dream that night I saw a shadowy figure, heard the sound of a shot and watched the young peregrine tumble to the ground. I watched as a bird that could only be Mistral's mate plummeted down towards him in anger and bank away at the last minute, never giving him time to take a second shot at the others. Then I was hurrying to the ledge to check on the two still in the nest, which had been in a direct line from the man as he shot from across the ravine. Their brother's body had sheltered them from the worst of the blast, but there was blood on them both.

I woke up with tears running down my face and a need to be sick. Yet I had the certainty that it had not been just a dream – so sure that there and then I made my plans for the morning and set out for the nest ledge the minute it was light, taking with me ropes and a rucksack. Half way there I stopped for a rest and closed my eyes for a minute, wondering if Misty was all right. Before I could even open my eyes she was there, calling in distress and I knew with a heaviness now to my tread, what I would find.

Climbing to the rocks above the nest took more than half an hour and then I had to haul myself from tree to tree until I was directly above the nest ledge. Once there I tied one end of the rope to the tree directly above and checked, several times and one extra for luck, that the knot was tight. I'm not good with heights, but there was no other way of finding out what was wrong at the nest ledge. It seemed further down than I'd thought, and I kept getting caught in the bushes that grew out of the rock.

At last I was there, my heart pounding in my throat and head with nerves. Finding a foothold just below the nest, I looked in. The first eyes I met were Mistral's. They looked blacker than usual but she met my eye and I threw all my love for her and as much reassurance, despite my vulnerable position, as I could muster into my gaze. I sensed a relaxation in her and she moved to one side giving me a view of her two youngsters.

Just as I had seen in my dream, the two younger eyasses were spattered with blood, but were very much alive, their frightened eyes following my every move, which wasn't difficult as I kept my movements to a minimum in my precarious position. The wing trailed on one of them – the female by her size – so there was no choice but to get them from the ledge.

The next bit was going to be difficult as I had somehow to get them into the rucksack and back up that rope. As my position on the cliff was somewhat insecure – and I'd seen too many films where ropes break just at that awkward moment – I wanted the task done with all possible speed. Determinedly not looking downward, despite the almost magnetic pull to my eyes of all those vertical feet, I transferred the rucksack to my front and, feeling rather like a kangaroo, placed each youngster in my pouch. They were sufficiently in shock not to protest, but Misty's gentle crooning also helped to keep them calm.

As I began the ascent, Misty flew down and gently touched the little dead male with her beak where he lay, the blood congealing and darkening on the ground around his body, as if asking why I wasn't taking him too. A scattering of feathers lay spread on the ground, bathed in blood and the creamy breast of the oldest youngster was sodden where the shot had penetrated deep into his body.

There was no choice now but to rely on the rope, and, with heavily beating heart, I carefully scrambled and hauled my way to the top. As soon as I was clear of the ledge, Mistral flew off to take her position on the outcrop of rock that they used to keep guard on the nest, and her mate took her place by the body. A few seconds later, getting no response from the dead youngster left there, he flew to join Mistral and a sadness and anger settled in my head.

I was too busy at the time to think much about the implications of the last few hours, and too busy later getting Misty's young checked and treated by Nigel. It was something Nigel said which made me realise I had to face what was going on.

"Let's get X-rays of them both," he suggested. "We'll have a better idea then what damage that bastard caused." Nigel only swore when severely upset, unlike me who managed it a lot more often. "Do you know who it was?"

"No, as far as I know no one saw him." I couldn't possibly tell him about the dream. "Only Mistral," I added.

"If only she could talk, eh?"

His words echoed round and round in my head as I travelled back home.

CHAPTER TWO

The news on the two young peregrines was better than I'd first thought. The female had a broken wing where the shot had cracked it, but not shattered it. But no shot had pierced the body, just a graze to her head, right down the middle just as though someone had parted it that way. It earned her the name of Rift that also brought to mind deep canyons where peregrines love to nest. Nigel was keeping her overnight to pin the wing and he was confident that it would be as good as new in a couple of weeks time. The male came off lighter, just a graze to his thigh and the leading edge of one wing, so I brought him home with me. Misty was waiting for us at the house. The sight of her lightened my heart.

Rift arrived back the next day but it was the little male who ruled the roost, despite being smaller. His favourite occupation was tearing up bits of newspaper and flapping his wings to fan the pieces into the air where he could chase them. Because of this and his size, I named him Scrap. He encouraged Rift to join in the fun, but, after her first clumsy attempt hampered by her bandaged wing, she left him to it. She bore it all with surprising fortitude, her gentle eyes tolerant of the behaviour of a loved younger brother. She put me very much in mind of her mother with this gentle acceptance and her very helplessness brought me closer to her. It would be only a matter of a day or two before the mischievous Scrap left to join his father, but Rift would be with me for a lot longer and I intended to enjoy every moment.

Once Scrap was able to fly free, he and Mistral slept most nights at the cliff with Mistral's mate, and once she was away from me, the flying dreams began again. I would wake in the morning feeling restless, unable to settle to my work and generally distracted. You know how a dream, sometimes one you can't even remember, flavours the day, either with a deep down happy feeling or a feeling of disquiet? Well this was like that, so I knew it must be the dreams making me restless, although I couldn't put my finger on it.

Soon after this, I dreamt I was flying with Misty and her mate, and he was trying to tell me something, but suddenly he was very far away, beyond sight, in darkness, with only the sound of his call to locate him. Misty yearned to be with him, but was held back by Scrap and Rift and also by something else. All of a sudden I could see myself as if I was in her dream and could therefore sense her feelings – and that other something that was holding her back was her love for me. I felt it flood the dream with light and I woke up in tears. I hadn't known she felt like that – that welling up of love was beyond anything I had ever experienced, certainly with humans.

I realised I had to face what could no longer be denied. I thought back through all the strange dreams since Mistral came to me and knew there was a bond between her and myself that went well beyond what was normal. I also knew she needed to go – somewhere – and I had to release her and had neither the knowledge nor the heart to do it. That one dream had altered my life – I'd never now be free of her in my heart. I never wanted to be.

With this knowledge came the realisation that I needed help. Already I was avoiding people, hurrying through the shopping, fearful of letting something slip which I couldn't expect them to understand. There was only one person I could trust with this precious secret and he was living in Australia.

I'd thought about Gabriel many times over the last two years, at first with bitter regret and later with an acceptance laced with hope that diminished as the months went by and I didn't hear from him. But thoughts of him kept intruding into my mind during this time.

Gabriel had been an environmental scientist and a spiritual healer when I'd first met him soon after leaving Art College when I was twenty-four. I'd persuaded him to help with the birds. We became a team, a good working team with his scientific knowledge and healing touch, and my day-to-day care. Then we became lovers and life was wonderful and fulfilling. Then suddenly everything changed.

A friend of his had died of cancer at only thirty-two. Gabriel had been to see her just before she'd died. When he came back, he seemed different – distant. He wouldn't talk to me about it and I felt pushed out from his life. Then one day he announced that he'd accepted a job at a university in Australia – and I hadn't even known he'd applied. I was devastated – the bottom fell out of my world. I didn't dare ask if he wanted me to go with him – I couldn't have borne it if he'd said no. And I didn't want to go to Australia – I'd made my life here in Mid Wales.

But now the desire to contact him was growing in me, even though I may be clutching at straws. I realised I'd never lost the hope that we'd somehow get back together again. The thought of hearing from him filled me with excitement tempered with dread – what would his reaction be after all this time? Was he perhaps married? But I needed to share the strange relationship that was building between Mistral and me. He was the only one I could think of who might understand, who knew me well enough and who might be able offer me some reassurance. If I mentioned it to any of my family they'd assume I'd lost the plot and take action accordingly! I was lucky to be living rent free in my grandmother's cottage with my parent's blessing because they supported the work I did with the birds – and because my father was responsible for bringing back the first bird I ever cared for – an immature kestrel – and from then I was hooked. So I definitely did not want to rock the boat by telling them.

Finding Gabriel's telephone number took me two days and then it was necessary to work out the time lapse so I could ring him at a reasonable time, not wanting to get off to a bad start by waking him at three in the morning. I sat, summoning up the courage, watching Rift balance herself while she exercised her one unrestricted wing. I wondered what would happen when the other wing was usable and the muscles in the good one were so much stronger in comparison. I remembered rowing, one oar each, with someone much stronger than myself and we just went round and round in circles. Poor Rift.

My stomach tight with nerves I reached for the telephone.

"Do I have the right number for Gabriel Rogers?" I asked the female voice at the other end of the phone – at the other end of the world.

"You certainly do."

"May I speak to him please?"

"Well, not just now, I'm afraid. He's in Great Britain, you see. I'm just house sitting for him."

"Oh." So she wasn't his wife. That was a relief. I couldn't believe, either, that he was so close, that maybe I could see as well as hear him. "Do you have a number I could contact him on?"

"Hang about – yes, here it is."

She gave me a number in Scotland and, not giving myself time to think, I rang the number straight away even though it was late in the evening.

"Hello, Callum McAllister here."

"I'm sorry to bother you so late, Mr McAllister, but do you have Gabriel Rogers staying with you?"

"Yes, I do. Did you want a word with him?"

My heart pounded. "Please," was all I could muster.

"I'll get him for you now."

It seemed an age before the phone was lifted again.

"Hello?" The tone was cautious.

Just the one word – but the voice, the deep, rich voice, brought it all back. "Gabriel?" It came out rather higher than usual.

"Yes, who's that?"

"It's Sara, Gabriel. Sara MacCallum – do you remember?"

"Sara – of course I remember. In fact, I was wondering when you'd ring."

In my nervous state I let that pass, not really understanding. "I tried you in Australia but here you are in Scotland."

"I'm over doing research for the University. I intended looking you up," for a moment my heart sang with gladness, "as I need some information on Red Kites and thought you were probably the best person for that."

That put me in my place. "Oh, yes, of course – I'll help all I can. Does that mean you're coming down here?"

"If that's okay with you?"

"Fine." 'Fine' – who was I kidding? "When's it likely to be?"

"Probably the day after tomorrow – if you're sure that's okay? I'll have outstayed my welcome here by then, I should think." I heard the sound of a protest in the background. "You should meet Callum sometime, Sara, he's another strange person like you – looks after birds."

"That's rich coming from a healer – or have you given all that up?"

I sensed a hesitation. "We can talk about that when I see you."

"I'll look forward to it."

"Good. Sweet dreams then, Sara. Bye."

"Bye."

In two days I'd have to explain why I'd called him – I'd made my bed – was I really ready to lie in it?

The dream that night confirmed I was ready. It only contained a jumble of images overlaid by that restlessness which had increased since Mistral's mate had left. Although Scrap was with her, she wanted to wait for Rift, wanted to stay with me, but something stronger was pulling at her – it was as if a whole universe called to her and she couldn't resist. The images were not clear enough for me to see what drew her, but I could feel her deep distress.

Suddenly a picture of myself came into the dream and it was as if I was there, thinking her thoughts and my own and she, in return, was sensing my thoughts. For the first time we met in her dream as two separate entities – we dreamt simultaneously. Turning to her, I met her eye and, flooding her with love told her to go where she was needed and I would care for Rift as long as necessary, until she came back. She leaned forward, preened my hair gently from my eyes, caught one of the tears that fell from them in her beak and flew off.

Now in my dream, not hers, I caught the feather that fell to the ground as she flew away. The overwhelming sense of loss woke me to the tears that were already falling and the cry I heard from Rift downstairs. As I hurried out of bed to go to her, a feather fell to the floor. Taking it as a sign that she would return, I tucked it carefully into the edge of the mirror where I could see it every day.

I brought Rift up to the bedroom to try and give her, and myself, some comfort. I knew for certain we were on our own now, that Scrap and her mother wouldn't be there in the morning.

And so it proved, but I had the thought of Gabriel's arrival to look forward to, despite needing to smother the apprehension it sometimes filled me with. What would he be like after all this time and what would his reaction be to me? What if I felt the same desire for him and he was married? Well I'd had plenty of experience in hiding my feelings.

The night before he was due, I sat staring into the mirror brushing my hair, not thinking of very much. Rift came and sat on my shoulder and I glanced at her reflection as she sat there. My eye was caught by hers and held there as she stared back at me. A feeling of detachment spread through me and I felt myself relax, despite my worries.

Suddenly I sensed a movement in the mirror, not caused by Rift or me – as though a wing had brushed over the surface of the glass leaving our images blurred and indistinct. Then a mist seemed to rise and I felt chilled as I continued to stare, hypnotised, into the glass.

Out of the mist came a mass of dark shadows that caught the sun as they swirled up through the haze. The sun shimmered on the surface of a throng of birds as they twisted and turned. Then, before the image became more distinct, it faded and there was just my own reflection again with Rift on my shoulder. Rift reached over to preen my hair as though reassuring me, but it took me a while to get to sleep after that.

CHAPTER THREE

There were just a few hours to go before I would see Gabriel – would he have changed? I realised I was placing a lot of hope on him being able to clarify things for me, but I'd seen the relief he was able to bring the birds – perhaps he could bring me the same relief – if he was willing.

He rang first thing to say he wouldn't be with me until late afternoon. Although this was disappointing it gave me the chance to take Rift to Nigel to have her wing checked and the bandage removed. She stood quiet under our hands just as her mother had.

"Yes, I feel quite happy with that," he declared. "I can feel a bit of a callous growing there which will give it strength while she sharpens up her muscles. There will possibly be a slight favouring of that wing but not enough to interfere with her flying."

"Thanks, Nigel, you've done a wonderful job – as always."

"Spare my blushes – please."

I gave him a hug instead, which really did make him blush. "How soon before I can release her?"

He smiled at me. "If it was me I wouldn't want to let her go, but I know you. Give her another week to sharpen up those muscles."

Rift was delighted not to be restricted any longer and spent the rest of the morning exercising her newly mended wing. She didn't try any actual flying so I couldn't test the theory of the rowing boat. I was too excited to eat much lunch and spent the afternoon pretending to work and listening nervously for the sound of a car.

My cottage is perched on the side of a hill with a quarter mile of track leading up to it that makes it easy to tell when I have visitors as they weave carefully between the potholes. One day I'd be able to afford to surface it properly, but, for now, all spare cash went on the birds.

I love the peace and quiet of this Mid Wales valley. It also suits the injured birds that come to me as it's such an ideal environment from which to release them. It is within a mile of all habitats – open moorland, wood, forest and meadowland. I love nothing better than to watch the buzzards as they soar, hanging so easily on the thermals, their broad wings outstretched, calling to each other their lovely mewing call way above the wood. They hang there whilst the ravens fly their dance below them in perfect formation, tumbling together with such accuracy you would think them a double image, their harsh cry a bass line to the mew of the buzzards.

It was nearly dusk when I heard the engine of a car and knew it must be Gabriel – late as always. I went out to greet him, shutting the door carefully on Rift.

There he was climbing out of the car, the same deep-set, blue eyes and dark brown wavy hair, the same wide, slightly teasing smile, the bump in his nose, (his reward for going to the rescue of a hedgehog being used as a football, aged eleven) and the same effect on my hormones. It seemed as if the years in between hadn't happened, as if he'd left the week before, but I realised we'd both been moulded by different experiences and all couldn't be the same. There had been too much pain.

Trying to subdue my first inclination to throw my arms around him and never let go, I held out my hand, but soon found myself pinned in the bear hug I remembered. It was as if nothing had separated us. I surfaced for air laughing.

"You haven't changed a bit."

"Neither have you, Sara. Except for the dark circles around your eyes."

"Oh, that's just lack of sleep," I replied flippantly, but he held me at arms' length and raised one eyebrow, a gesture that I both loved and was irritated by – mostly because I couldn't do it myself.

"Is that why you wanted me to come – to help you sleep?"

I felt myself blush at the implication. "Excuse me, I think it was the other way around – something about you picking my brains?"

"Well, there's that as well."

"As well as what?"

"As well as wanting to see how you've managed without me all this time, of course."

"Very well thank you," I replied defensively.

"Then why did you call?"

"Maybe I just wanted to see how you'd managed without me."

"You can't have changed that much, Sara. Don't forget – I know how independent you are." I heard the grievance in his tone and wondered if this was why he'd become distant before. "You'd never have called me after all this time unless you really needed help. So – why did you call?"

I resented the fact that he was right, but didn't want to admit it. "Let's go in – it's getting cold."

Bran was barking from inside the house. As I opened the door he came bounding out to greet Gabriel, whom he obviously recognised even after all this time.

We went through to the kitchen and Gabriel sat at the kitchen table while I made some tea for me and coffee for him. He put his chin in his hands and looked at me with the expression I remembered so well. It was a kindly expression but mixed with a spot of exasperation behind the blue eyes.

"Okay, let's have it."

Putting the mugs on the table I sat opposite him and answered his quizzical smile with a resigned one of my own.

"You asked why I rang you just now, out of the blue like that. Well you were right – as usual – I do need help from someone and, basically, you were the only one I could think of who might understand."

"Well, that's very flattering, but not very revealing."
"I know, I'm sorry – but it is a bit – well – strange."
"Where's the change there, then, Sara?"
"Well, thanks for that vote of confidence – and you think being a healer isn't strange?" I saw the look on his face and hurried on. "Okay – don't answer that – but this is different, honestly."
"Go on, then."
"It's not that easy." The raised eyebrow did it. "Okay, okay – it's Mistral, the peregrine."
"Is that the one I saw in the aviary as I came in?" Gabriel asked.
"No, that's her daughter, Rift. She was shot by some bastard, but her wing's fine now."
"Okay – but what about Mistral, then?"
"Well she's so unlike any other bird I've ever handled." I lifted my head, determined to meet his eyes so I could see the response in them – those beautiful blue eyes. I hurried on – "Do you think it's possible to share someone's dreams, Gabriel?"
"It has been known." His tone was neutral.
I looked down at my hands, unable any longer to meet those eyes whilst I asked, "But not with birds, surely?"
There was a slight hesitation. "So, let me get this straight, you're saying you think you share your dreams with Mistral?" Somehow he managed to keep the incredulity out of his voice.
"Well, more that I dream with her – only lately – well it's changed a bit and now it's like I'm aware of her all the time – even though she isn't here." I was beginning to regret having started as Gabriel remained silent. "Or do you think I'm just going crazy?"
This prompted him into speech. "Well I do always remember you as being a bit odd."
"Thanks," I muttered. This was not going well, I felt, but what else had I expected. Maybe I'd made a terrible mistake.
"But not crazy the way I think you mean, Sara. From what I know of you, you have your feet planted too firmly for that." I couldn't tell from his tone if this was a criticism or not. He leant back in his chair and folded his arms. "But you must have been aware, Sara, that a lot of the healing that went on when we were together was down to you, not just me?"

"Well, I fed and watered them, if that's what you mean."
"No – it was more than that. You've always had a remarkably close affinity with the birds." He took a sip of his coffee. "But now I want you to tell me more about these dreams."
At least he wasn't rejecting me out of hand, so I told him how it had all begun and how the restlessness I'd felt in Misty had transmitted itself to me. At the same time I was trying to absorb what he'd just said about the healing.
"So you believe them utterly?" he asked. "There's no room in your mind for doubt?"
"Well, of course – I'm not that 'odd', as you put it, but I have no other explanation. You know how difficult dreams are to describe." I saw the look on his face. "You think I shouldn't believe them, then – that I am going crazy?"
"Come on, Sara, – that's not what I said. Perhaps you're just too close to this particular bird and just don't want to let her go."
I looked down at my tightly clasped hands. So much depended on me being able to convince him. Through clenched teeth I answered him. "One way I've definitely not changed is holding onto a bird longer than is good for it. Anyway, I've already released her so that's definitely not it."
"Okay – so what do you feel is happening?"
"Oh – I don't know." I was conscious of playing with my hair, which I only did when particularly nervous, but I tried to keep my tone casual. "Perhaps I'm sharing her thoughts through my dreams – that it's some form of telepathy?"
"Well, I'm not the one to say anything is impossible – if I've learnt anything over the years it's to have an open mind. I've certainly come across plenty of unusual things of late." He rubbed the bump on his nose as he always did when thoughtful "But personal experience leads me to warn you not to mention this to just anyone. People can be cruel if they feel ignorant, so just be careful."
"Or the men in white coats will come and take me away?" My heart felt lighter – he wasn't just rejecting it out of hand.
He felt it necessary to rub it in. "I know you've always preferred your own company, Sara, and those of the birds, but we all need friends, true friends."
This was a little hard to swallow as it had been Gabriel who'd

left me at a time when I had considered him a very true friend, but I didn't want to alienate him now he was back, however temporarily, in my life.

"Okay, I know what you're saying, but are you willing to help me try and get this thing straight?"

"Of course I am, Sara. Curiosity – scientific, of course – wouldn't let me do otherwise." I had rather hoped it might be more personal than that, but there was still the rift of the past between us. He grinned. "So, not so independent after all?"

I gave him a certain sign and then took the empty cups to the sink.

We were late getting to bed that night. Rift slept contentedly in her aviary as we talked and talked, catching up on the past years but skirting around the issues that had divided us. We also discussed what to do about Misty, Scrap and Rift.

"It's odd, really," Gabriel said, "as it's birds which brought me here in the first place. I've been doing studies into declining numbers of Red Goshawks for the University. My trip to Scotland was to study the reintroduction of the Sea Eagle and Red Kite there – not that I think it's an option with Goshawks – their feeding habits are too different – but it was a good excuse to come back for a bit. And it seems I arrived just about in time."

"Meaning?" I asked, needled.

"That I may be of some help to you, of course." I was relieved to hear it. "Do you believe in synchronicity, Sara?"

"Coincidence, you mean?"

"More than that. Things happening together for a reason, as if we're connected on a level we're unaware of, drawing people together?"

"I've not really thought about it. There are an amazing number of coincidences which I hear about in this area, people meeting someone from here in the middle of Australia or on holiday in Egypt – things like that."

"That's an indication of it – the interconnectedness of people – of us all, but I think it's more than that." He yawned. "Anyway, I don't know about you but I'm ready for bed."

"Sorry, Gabriel – I forgot you'd driven all the way from Scotland. I shouldn't have bothered you with all this."

"But you needed to bother me with all this, Sara – and I'm

not complaining, but I am tired!"

"I've got the spare room ready for you," I didn't want him thinking that I'd other ideas in mind, even though I'd thought long and hard about it. I'd decided it'd have to be one step at a time. "But it's a bit cluttered." I added giving him the chance to take the initiative.

"Sleep is all I want, Sara, and I don't care where I do it. This sofa will do."

"There's a perfectly good bed in the spare room, if you can remember where it is."

That night I dreamt of flying over the cliff just as I had done so many months ago. I was tired but happy and filled with a feeling of anticipation. I awoke with a conviction that Misty was back.

CHAPTER FOUR

Gabriel came down when I was half way through preparing breakfast and I told him about the dream and my conviction.

Any doubts we may have had were quickly dispelled by Rift, who set up a screaming call and dashed at the outside aviary door. I'd remembered to shut it, fortunately, so she was brought up short by the netting. We ran outside just as Mistral started up a din from the roof. I called to her, thrilled to see her again, and held up one arm in an invitation for her to come down, somewhat unsure she would with Gabriel by my side.

Gabriel gave my shoulder a squeeze. "I'll go into the house to give her a chance to come down."

"No, wait here for a bit. Let me just call her and see what happens."

It was so wonderful to see her again and in such good health. The blue black of her head shone against the white of her cheeks and threw the black moustache into sharp relief. The cere around her eyes and beak was a rich deep yellow, not the pale colour it had been when she first came to me.

She made a gentle glide onto my fist and sat there looking

happily into my eyes for a few seconds, renewing the bond. She then turned her gaze on Gabriel. He met her eyes and a change come over him. As the surprise left his face, a gentle smile took its place and the slight tension in Mistral's talons drained away. Any further communication between them was interrupted by Rift, who set up her keening again.

Misty flew to the ledge outside the aviary and I opened the door, knowing that Rift would be cared for now if she did fly out. Instead she nuzzled her head under her mother's breast as she used to do as a tiny fledgling. Misty tweaked the feathers on her back and crooned to her quietly. Being young, Rift couldn't stay quiet for long, and she was soon chattering again. Tears pricked the back of my eyes to see them together.

My responsibility for Rift was now at an end and I knew with a heavy heart that she and Misty could disappear at any time. I couldn't be sure that Misty would ever come back once she had Rift, well and ready to fly. She'd returned without Scrap and I did worry where he'd gone and whether he was safe. In the dream last night, that had told me she was returning, I hadn't seen Scrap so I hadn't expected to see him now. A shiver ran through me as I realised now how utterly I believed the dreams.

Gabriel and I went into the house leaving the two birds together.

"That is one very special bird, Sara. Would she let me get close to her, do you think?"

"I'm not sure. She might. Why?" Suddenly I found myself reluctant to share Mistral even though I knew this was selfish.

"Just something I can't quite put my finger on. I'd really like to try, Sara..." he saw the doubt in my face. "Only in the cause of science, of course!" He was deliberately teasing me – I'd always found it incongruous that someone who undertook scientific research for a living could also be a 'spiritual' healer.

I couldn't deny him the chance to experience what had become so precious to me over the last few weeks, so we went out to find Misty. We could hear Rift calling from a tree across the valley, and then saw the shadow of Misty as she flew in front of her up and down the valley, teasing Rift into following her. She'd wasted no time getting Rift into training and I could feel the restlessness in her stronger than before. What was compelling her, I didn't know – the cold of winter was still a few months away, so it was no migratory instinct.

We sat and watched them for a bit. It was a stunning sight to see Mistral jinx and turn at such high speed, so close to the ground. In all the hours Gabriel and I had spent guarding the nests of peregrines all those years ago, we had never seen a display like this. But Rift was not to be tempted. She'd got that far and that was where she was going to stay.

After twenty minutes of trying Mistral decided she'd had enough for one day and came and perched in the branches above us. I invited her down with some meat and then passed the glove and the next piece of meat to Gabriel and told him to call her. She didn't hesitate, and I felt a slight jealousy that she should share her affection so readily but put it down to her being pretty hungry after her long journey.

Only when she'd finished eating and had wiped her beak carefully on the glove, did she turn her attention to Gabriel. I remembered well the deep look she gave him then and wondered what effect it was having on him. It was just as if they were silently communicating together. Remembering his ability to heal, I wondered if Gabriel was able to see deeper into Misty than I could. This thought gave me great pain and I realised how dependent I'd become on the close contact the dreams gave me. I went into the house to get some more meat.

When I came out again Misty had flown off to join Rift.

"Well?"

"Well, what?" he teased.

I didn't bother to reply, just gave him a look and threw some grass at him.

"Okay, okay, I give in." He settled himself more comfortably and took off the glove.

"Well, she doesn't need healing physically – you did good work with her there." He stopped as if exploring what he'd seen. "Her eyes followed you as you went into the house, you know. She has a great need of you and it doesn't seem to be physical – I don't really know what it is." Again he stopped and stared into the distance.

"What's happening, Gabriel? This just isn't normal."

"What's 'normal'? If we only believed in what we can see in black and white, we'd have no religion, no faith, no spirituality, no myths and legends. Let's just accept it for now. It's happened and if I'm right it isn't over yet."

"You mean she isn't going to go away?"

"No, Sara, that's not what I said." His tone was abrupt and I noticed his blue eyes darken to deep sapphire as they used to under stress. He must have seen my face so he softened a bit. "I know you don't want her to go, but you've always given her her freedom – and she's always come back. And you mustn't forget the dreams."

He was thoughtful for a moment, rubbing the bump on his nose. "You know what we were saying about synchronicity – well, I don't want you taking this the wrong way, Sara – but I've been having dreams lately too, strange dreams and you've been in some of them. That's why I wasn't too surprised when you rang – it sort of followed the pattern."

"What sort of dreams? The same as mine?"

"Nothing like the birds – and yet -"

"Yes?"

"Oh, I don't know – you know what dreams are like – something you can't quite put your finger on. But it's one of the reasons I came over here."

"I'm flattered."

"Don't be," he replied somewhat brutally. "It wasn't just you I was dreaming about." It was as though a barrier came suddenly between us and it took my breath away. He hadn't been prone to such mood swings in the past.

Hurt, I left it at that, but then what else had I expected – I didn't know a thing about his private life and decided that now may not be a good time to ask. Instead I went and found Gabriel the data on the Red Kites I'd collected over the years. I'd always enjoyed handling Red Kites. Their tendency to play dead meant you could pick them up readily without being injured, as they never used their talons in defence. To watch them in the aviary slowly fall off their perches in a parody of death as you approached was a joy to behold – and, as you crept away, they'd return to the perch with a quick ruffle of their glorious russet feathers as if nothing untoward had happened.

I gave Gabriel the freedom of the phone and left him alone.

Towards the middle of the afternoon, Rift found her way back to the aviary and I fed her. If she was going off with Mistral I didn't want her to go on an empty stomach. I talked to her quietly as she ate, wondering if it might be the last time. Mistral knew her way around out there, but Rift was completely inexperienced and not yet fit. If she got separated from Misty there was no knowing what trouble she might get into, but she was still there that night, and Mistral was there on the roof. So it wasn't to be tonight then.

It seemed I'd no sooner fallen asleep than I was awoken by a bright light shining into the room. As I looked, bleary eyed, I realised that the moon was shining full onto the mirror and filling the room with light. I got out of bed and went to the mirror to move it so that the moon was not shining directly onto it. As I reached forward, my hand brushed the feather there and heat seared my hand. I withdrew it quickly, bewildered. I felt light-headed and dazed with sleep, but was compelled to sit in front of the mirror and see if I could find an answer to the heat in the feather.

All I could see was a golden expanse, as though reflected from a golden stone wall, with the dim outline of my own face fading into a haze. Then a faint dark outline came into the mirror staring out across the gold. For a second the image sharpened and I saw a brown-black head with white cheek patches and dark moustache below the eye. In that second I knew I was looking at Scrap, a Scrap all alone, bewildered, in a land filled with golden sand and rock. Without taking my eyes from the mirror I called loudly for Gabriel, but he didn't hear me. As I rose to go and wake him, the image faded from the glass and all that was there was my own reflection in the mirror. I reached out tentatively to touch the feather and it was cool once more. Had I imagined the heat?

I couldn't settle, so took the torch and went to see if Mistral was still on the roof. She was, looking ghostly bathed in the moonlight and I wondered if the image of Scrap had come to her as well, but she gave no sign of it. Rift, though, was wide-awake, and she flew onto my shoulder and moved from foot to foot in agitation. I spoke to her quietly, telling her that Scrap was alright, that she didn't need to fret. Eventually she settled down and I was about to return her to the aviary when Gabriel called from upstairs.

"Sara, are you okay?"

"Yes – just checking on Misty." I hoped that would satisfy him and he'd go back to bed. The coolness that had come between us had only eased a bit and I didn't fancy trying to explain to him about the mirror – I was no longer sure what his reaction would be.

It didn't satisfy him, though and he came down to the kitchen where I was making a cup of hot chocolate, Rift still clinging to my shoulder. His hair was all tousled and sticking out, tangled where it rested on his shoulders. The sight warmed me and reminded me of past years – of past longings.

"Do you want a cup of chocolate?" I asked

"Yes, I would, now you've woken me up."

"Sorry, grumpy."

"I thought I heard you call me – did you?"

"Yes, but you didn't hear me in time."

"In time for what?"

I'd have to tell him about the mirror. If I wanted his help – I'd have to tell him everything.

I sighed, seeing difficulties ahead. "To see Scrap in the mirror."

"To see Scrap in the mirror – sorry, you've lost me – what mirror?"

"The one in the bedroom. Rift can see it too."

He groaned. "Just what can Rift see?"

I blushed. "Well, I don't know exactly, obviously – I only know what I've seen."

"Which is?"

I explained what I'd seen in the mirror and the heat from the feather.

"And the feather was really hot – that couldn't have been imagination?"

I felt the area of skin that had come into contact with the feather and it was slightly tender. "No, I don't think so." He could hear the uncertainty in my voice.

"Is it worth going to have a look?"

"I doubt it – but we can if you like." I knew I was clutching at straws but what if he could see something?

"Right, come on then. This I'd really like to see."

We went back upstairs, me now feeling a little foolish. If only he'd woken before I'd had to take my eyes off the glass, maybe he would have seen it too. He said he couldn't see the same dreams, but perhaps he could see into the mirror with me and help me unravel the tangle. I settled in front of the mirror without much hope of it revealing anything.

Gabriel stood behind me with his hands lightly on my shoulders and all the old feelings I'd had about him flooded back and I shivered.

"Here put this on." He pushed my jumper into my hands. He'd misunderstood the shiver and I was glad about that. I wanted to place no emotional ties on him at this moment – I needed his help too much. Anyway, his presence here was more to do with his own strange dreams, I now knew, than any special feeling he had for me.

I turned to look again into the mirror, accepting his hands on my shoulders. A feeling of disconnectedness came over me as I stared into the glass and I felt very far away, my body heavy. Then suddenly an image sharpened in front of my eyes – no bird this time, although the sand was still there. This time a man stood before me, dark skinned, eyes deep brown and kindly in a lined face. In his hand he held a feather and, as he tossed it into the air, a curling desert wind took it and spiralled it skyward. He watched it until it was out of sight then he turned round to face me and stared as though right into my eyes. He framed one word, which I didn't understand and held out the hand that had contained the feather towards me. Then the image faded and I could once more see my face, pale as the moonlight that shone onto the mirror.

Glancing at Gabriel, I caught a look of confusion on his face and knew, with a deep sense of relief, that he'd seen something. We stared at each other in the glass and I reached up my hands to grasp his where they lay on my shoulders. He leant his chin on top of my head, still staring into the mirror, then placed his arms around me and hugged me to him.

"Come on, let's talk about this away from that mirror." He helped me to my feet, which I was hardly surprised to find were unsteady, and we went down to the warmth of the kitchen.

"What did you see, Gabriel – you saw something – judging from the expression on your face."

"I didn't see any birds, Sara, but I did see the sand and rock you described, and I saw – someone. I could see he held something, but it was only when he tossed it in the air that I could I tell it was a feather. He said something too which I didn't catch. So what did you see?"

"Just the same." I had my arms folded closely to my chest to try and stop the shaking. "Except I'm pretty sure the feather was from a peregrine. I didn't understand the word he spoke either." I took a deep breath. "So I wasn't imagining all this. If you can see it too – just – what – is – going on?"

He shook his head. "I really don't know, Sara. When I started having those dreams in Australia and the next day came across a photo of you, I did feel a compulsion to come here. Now I'm here, I'm just as confused."

"You don't think that feather might have been Scrap's do you – that some harm has come to him?

"I don't think so. It certainly wouldn't have been by that man's hand." He was very sure, but I was still shaken by the whole thing.

"What if someone has taken him as a falconry bird – somewhere it's too hot for him? Our peregrines have always been popular in Arabia because they're bigger. You don't think that's what may have happened to Scrap do you?"

"No I don't, Sara. That wasn't anywhere in Arabia, I'm sure. Anyway, did Mistral seem concerned when you went out just now?"

"No – I didn't get the sense that she had anything to do with tonight's 'visions'."

"I think she'd know if anything had happened to Scrap don't you?"

"I suppose so. But what if he keeps Scrap?"

"He won't, don't worry." He became brusque again. "Well there's not much left of the night so I suggest we try and get some rest. Things may look different in the morning – they usually do."

I lay in bed for a long while, waiting for sleep to come as my mind raced. Why was it that Gabriel could also see into the mirror, I wondered? Was I transmitting the images for him or was he somehow involved with the birds? I could still feel the warmth where his hands had rested on my shoulders and still see the face of the stranger. Both sensations made me restless, so I didn't drop off to sleep until five o' clock and woke to find a cup of tea by the side of my bed. I couldn't remember the last time anyone had brought me a cup of tea in bed and it reinforced the feeling that I was no longer alone. Up till now I'd been happy with just the company of my birds and animals, but now I needed the reassurance of my own kind. But how long would Gabriel stay?

After last nights experience I decided to keep Rift in for a little longer. I felt a bit selfish keeping Misty from taking her off, but I still had this deep feeling that something was imminent and I needed them all here while I sorted it out. A restless compulsion seemed to be leading us all and only time would tell where it would lead.

CHAPTER FIVE

A brown A4 envelope came for Gabriel by the morning post, sent on from Scotland. It looked innocent enough – it contained a programme for a conference taking place in Canada on 'Raptors as Early Warning Systems' – but it turned out that it also contained a part of the mystery. Gabriel handed me the programme to read but kept the hand written letter that had come with it and slowly read it. I'd stolen a glance at it and it looked very like feminine writing to me and I wondered again if Gabriel was involved in a relationship – and, if so, how deeply. The thought depressed me, but I didn't want to ask. I picked up the other letter that had been in the envelope and had fallen on the floor. I went to hand it to Gabriel but he was too busy reading the first letter, so I just put it on the table and forgot about it.

The conference was to be an International affair, bringing to people's attention the plight of our eco-systems and how raptors, as predators were good indicators of the health of a habitat. Being at the top of the food chain any lessening in their numbers could indicate a break in that chain, whether caused by pollution, over hunting, loss of habitat or some other cause.

There were to be a number of speakers, some of whom I had heard of within the world of birds.

"This looks really interesting, Gabriel. Are you going?"

"I hope to. The University has agreed to sponsor me. There are going to be a number of smaller seminars and I've been asked to talk at one of them."

"Wow, so you get all expenses paid, do you?"

"Pretty well. One of the reasons I'm over here now is to research for that talk." He hurried on briskly, "so I'll need to follow up those contacts of yours today. It's less than two weeks till the conference, so I may be away a night or two. Is that okay?"

"Well I've managed alright up until now," I replied rather tartly because of the hollow feeling at the thought of not having him there. He'd entered my life again to fill a void and now he was going just when I had the greatest need of him. It was awful being afraid and not knowing what I was afraid of.

"In some ways it seems." He smiled. "Is there any chance you could type up some of the notes for me – for the talk – they're pretty well in order?"

I sighed. "Leave them with me, then – I'll see what I can do." I felt the need for some revenge, so added – "But I'll have to charge – it is, after all, partly how I earn my living."

"That'll be fine – the University will pay."

Gabriel's absence gave me time to catch up with some work, before starting on his notes. I'd had no new injured birds in for the last four days, so would be able to catch up on some of the jewellery I'd been promising I'd make for my own pleasure rather than to keep the wolf from the door. I had started work on a quarter size silver figure of a peregrine that I was building up feather by feather and it was at quite a critical stage. But before starting work I went with Misty and Rift for a walk, not daring to let them go together on their own – I needed a lot more answers before I risked Misty taking Rift off with her.

As we neared the cliff – Mistral gathered speed and Rift joined her to sail over the rocks calling to her mother as she tested her newly strong wing. I was reminded of Mistral's mating flight I'd witnessed three months ago now and wondered what had become of her mate. I had no doubt that he'd be back next year to claim Mistral, should they both live until then, but where was he now?

After chasing her mother for a while, Rift went to settle on the nest ledge. The skeleton of her dead brother had gone now, taken by some predator, but Rift poked around in the debris left in the nest as if seeking something. Eventually she came to the edge of the ledge and looked around. Seeing Misty she called to her, a gentle reassuring tone. She then looked down at me and dived off the ledge straight to where I sat on the rocks watching them.

She landed beside me, all childish gawkiness gone. She reached over and, as I put out my hand, she dropped a feather into it, a delicate curling feather, such as can only have come from the breast of a juvenile peregrine. I tightened my fist gently around it before it could blow away and then carefully tucked it into the top pocket of my jacket. As if satisfied Rift joined her mother in the air while Bran and I made our way back along the path.

Bringing Rift into the house, but leaving Misty outside, I settled down to work. Rift watched for a bit and then flew over to my jacket that hung over the back of a chair where I'd chucked it. Very delicately she reached into the top pocket with her beak and found the little breast feather she'd given me. Holding it carefully she brought it over to me and dropped it on the bench where I was working. I turned my head to look at her and, as with her mother, felt myself swim in the depths of the deep brown eye.

Unbidden into my mind came the image of a silver pin holding the feather which lay on my bench, and the sun shone through its delicate veins. The shape that held the feather was like the talon of a bird of prey, suspended from a carved bead of a shiny black stone. In my mind it twisted in the breeze and revealed itself as an earring hanging alongside a brown-skinned cheek.

The image was so clear that I quickly drew paper to me and sketched out the shape I'd seen. As I worked out the design, I decided to make it as a symbol for Rift of her lost brother and couldn't resist starting work straight away. The black stone was a problem as I didn't recognise it – black obsidian was the nearest I could think of but the texture of its surface didn't seem quite right, nor would it be easy to carve.

Rift remained at my shoulder the rest of the day, sleeping, watching and preening. It took me a couple of hours to get the shape of the earring, hammering the metal thin to catch the light. By the end of the day all it needed was the black bead to complete what I had been inspired to see in Rift's eye that morning.

Despite my hope that he would, Gabriel didn't ring that evening to let me know how he was getting on. It was odd how empty the place seemed without him considering how short a time he'd stayed. I worried also what would happen tonight, if I would be visited by dreams again and what they might portend. For the first time I felt insecure being here in my home alone. Bran brought the solace of companionship and early warning of any human visitors, but the dream visitors were something unpredictable. I knew they were important but had no idea in what way. When Mistral had first visited me in my dreams it gave me a feeling of privilege and exhilaration. Now, though, I felt something was being asked of me, and doubted myself adequate to the task.

But it wasn't to be a peaceful night. It was as if I had a fever when dreams take on an exaggerated effect and ordinary things go round and round totally out of proportion in size. I dreamt that the earring I'd made that day was slowly swinging from side to side suspended from the beak of a raven perched high on the top of a carved pole.

Ten times its actual size the earring swung slowly, hypnotically from side to side and I felt myself slipping away up into the sky beyond. As I passed the raven it gave a loud cackle and dropped the earring and a drop of blood fell on it from the raven's tongue. As it plummeted downwards a dark shadow fell at great speed from the sky and caught it before it reached the ground and swooped back up with it in its beak, labouring under its weight. As it neared me I recognised the shadow as Mistral. She dropped the earring in my hand and, as I closed my fist around it, it returned to its normal size, just a small earring, only now it had a softly polished, carved black bead dangling from it.

At this point I must have stirred because the dream shifted and this time I was over an expanse of ice and snow, following a trail of drops of blood, flying low over the cold blue ice.

Suddenly I came to the edge of a forest growing out of the ice, the trees rich and green, surrounding a lake of blood red water. Here the trail of blood stopped and I passed over the trees until I was peering down into the middle of the forest. There was a huge dome, marble white with streaks of red-brown veining. As I watched, the dome started to shudder and cracks appeared on its surface heading out from the middle until the whole surface was criss-crossed with jagged lines. Then a point appeared at the centre and began to push upwards. There was a loud screaming in my ears that became too piercing for me to bear and I woke up sweating.

It was already dawn so I went downstairs as it was unlikely I'd get any more sleep now, and fed Bran and Rift and took some food outside to see if Misty needed anything. She wasn't there. I knew I should give Rift the freedom to go off with her mother, but there were too many unanswered questions. All my judgements in the past were based on the normal laws of the wild where the birds were concerned, but these were not ordinary birds. They were so special it sometimes made my heart ache and other times I doubted the sanity of it all. Gabriel wasn't here – had he ever been here – had I dreamed that too? I shivered with apprehension, wanting at that moment only to be free of the responsibility of it all.

Never before had I been so aware of my desire to fit in with the rest of the crowd, not to be conspicuous in any way, just to be left alone to lead my life as I wished. Yet I knew I wouldn't sacrifice the special bond I had with Misty, Rift and Scrap, just in order to appear normal in anyone's eyes. Take me as I am or not at all.

At twelve o'clock the phone rang. It was Gabriel.

"Sara, I'll be another day yet. Is everything okay your end?"

"Yes, fine, thanks, Gabriel. I'm catching up on a backlog here"

"Okay. See you tomorrow then. I hope to have some news for you then."

"What sort of news."

But he wasn't to be pushed. "I'll tell you then. Bye."

The whole conversation was rather terse and I felt there was something wrong.

Late in the afternoon I set out for a walk to the cliff to see if

Misty was there, leaving Rift at home. When I reached the cliff I was relieved to find Mistyl flying overhead, but she seemed distracted as though waiting for someone or something at the cliff face and I wondered if it was for her mate, or perhaps Rift.

We sat for a while at the top of the cliff, just staring out over the hills and valleys. From this position you could just see the sea, and the forest protected our backs from the wind. The hillside was lush with bracken contrasting with the grey of the rocky slope. The tops of mountains, misted by distance, seemed closer than usual in the clear air and I had the old sensation of wanting to jump towards them and test my dreaming wings, but I stayed where I was, only too aware of what would happen.

"What is it, Misty?" I asked, stroking her breast gently. I felt the deep layers of feathers that kept her warm and my finger sunk into the soft downy layer that protected her delicate skin. I wondered at the perfection of each such tiny feather and imagined a bird a tenth her size and how minute each of its tiny feathers would be yet just as perfect. Truly a miracle of nature that could produce such miniature, yet perfectly designed things.

I was distracted from my musings by Misty's sudden alertness of stance. Then she started a keening sound and then a loud call issued from her, coming from deep from within. The sound reminded me of my dream and I shuddered. She turned to me, her eyes pleading.

"But Misty, I don't yet understand."

She tweaked at the pocket of my jacket where Rift had placed the feather. She then tugged at the sleeve with her strong beak.

"You want me to come with you?" I looked deep into her eyes and the answer formed inside my head – "Yes". I shivered. That "yes" reverberated round my mind and made me feel light-headed. "But I don't know how – or where." I cried in despair. "I can't fly – only in my dreams." "Yes" – it came again. "No!" Now I was afraid, unsure what she was asking of me.

Suddenly she turned her head upside down in the gesture that I loved so much and the atmosphere relaxed. My mind opened and again I heard her in my head. "You will be shown the way. Follow your heart."

With that she'd gone.

I trudged back, desolate. Unless I could follow her, I may never see Misty again.

So I was left without Mistral and without Gabriel, both of whom had become central to my life. Bran and Rift did the best they could to comfort me, but I felt dreadfully alone. That evening, I decided to try and reach Misty. Sitting relaxed, I searched for her in my mind. I could feel her spirit was there but it seemed a long way off, not in distance but in attention. It was enough, though, for me to know she was still in touch with me. Only later I began to worry about how I was to follow her and why. I decided that I couldn't wait for Gabriel to come back – I had to find an answer in the mirror if I could.

Rift sat on the back of my chair as I stared into the glass. For good luck I touched the feather still in the corner of the mirror and was reassured to find it was a normal temperature. At first I saw nothing, only our reflection, Rift's and mine. Then it became misty and I had that light headed feeling which was now becoming familiar. As the mist cleared Mistral was there and she was hurtling towards a dark shape in the sky, which I thought might be Scrap.

We waited, Rift and I, for what seemed an age, neither of us moving.

Then through the dark mist came the image of a face, indistinct, but with a look that made my flesh crawl and involuntarily I moved my head back out of his vision. It was a look of gloating, made worse by the image taking up the whole of the mirror and blocking out the light that had begun to creep in. Desperate now because I couldn't see Misty or Scrap I dragged my eyes away. Instantly the face disappeared and the mirror once more reflected only my pale face and that of Rift, who was leaning forward slightly as though still gazing into the glass. A soft crooning came from her throat and I noticed her eyes were not focused on the glass – she was gazing rather into the distance. I wondered then if she could see what was in the mirror, or she saw the images in her head and transferred them for me onto the glass, like her mother did in my dreams.

Try as I might I couldn't find Misty and Scrap in the mirror again, perhaps because I felt too tense. There was nothing more I could do. Maybe Misty would come to me in my dream tonight – I longed to fly with her, feel her near me and be reassured by her.

Before I went to bed that night the phone rang. It was Gabriel.

"Sara? Look, I'm sorry but I've got to fly back to Australia first thing in the morning. I can't explain now, but you've got my number there. Any problems just ring."

"But, Gabriel, I ......" – I was about to say 'I need you here' but I couldn't. "Okay, but when will you be back?"

"I don't know. I might have to fly out to Vancouver without seeing you first. I'm sending you some notes I've made over the last couple of days to add to the ones I left with you. I'd really appreciate it if you could run over them and see what you think. Any chance you could type them up for me too?"

"If I get time." I replied feeling very let down – so now I was just the skivvy.

"Any news on the Mistral front?" he asked as though humouring me.

"No." I lied. What good would it do to tell him now? "Well I'll see you whenever then."

"I'll try and make it before I go." I knew it was unlikely as he was nearer Vancouver from Australia than coming via us. "I'm really sorry to cut things short like this."

"Yes, well so am I, Gabriel."

"It was really good seeing you again, Sara." Some warmth had entered his tone.

"Yes," was the most original reply my confused brain could come up with. "Good-bye, then, Gabriel. Good luck." And he was gone – my life-line was gone.

A feeling of depression fell on me when I came off the phone and I longed just to weep, but felt too low even for that. I did what I perhaps shouldn't have and drank a couple of double vodkas, one after the other – you know how it is – it just seemed a good idea at the time. Then I put Rift to bed and staggered to bed myself. The alcohol dulled the feeling of despair, but emphasised the feeling of loneliness. It also led to a jumble of dreams that did nothing to put my mind at rest about Misty and Scrap.

Faces kept whirling round in my head, a spiral of confusion.

Then another circle joined, this time a swirl of birds, then another. I could see through to the centre and there was a huge Raven circling the face I had seen wearing the earring and, in the background, another familiar face – Gabriel – a Gabriel so remote I couldn't reach him. As I stretched out my hand towards him, I felt myself tumbling and woke up giddy and sick. That'll teach me to revert to alcohol, I thought – for now, anyway.

It was nearly dawn when I woke. A headache kept me wide-awake, so I decided to watch the sun rise as the air was clear and the moon just fading. I left the track and walked a little way towards Mistral's cliff, half hoping she would be there. The sun was rising, filling the sky with soft pink-orange light. I stopped to watch the glory of the start of the day, leaning with my back against an oak tree, feeling its strength. Above the slight breeze in the leaves parched by the heat, I heard a familiar cry. My heart gave a lurch as I looked towards the direction of the cliff and saw a dark anchor shaped shadow. Too small for Misty – could it be Scrap?

I stepped out of the shade of the tree and called, hoping against hope he'd remember me. There was no hesitation; down he came, swerving at the last minute to sit in the branches of the oak I had been leaning against. It was Scrap – my heart lifted.

Together we hurried back to the cottage and we could hear Rift shouting as we neared the house. How close these two were to always be able to sense each other's presence, even over hundreds of miles. Did humans have this same ability, but overlaid now by thousands of years of civilisation?

They spent half an hour preening and inspecting each other. The size difference was quite marked now, but Scrap had solidified and grown up in the last few weeks and looked harder than Rift who had yet to be tested. I let her out to fly with Scrap and they played sky games for an hour before Rift tired and came asking for food.

When she'd finished she hopped up onto my knee and tipped her head to one side as she looked up at me. She then flew into the house very purposefully. Something told me not to follow her. She came out in a short space of time and in her beak she carried the earring with the little breast feather on it. Whether or not this feather came from her dead brother, I don't know, but I think she believed it did. She placed it on my knee and, as I put my hand over it, she tucked it further under my hand as though leaving it in my safe keeping. I knew then that she was going.

I looked at her with tears in my eyes. "Please don't leave, Rift. Please." But her words were inside my head "I have to go – you have to let me go." And like her mother she caught one tear as it fell and flew off to where Scrap was waiting for her. She flew down once to my shoulder, rubbed her head gently against my face and was gone.

I was devastated. In the space of twenty-four hours I had lost four of my closest friends and my mind was in such turmoil, I needed their guidance. Bran pushed his cold wet nose into my hand to comfort me and I bent and wept into his curly black coat.

The papers came from Gabriel the next day. He'd certainly been doing some research and his rather random handwriting did nothing to make my task easier. There were a number of maps and aerial photographs which needed inserting in the right place and a fair amount of typing. Fortunately I had a computer, on which I put the information on each of the birds I had in to care for, so it wouldn't take me that long. At first I felt resentful that Gabriel had dumped this job on me and scarpered back to Australia just when I needed him, but the details on the bird releases was so fascinating I soon became absorbed in it.

There was a short note from Gabriel in the envelope explaining that there had been an accident that he needed to sort out, but nothing more, except a cryptic note at the bottom that was not very informative.

P S I'm still having dreams.

So was I, I thought. Obviously it was up to me to sort it out – how – well that I didn't know.

But that didn't mean they were going to stop. That night, I dreamt that I was flying over a lake with forest all around, a huge egg shaped rock on its shore. I heard a shot ring out and felt the hot stream of pellets shoot past me, but none of it touching me. Looking downward I heard another shot and then saw a dark pool of blood ebb its way into the waters of the lake where it sank as though solid.

Suddenly the water erupted from that spot and a figure shot from the depths skywards, hands at its side diving heavenwards. I peered into the lake and felt myself falling inwards and, as my face hit the water, I woke up in panic.

CHAPTER SIX

So many disturbed nights were taking their toll and I had to concentrate hard on collating Gabriel's notes and slides. Time was running short and I felt myself trying to speed things up, compelled to do everything quickly. The conference started in under a week and I'd still got to get the notes and slides to Gabriel.

The thought had occurred to me that I might offer to take the notes out to Canada for him. Although it was a long way, I needed a holiday and the conference would be a good excuse.

I'd also been doing some research into different species of peregrine falcons. The peregrine is widespread throughout North America, although as a slightly darker version of our European Peregrine. But there is a breed of peregrine that occurs on and in the vicinity of the Queen Charlotte Islands, not that far distant from Vancouver. The description could fit Mistral's mate. The possibility of getting a glimpse of this bird, peregrinus pealei, was irresistible. A species special to such a small area and yet a larger bird than its cousins was well worth seeing, I reckoned.

But it was pretty scary to think of flying that long way on my own without knowing what I was likely to find at the other end. But, putting aside the mere practicalities, the idea appealed to me. If there was a chance of hearing some of the seminars at the conference I'd be in my element.

As I was sorting through the maps and aerial photographs that afternoon, spread out on the kitchen table, I came across the letter that had come for Gabriel from Scotland, tucked under some papers, unopened. I'd forgotten to give it to him. What if it was something important – the postmark was Vancouver. He'd not be pleased I'd forgotten to give it him, I didn't think.

There were two things I had to do – ring Gabriel – then try and find out from Misty whether I was doing the right thing. The words of hers I'd heard in my head just before she left, returned – "you will be shown the way." I laughed. If indeed I was to follow what better way than by aeroplane? Other than hang-gliding and ballooning it was the only practical way I had of following her. I had a friend who learnt to hang-glide so that he could fly with his Red-tailed Hawk. The idea had always appealed to me, but maybe now wasn't quite the right time to learn.

I put in the call to Gabriel, wondering how he would take my suggestion. He'd seemed so distant the last time we'd spoken on the phone. Then there was the dream. Well, I had to try.

A woman answered.

"Could I speak to Gabriel, please?" I asked nervously.

"Sure, I'll just get him for you. Who shall I say's calling?"

"Tell him Sara and it's urgent."

"Will do."

Then I heard his voice and an overwhelming desire to cry welled up in me. What was the matter with me – it wasn't even the wrong time of the month? I was behaving like a child not like someone who planned to fly half way round the world after a dream.

"Sara – what's wrong?" He sounded concerned and harassed at the same time.

"Nothing's wrong, Gabriel."

"Well, you said it was urgent, didn't you?"

"Yes, it is. In case you hadn't noticed it's less than a week until the Conference and I've got to get these notes to you yet."

"Yes, of course – I'm sorry, but things are a bit difficult over here just at the moment. I'm not absolutely sure I'm going to be able to make it after all."

"Oh no. But, Gabriel, you can't miss it – you're giving a talk."

"God knows I don't want to. Look, I'm not about to burden you with my problems ..."

"I burdened you with mine." Not that he'd been a great help to date.

"That's different, but this involves someone else, so it's nothing I can really share with you. You're better off out of it anyway." The tenseness had returned to his voice.

"Okay, if that's how you want it."

"Oh, Sara – I'm sorry. I know that sounded bad, but you've no idea what's going on."

"Maybe my idea of bringing the notes over personally is not a good one, then."

"What, here to Australia?"

"No straight to Vancouver. I need a break and I'd love the chance to hear some of the speakers." I was aware that a note of pleading had entered my voice and didn't much like it. I felt hollow to think that I might have to make the journey all alone and then arrive knowing no one. But the last few hours had convinced me that it was the thing I was meant to do, I just didn't know why.

There was a pause at the other end. "That actually seems a great idea to me, if you're sure you can afford it. It would be a load off my mind and there'd be no risk of the notes going astray. If I can't make it you can give the talk instead. How does that sound?"

"Terrifying." I replied. "In front of all those knowledgeable people."

"You can do it."

"Mmm." Now for it. "One more thing, Gabriel – I'm afraid I forgot to give you a letter which arrived with the stuff from Scotland."

"What letter?"

"Well – it dropped out of the envelope and fell on the floor – I was going to hand it to you – but you were too busy reading. Then I forgot – sorry."

"Oh, Sara!" I could hear the familiar exasperation.

"Do you want me to open it – it's from Vancouver."

"Handwritten?"

"Yes."

"Then you'd better open it, Sara." His voice was low and very tired.

I tore open the envelope and a feather dropped out onto the table. I picked it up and examined it. It appeared to be a secondary feather from a wing, but the structure and texture didn't look quite right. I pulled out the paper inside the envelope and my stomach lurched as I saw the photographs contained inside.

It was the lake from my dream – I was sure of it. The shore was rugged with deep inlets interspersed with narrow stretches of gravely sand bounded by tall trees, with the egg shaped boulder on the shore. One of the photographs was taken from the air – the trees looked denser and foreshortened, but it was exactly the angle I had seen it in my dream as I'd flown over it and had heard the shot. It was the feeling of certainty that took my breath away. After all, many lakesides must look the same – but I had no doubt – I'd seen this place in my dream, from this angle.

I didn't say anything to Gabriel – he wouldn't believe me, but my hand shook as I read the letter with it. It was a report from a microbiology department with a scribbled note on the bottom.

'No time to explain – but if anything happens to me, please, please look after Kate. It's up to you what you do with enclosed – Paul.'

I read it out to Gabriel. "Do you recognise the feather, Sara?"

"No, I don't – it's like nothing I've ever seen." I described it to him.

"Does it say what the report is about?"

"The feather as far as I can tell – it says... species unlisted."

I heard Gabriel's sharp intake of breath. "So that's it. Look, Sara you need to keep that feather and the photographs safe – bring them with you to Vancouver and I'll do my best to be there."

"Do you know where the photographs were taken, Gabriel?"

I asked anxiously.

"If it's connected with Paul, then it's likely it's not a million miles from where the Conference is being held. Why?"

"Oh, nothing." My instinct had been right. "Look – I'll ring you in a couple of days and let you know if I've managed to arrange a flight."

"Thanks. If you do give the talk, I could perhaps swing some expenses. Would that help?"

"Tremendously."

"I'll see what I can do. Sorry if I'm a bit tetchy. I'm just very tired."

"I can tell. Take care, then, Gabriel. Bye."

So I'd made the decision – I was going to Vancouver – if I could get a flight. I made sure there was enough food for the birds, and asked Ted, who ran the farm next door if he would be able to feed for me.

"Where are you off to then, cariad?" he asked.

Feeling guilty for being evasive I replied, "I'm not sure yet, Ted. I just need to get away for a few days. The RSPCA will take care of any new birds and the rest just need feeding for now."

"Now don't go worrying. I can manage – you just go off and enjoy yourself. Take your time. We'll be alright."

"If a peregrine comes to the house – could you feed her too, Ted. She'll come down for the food – and her youngsters." I wasn't ready to believe in the dreams without some contingency plan. It wasn't until then that I realised how wrapped up I'd been in the falcons – normally Ted would have known all about them.

Bran would go to a college friend of mine where he was always happy, mostly because they spoilt him rotten and fed him to the point of obesity. As my father was unwell, I didn't want my mother to have the added responsibility of a dog. Besides, Maggie and John lived nearer and time was of the essence now.

I spent the rest of the afternoon finding out the cost of flights to Canada. Being late summer there were still flights available and they weren't as expensive as I had expected despite the late booking. With butterflies in my stomach at the step I was taking, I booked a flight that would get me to Vancouver the day before the Conference started. I booked one night's accommodation and then I would find something as cheap as possible when I got there. I had enough money to see me through about a week but had no idea if that would be long enough.

So now I was committed. That night I tried contacting Misty in the mirror, not daring to rely on the luxury of seeing her in my dream. I had to let her know what I'd done, and hope she would be able to show me if it was right. There was only mist and ice and snow in the mirror, at least that is what it looked like. The fact that I felt the cold only confirmed this. I saw neither Misty nor Rift. I found this worrying – the last thing I needed was to lose contact with them now.

Suddenly the idea of flying all that way on a whim overwhelmed me and I felt lonelier than ever. What if none of this was other than a mirage, all just in my imagination? Was Gabriel just humouring me? Where was it all leading? Depressed, I went to bed, taking Bran to keep me company.

Next morning, after a dreamless sleep, I woke refreshed and started my plans for the holiday – in four days time. I determined to put aside any thought of it as other than a holiday. One day I'd always intended to go to Canada and Alaska, since seeing a holiday programme that had included a trip to a Bird Sanctuary like my own. Now was my chance. It was also educational – if I could bribe my way into any of the seminars.

Taking Gabriel at his word, in case I had to give the talk on his behalf, I went through the notes several times. Fortunately he'd included the work he had done before he left Australia to come to Britain. I was used to giving talks, but mostly to people with very little knowledge of the work we did with birds – so a little exaggeration went a long way, but these people would be far more knowledgeable.

It was as I was going through the notes that Gabriel had done prior to his visit that I came across the name of Paul Bates, among the acknowledgements of those who'd helped with the research. Was this the Paul of the note? Delving deeper into the text I found another mention, this time on the prehistory of birds and how many species had died out over the last few thousand years.

It was frightening to see how many species we'd lost during that time, and how that loss had accelerated as soon as humans came on the scene. Now we were losing as many as two or three species a year. These all as a result of pressure from humans, either directly or as a result of the introduction of creatures such as rats and cats. This was why Gabriel was so interested in how the reintroduction of species, once endemic, worked – whether the environment was now suitable, or whether further interference by us just made matters worse. Inevitably any change in the level of any species was going to have an affect on the indigenous population and this needed careful monitoring.

Back in the sixties the numbers of peregrines had dropped dramatically. This fact was only discovered after complaints from pigeon fanciers that peregrines were taking thousands of their birds. A survey was done and far from their claim being substantiated, the drop in numbers of peregrines was so catastrophic that an immediate rescue plan was put into operation!

This decline was accounted for by the chemicals used to dress seed that the wild pigeons were eating and the peregrines ingested, leading to thinning of their eggs and a drop in successful breeding. Adding to a decline in their numbers was a campaign to eliminate the peregrines on the south coast during the Second World War because they relied on pigeons for their source of nourishment and didn't differentiate between feral and carrier pigeons – nor racing pigeons. This made them the farmers' friend and pigeon fanciers' enemy, even though – in straight flight – a pigeon can out-fly a peregrine. But not when they stooped out of the sun at over two hundred kilometres per hour!

How sad it is that a bird of such stunning beauty should be killed when survival is the only thing on the peregrine's mind. Only a very small percentage of the losses of racing pigeons can be attributed to peregrines, their chief enemies being the domestic cat and weather conditions.

So, putting all doubt out of my mind, I started packing. I rang Gabriel to let him know I'd managed to get a flight.

"That's good. I'm still not sure what's happening this end, but you've got all the notes. Do you think you'd be able to do the talk?"

"I don't know but I'll do my best. I'm sure they won't mind me reading most of it out, will they?"

"I shouldn't have thought so. Look, Sara, I really do appreciate this. I'll make it up to you sometime, really I will."

"I'll let you know if I run out of money, then." I said jokingly, but aware I might have to.

"Do that. Anyway I hope to see you there on Friday. If you don't hear from me go to the Conference Centre and ask there. If I'm not coming I'll let them know you're able to give the talk for me. Okay?"

"Okay and – Gabriel – take care, won't you?" What did I want to say that for when it was me travelling half round the world on my own, not him.

"You too – and, thanks again, Sara."

"Croeso – you're welcome. Bye."

Hearing his voice over all those miles made me realise how much I wanted to see his face, feel his touch on my arm, my shoulder .... Shaking myself, I got on with the work I needed to finish before going.

The earring with the feather on it that Rift had given to me lay on my workbench. I picked it up and looked again at the little feather and felt great sadness. If it was from her brother, this was all we had left of him, because some selfish person had considered he had the right to kill. I hated the injustice of it and the need to enlighten people of the damage we do to all the wild creatures around us for our own selfish ends.

As I tightened my hand in anger around the feather a sharp piece of silver dug into my palm and drew blood. I stared at the droplet as it grew and saw again the blood on the corpse of Rift's brother. The drop of my blood seemed to grow as I stared at it and I saw again the blood around the lake and the blood that seeped into the water from the shore. Then I saw Gabriel's face as though it swam in the lake of blood and my heart pounded. It had been clear over the phone that he was in trouble – this, and the fact that he wouldn't share whatever it was with me – added to my concern. If only he would come to the Conference.

Carefully I wrapped the earring in tissue and put it in my bag. It was Rift's parting gift and I was taking it with me to wherever I might be going. I still felt that this trip was for a deeper purpose than giving a talk at a seminar.

I decided to take another talisman with me and went to fetch Misty's feather from the mirror. I'd pushed it hard into the frame and had to tug to release it. As it came free, the mirror was suddenly washed with light. I heard a sound of faint music, pipe music, with a soft gentle rhythm, haunting in its melody. I held my breath in case it went away as I sat down at the mirror and peered into the light.

Although the sound came from a human instrument, it was the birds I saw. Misty, Rift and Scrap were there and they soared and twisted through the air as though in time to the music. Misty was the first to settle and she sat part way down a towering cliff with what looked like images carved into them. As I looked, the picture sharpened and my eye was drawn in to the carvings. Each depicted a different bird. As I looked closer a living bird of that species was visible standing in front of the image of its own kind. There were birds I could not recognise, but many of these had no living birds standing in front of them. I began to feel dizzy as my eye was drawn to so many, many birds. There were perhaps thousands there – they seemed to stretch for miles and I could not possibly see them all.

My eye returned to Misty and I could see her looking towards me. She seemed to want to show me something, so when she turned her head, I followed her gaze. Not far from her stood another peregrine, bigger than her with a more heavily barred chest and a bloom to her feathers unlike Mistral's. I knew straightaway that this was Peale's Peregrine, the one I hoped to see if I could get to the Queen Charlotte Islands when I was in Canada. With a rise in my heart I felt this to be Misty's way of indicating that I was heading in the right direction after all. I was answering her summons, as surely as if she'd dictated it, which, in her own way she had – I'd never really had an option to refuse her.

Misty turned her head once more and gazed skywards and I felt a softening in her. She was watching Rift and Scrap who continued to weave their dance in the sky together, Rift more sedate than her brother, her wing slowing her only a little. Mistral was proud of these two. They had been tested and not found wanting. Wherever she was, and I sensed it was far away, they had come with her, never hesitating when she called. As with all children they continued to play, unaware yet what was really expected of them – just like me.

At that moment I knew that Mistral was guiding my spirit, that she was the stronger and I was following, not just from love of her, but because without her I was not complete, not at rest. This was at once both frightening and exhilarating. I had dreamt of a bond as complete as this, but had always imagined it would be another person, even at one time that it might be possible with Gabriel. Never would I have believed it would be possible with a wild creature.

My eyes wandered over the cliff face, wondering at the beautiful carvings, and, as they reached the summit, I saw the Raven standing there, above the rest, watching as the sky filled with all the birds I could see carved on the rock. As his head turned my way the image faded and the mirror went blank

I still had Mistral's feather in my hand, so went and put it with the earring in my bag. If it could work here I may need it on my travels to keep in touch with her.

That night I dreamt dreams of my bird family, but they were vague dreams. They wove in and out, flying through my subconscious, as though leading me on, but with none of the views and sequences I usually had. They were just there, warming my heart, so that when I rose the next day, I felt rested and cherished, as though they were really here with me and I only had to reach out my hand.

I went for a long walk with Bran – the last for a long time, I knew. I felt bad about leaving him behind, we were so rarely parted and he'd seen me through so many difficult times with his gentle love. He knew my friends well, though, and loved them both, but he knew I was going and dogged my heels all day, looking concerned.

The car was packed and I turned to take one last look at the cottage, wondering when I would see it again. The fear at what I was doing almost made me turn back, but I knew I was committed. So I set out for the first, and shortest, part of the journey.

It was good to see John and Margaret again. I'd been at College with Margaret and we'd re-established our friendship when she'd moved back to her native Mid Wales. I'd arranged to spend the night with them and go on to the airport from there as they were fifty miles closer than me, so I had a quiet relaxing evening catching up on gossip with little time to think about the impending trip, except when reminded.

"I do think it's brave of you going all that way on your own." Margaret was not a great traveller – two children kept them on a pretty tight budget. "Whatever brought on this wanderlust?"

"Oh, I don't know." I prevaricated. "The signs of oncoming age maybe. If I don't go now, goodness knows when I may get the chance again."

John snorted. "Age, indeed – you wait till you're the great age of thirty ... something like me." He patted his less than slim stomach. "You wouldn't think it would you?"

"More like forty something, I should think." Margaret winked at him. It was good to be in the company of two people so content with each other and their life together. "Won't this Conference be a bit dry, though, you know, all academic people?"

"It may be, but if I do end up giving this talk, I may be able to swing some expenses out of them, or Gabriel."

"I haven't seen Gabriel in ages – how is he?"

"Much the same really, I suppose." I replied evasively.

"Still as attractive?" Margaret asked mischievously. We'd had very few secrets from each other – she was a good listener.

"I suppose so." I could see from her expression she took this with a pinch of salt. Perhaps she was right. Seeing Gabriel again had done nothing to allay any ghosts of the feelings I'd had for him.

The children came to say goodnight and the conversation shifted to College days, much to my relief. I felt I was cheating them not giving them the full story but John was far too down to earth to understand anything of what was happening to me. Margaret, being a fellow crafts person, may have had a better chance of understanding but I didn't want to stretch their friendship.

Next day I rose early and took Bran for a quick run. By the time I got back Margaret had cooked me some breakfast. I didn't really want it as I was feeling nervous about the day, but didn't want to offend her and, after all, the meals on aeroplanes are not known for their great substance or gastronomic delight.

"Are you sure you wouldn't like us to run you to the airport?

The children would enjoy it and it would really be no trouble, Sara." John was up by now. I gave him a big hug.

"No, thanks, John, really. I'm not sure when I'll be back, as I mentioned, so it'll be easier for me to have the car at the airport. You're doing enough looking after Bran for me. I really do appreciate that. I know he'll be spoilt rotten by the kids and have a whale of a time just so long as he doesn't end up a whale of a size!"

"As if. Well, you've got our number if there's anything you need, Sara. We'll do what we can, you know that."

"I know you will, John. And I go forth with a lighter heart knowing it!"

"Cheeky." But he never minded being teased. He was a big, untidy man with a child's way about him that hid a shrewd brain. He and Margaret were one of the happiest couples I knew. "Just make sure you ring us when you get there safely."

As I drove away, waving to the family until they were well out of sight, Bran sat at the end of the drive staring after the car, his head on one side.

As I rounded the corner and they were all out of sight, the feeling that I'd well and truly committed myself hit me and for a minute I panicked. Then a picture of Mistral as I had first seen her came into my mind and I remembered the magic we'd woven together then – and since, and I was thankful that it hadn't ended there, that she was still with me if only in spirit. With a lighter heart I set out on the longest journey of my life with little idea what lay ahead.

CHAPTER SEVEN

It was certainly a very long journey and I was very thankful to reach Vancouver nine uncomfortable hours after leaving Britain as I hadn't been able to afford any extra leg-room. I caught up on some reading on the plane, between dozing. I went through Gabriel's notes a couple of times, hoping it would act like crossing my fingers – if I knew them well and could therefore give a good representation then I wouldn't be called on to do it. But if I didn't know them then sod's law would apply and I'd be asked to do it! I did so hope that Gabriel would be there.

As we began the descent to Vancouver we got spectacular views of the Rockies with their tall rugged peaks topped with the snow still lying in crevices down the sides of the mountains, wisps of clouds floating round the tallest peaks. I wondered if there'd be a chance I could take the train that ran through the Rockies. All the possibilities added to my feeling of excitement and inevitably my nerves, so that it was with a feeling of relief and trepidation that I descended from the plane at Vancouver.

Whilst we waited for the luggage to arrive on the carousel, I put a call in to my parents – to let them know I'd arrived safely. As I was walking back to collect my luggage I heard a message over the loudspeaker.

"Would Sara MacCallum please go to the enquiries desk."

Hurriedly I grabbed my bags and made my way to the desk where a letter was handed to me. I opened it straight away being uncertain what it might contain. It came from a secretary at the Conference Centre saying accommodation had been booked for me a little way out of the city and giving me directions to reach it. I was touched by their thoughtfulness, and pleased to see that it was University accommodation and, hopefully, cheap. Although I was glad that Gabriel had thought to ring ahead, this probably only confirmed that he was still in Australia.

Everything was too exciting to be upset by this, so I set out for the accommodation. I gleaned various bits of information from the cab driver, such as the best, and cheapest, places to eat and the places I must visit while in Vancouver. He knew little about the Queen Charlotte Islands other than I would have to take a ferry from Prince Rupert to the north if I didn't want to fly.

It was getting dark as we drove through Vancouver and I looked forward to seeing it better in daylight. I'd been told it was a beautiful city but exploring it would have to wait until tomorrow. A meal, a nice hot bath and early to bed was what I was looking for. Despite all the excitement I hadn't forgotten I needed to keep in touch with Misty. The journey had started on a whim, but this was the reality. I was here in Canada and tomorrow there was the possibility of seeing Gabriel.

I rang the bed and breakfast I'd booked and they were fine about me cancelling. Despite it still being early in the evening Canadian time, tiredness got the better of my worries almost straight away and I fell asleep. It seemed like only minutes after I'd dozed off that I started to dream. I was back on that shoreline, but this time on the ground and, as I looked up there were Misty, Rift and Scrap flying an intricate dance in the sky above my head. Then, one by one, they came and stood on the rocks beside me so I was able to stretch out my hand and touch each precious breast. As I sat with them we were joined by another, larger peregrine, but when I stretched out my hand to this bird, my touch turned it to stone. As I withdrew my hand in shock, Mistral came and sat on my shoulder and spoke into my ear.

"So is beauty made from beauty – to live forever."

Then I felt myself drawn into the sky and I flew with them over the lake, the dense trees and far into the heavens, my heart filled to bursting with the sheer joy of feeling the wind below my wings, the elation of slicing through the air, and the joy of flying at last with my special family. I knew then that they were closer to me than they had ever been, Misty, Rift and Scrap. Although I didn't know how many miles divided us, I felt them with me in a way that I hadn't before and the warmth of it filled my heart.

I slept deeply after the dream but woke early, my time clock all to pieces. I lay and dozed and fell into a light on and off sleep. I dreamt about Gabriel and woke convinced he wouldn't be there in the morning.

There were quite a few people staying in the University rooms I'd been booked into. I was relieved to find the rate was quite cheap as it was student accommodation and I blessed whoever had had the forethought to think of my finances. I wondered if the other delegates were accommodated in plush hotels paid for from expenses. I didn't mind. I felt very much at home here and it was only a twenty-minute journey to Vancouver centre on the bus. The grounds of the University were pleasant to wander around in and I was determined to get out and about, so I probably wouldn't be here very much.

It took me over an hour to find my way to the Centre, but I had time on the bus to search out the places I wanted to visit from the tourist sheet I'd picked up at the University from Tom, the porter. In doing so I found out that Prince Rupert was more than four hundred miles away to the north and was known as the City of Rainbows, which didn't bode well for the quantity of rain, but at least there had to be sunshine to create the rainbows. The crossing to the Queen Charlotte Islands would take six hours by ferry. Somewhat daunted by these miles I very much doubted if I would get my longed for glimpse of Peale's Peregrine after all.

The Centre was a huge place down by the docks, which contained a shop and a restaurant as well as a hotel. I found my way to the right enquiry desk and was welcomed by an efficient middle-aged woman, (Mrs Stewart it said on her badge), who immediately made me feel at home. She was obviously used to dealing with all sorts of foreigners and their problems and ordered a cup of coffee for me whilst we went through the agenda. Gabriel had been in touch with them and asked them to look after me as his representative.

So I was issued with a badge and a pass and was told I could sit in on any of the seminars provided I let them know in advance. I went through the list and chose the ones that sounded as if they touched on the areas I was most interested in. I didn't want to spend all my holiday in lectures, so ended up choosing about five. Gabriel's talk was scheduled for three days time. Mrs Stewart showed me the room it would take place in and gave me instructions on the use of the overhead projector, but let me know that there would be someone there on the day to help out with technicalities, thankfully.

As we returned to her desk in the foyer, a man was looking through her list of delegates. Mrs Stewart hurried over to help him, taking the list out of his hands, and I returned to the desk to pick up my pass. The man glanced at it as I picked it up and then looked up at me. He was a man of medium height with the start of a paunch complemented by the end of most of the hair on his scalp. What was left was scraped over in an attempt to make it more than it was, but only emphasised the lack. The look in his eyes, that were small and watery blue, was calculating and left me feeling uneasy, I don't know why. He showed no sign of moving so Mrs Stewart introduced us and mentioned I was here as substitute for Gabriel.

"How interesting," was the calculatingly bored reply. "Now if you will excuse me I have a lot to arrange."

With that he hurried off in the direction of the Conference Hall. I stared after him, taken aback by his rudeness. Mrs Stewart smiled at me.

"Don't mind Dr Long. He's responsible for the first lecture this afternoon so that's probably why he's a bit tetchy."

"Perhaps I'll just make a point of keeping out of his way, then. I haven't chosen to attend any of his lectures have I?" I asked.

She smiled with understanding and checked my list. "No, it

looks like you're safe there. His are mostly about palaeontology. The first one you've chosen is tomorrow, so what are you going to do the rest of the day?"

"Wander round your lovely city, I think." I replied. "Is there anywhere in particular you'd recommend?"

"Well, now, there's the Museum of Anthropology if you're interested in that sort of thing, and it's close to the University where you're staying. They deal with the art and history of the native Indians in these parts."

"I'll give them a try, then. Do you know anything about the Queen Charlotte Islands?" I asked. "Only I have a special love for peregrines and they have a particular one there I'd very much like to see."

"Well, now, I can try and find out for you. If it's about birds there's sure to be someone here at this Conference who can help, wouldn't you think, now?"

I laughed. "Just so long as it isn't Mr. – sorry – Dr. Long, I don't mind." She grinned back at me.

As I walked away I realised that I hadn't altogether been joking about not asking him – I hadn't at all liked the look in his eye.

I spent a lovely leisurely morning, soaking up the sun and the atmosphere of the city. Being a country girl by birth – and inclination – it was always exciting to be amongst the bustle and energy of a city – tiring but invigorating. Then I set off for the University as jet lag was catching up with me and I wanted to see the Museum of Anthropology before having a sleep. I wanted to get a feel for the country I was visiting and had always had a fascination for the people and things of the past. If I'd had more patience I might have been tempted to become an archaeologist, but enjoyed instead seeing the results of other peoples' hard, patient work.

As soon as I walked into the grounds of the Museum and saw the totem poles looking as if they were growing there out of the ground, I recognised them. The carved faces, the pole the Raven sat on – it was all there before me. I stood there in shock realising they were another part of the unfolding of the dreams – I was in the right place – I'd been right to come to the Conference. As the thought came to me I saw in my mind a picture of Mistral, serene and majestic sitting on the rock in front of a carving of a peregrine – not wood like these superb carvings – but living rock.

The Queen Charlotte Islands were obviously on my mind as an information brochure containing a short history of the magnificent totem poles caught my eye. Although many of the poles, which had graced the deserted villages on the islands, had mouldered into dust, some of them had been preserved here at the Museum and outside. European influences, most noticeably the smallpox that had decimated the local Haida population, had led to the desertion of these once proud villages. My curiosity was fired, particularly by the description I read that – 'they lie on the edge of the province's collective memory like a dream scarce remembered, mythical and elusive, full of meaning and beauty ...' Who could resist such an alluring image.

Feeling this was probably enough culture for one day and still lagging a bit behind the time, I returned to the University. There was a note on my door that came as a bit of a surprise. I could only assume it came from Mrs Stewart.

I took it into my room along with my shopping. The beauty of being in the University accommodation was that there was a shared kitchen so I could save money on food. I opened the note that had been stuck with tape to the door – its message was bald -

RING GABRIEL URGENTLY

Nothing else. I knew Gabriel well enough to know that he wouldn't say urgent unless it was, so I went down the corridor in search of a phone. As I approached the entrance hall to the block, I heard someone arguing with the porter, Tom. I'd taken to him straight away, particularly as I found he was a fellow peregrine devotee. He'd been very helpful when I needed to know where the buses went from and even found me a timetable, so I felt rather sorry for him being harangued. Always one to keep out of trouble, though, and other people's business – when the temptation isn't too great – I hung back in the corridor. It was lucky I did – the raised voice belonged to Dr Long!

"What do you mean you can't – won't more like." I could imagine the veins standing out on his neck in anger at being thwarted.

"I'm sorry I am not in a position to release that information, sir." Tom was being ultra polite, but I could tell Dr Long had got under his skin. I couldn't blame him – I had disliked him on sight.

"Well, I'll just have to take this up with your superiors, then. You do know who I am, I suppose?"

"Yes, Dr Long, but I'm afraid that makes no difference."

I heard the door bang as Dr Long slammed out. Hoping it was safe to emerge, I popped my head round the corner.

"Is it all clear?"

Tom smiled. "Yes, he's gone. Wow, was he livid though. What have you done to him, eh?"

"Me?" I asked astonished.

"Well, he was asking which room you were in." He must have seen the shock on my face. "Now don't worry – I didn't tell him. Oh, I could have done, but I just didn't take to his attitude."

"Me neither and I've only met him once. What do you think he wanted?"

"I don't know but if his intentions weren't honourable I didn't want to be responsible."

"I really appreciate that, Tom. I hope he won't really take action against you."

"Don't you worry your head about that. I've done what I thought right and I guess there's no-one going to get into trouble for doing that, now, is there?" His smile was untroubled, so I smiled back and then remembered what I had come for.

"The phone – well there's one over there, but it's not very private, and if HE comes back – well he'll see you for sure and I gather that's not quite to your liking."

"You're right there, Tom, I didn't at all like the way he looked at me when I saw him at the Conference Centre – and he was very rude."

"Sounds like him. He's only been in the city for a while, but thinks himself a hell of a bigwig. Maybe he is brilliant at his job, but that's no reason to go around with that attitude. No, what I suggest is that you use the phone in my office at the back here."

"I'd really appreciate that. I've got a phone card."

He led the way into the office and found the code I needed for Australia and then he went out, discreetly shutting the door behind him. It took a few rings before Gabriel answered and

I became anxious he wasn't there. The incident with Dr Long had put me on edge and made me feel vulnerable which made me all the more eager to hear a familiar voice. Eventually, thankfully, he answered.

"Sara, thank God you rang. Look, there isn't time to explain, but I think you should leave straight away."

I gasped. "But, Gabriel I've only just got here. And why should I leave?"

"Do you remember the photographs and the stuff that came from Paul – the feather? Well, it's best they don't come into anyone else's hands, Sara, and the only way of guaranteeing that is for you to leave."

"Can't I just post them off somewhere."

"I wish it was that simple. I know how much this trip means to you and I'll reimburse all your costs, but I think someone already knows you've got the feather and photographs. Don't ask me how."

My stomach lurched as I thought of Dr Long. Could his strange behaviour be something other than someone with a roving eye?

"What's so special about them?"

"I don't want to go into that over the phone. Just get out of Vancouver and make sure no one knows where you're going. Please, Sara. I'm sorry to have you got you into all this – but I think you'd have been involved anyway."

"Does this have something to do with the birds, then?" I asked.

"In a way. This is important, Sara – can you still follow Mistral in her dreams?"

"A lot has happened since you went, Gabriel."

"I knew I should have kept in touch but with Paul's ......"

"Paul's what, Gabriel?"

"Never mind that now. What's been happening – have you contacted her since you arrived in Canada?"

It was so strange to hear someone talking so matter-of-factly about something so odd.

"I haven't really tried, Gabriel, but I'm as certain as I can be that this is where I'm supposed to be. That's why I asked you about the photographs – where they were taken."

It was his turn to gasp. "You mean you've been there?"

"Only in my dreams. I sort of saw the lake in the photo and heard shots and then the lake filled with blood and ..." I trailed off – it was all so tenuous.

I heard him groan. "This is getting a bit beyond me. Look, Sara I don't want you looking for this place, not until I get there, anyway."

My heart lifted and a feeling of relief flooded through me. "You're coming here, Gabriel?"

"I'm going to have to. Kate will manage until I get back."

I wondered who Kate might be. "One thing before you go, Gabriel. Do you know of anyone called Dr Long, a palaeontologist?"

"Yes, I most certainly do. Why do you ask?" I explained. "That confirms it. I want you out of Vancouver within the next hour. Is that clear?"

"Okay, okay, anything for a quiet life."

"It won't be if you don't do as I ask."

"But where should I go?"

"I've friends in Prince Rupert I'd like you to go to. I've already been in touch with them and they'll put you up until I get there."

Wheels within wheels, I thought, that's where I was heading anyway, but I didn't say anything.

"But it's over four hundred miles away, Gabriel. I can't afford the air fare and it'd take two days to drive it on my own."

"You're very well informed, Sara," he observed suspiciously but I kept quiet. Now was not the time to tell him I wanted to go to the Queen Charlotte Islands. "Look – if you can book the flight with your card for now I'll repay you. I'd rather you got there as soon as possible."

I took down the address of his friends and rang off. Once the sound of his voice had gone and I'd thought over what he'd said I began to feel very alone and vulnerable. I got the bus timetable in my bag, so checked it for buses within the hour.

I went out to find Tom.

"Thanks again, Tom. I'm going to have an early night – I've still not got used to this jetlag."

"It affects people all different ways. Well, I'll say goodnight, then. Sleep well."

"Thanks, Tom. See you."

It was horrible having to deceive him, but the one thing that Gabriel had managed to drum into me was that there was no time to lose and I was in danger where I was. I hurried back to the room and packed my bag, leaving some of the food and my dressing gown on the unmade bed to make it look as if I was coming back. It might not buy me much time but it might be enough. Fortunately the accommodation was on the ground floor so I was able to heft my luggage out of the window and then follow it – undignified, but then I had no pretensions to being a lady at that moment – or any other, I suppose. Dusk hadn't yet fallen so I just hoped that the shadows of the buildings would hide my exit.

CHAPTER EIGHT

I felt the need for hurry deep inside in a knot in my stomach and I knew I didn't have much time if Dr Long was involved. Failure wouldn't sit kindly on his sagging shoulders, he would be certain to have approached someone who wouldn't refuse him the information he obviously wanted of my whereabouts and how to get his hands on the photographs. Gabriel hadn't said in so many words that he was involved but I could put two and two together. I had been known to make five, but I was sure this time it was four. There was just something very unpleasant about the man.

There seemed to be a lot of coming and going generally about the campus, so I hoped I wouldn't look conspicuous carrying my suitcase and rucksack. I could feel the rucksack burning a hole in my back where the notes containing the photographs and feather rested.

It was now the middle of the afternoon so I decided my best bet was to stay in a hotel near the airport and fly to Prince Rupert in the morning if there weren't any flights that night. Dr Long would have no way of knowing where I was going and would surely give up once they'd found I'd gone from the University.

As the bus approached I saw a car overtake it and turn into the campus. The face of the passenger was that of Dr Long. He'd wasted no time and suddenly I felt very cold and vulnerable. Up until then I had not really been sure this was serious, but the speed with which he had presumably found out what he wanted to know, and returned, showed how serious he was. Did he intend just to ask me for the photographs or wait until I was out and steal them? Getting no answer would he force the door and find me missing? How long would it take Dr Long to find I wasn't actually there? How long would Tom be able to stall him? All these were rhetorical questions. I didn't have the answers and hoped not to be around to find out. The over-riding question, though, was what had I got myself mixed up in and how quickly could I get to Prince Rupert?

Thankfully I got on to the bus. Only when I looked again at the timetable did I realise I was on the wrong bus, I shouldn't be heading back to the Centre, but out to the Airport. I got off at the next stop and decided the only thing to do was to call a cab. I found a telephone booth in a café and rang from there and then found the number for the airport. There was a flight to Prince in Rupert in an hour's and a half's time – I should just make it. I waited there until the cab arrived, looking round at the least sound and alternating between feeling stupid at being so cloak and dagger and just plain scared. Everything was so alien, the accent and the bustling traffic, even the food seemed to be mostly Chinese. I felt rootless and alone and I longed to be back in Wales in a familiar environment, amongst friends.

With a great feeling of relief I saw the cab arrive. I climbed in and asked to be taken to the airport.

"You from England?" he asked

"Well, Wales, actually."

"I've an aunt living in Swansea, South Wales. Anywhere near there."

"No, not really."

Is this what it feels like to be on the run, I wondered? I'm not a naturally cagey person and the driver was only trying to be friendly. I smiled to myself when I thought that to him the hundred odd miles to South Wales was probably a drive to work for some of the people living in this huge continent, yet I'd just said 'not really' and meant it.

"Do you want internal departures or international?" he asked.

"Internal, please." I would have liked to have asked him where I needed to go for Prince Rupert, but held back.

Thankful I was travelling light I made my way to the airline flying to Prince Rupert. There was quite a queue and only half an hour before the plane left. I noticed several people at kiosk type machines obviously keying in card numbers and other details. This looked like a quicker way to book your ticket if you were paying by credit card but I had no idea how to use it. There were airport staff showing people how they operated the machines, but no one available for me to ask how to use the one I was staring at bewildered. Should I join the queue at the manual desk?

Before I had made up my mind, a voice behind me spoke.

"Do you need some help with that machine?" The tone was impatient. I turned to see who had spoken. A man stood there leaning on a luggage trolley. He was a man in his mid thirties with light brown hair and sunburnt skin that made his hazel eyes look paler. "Only my plane leaves in half an hour."

"Mine too." I replied tartly

"Prince Rupert?" he asked. I nodded. "Right then let me show you what to do." His tone had softened a bit.

When we had both got our tickets he showed me the way to the luggage check in. As I got my passport out, the pass I'd been issued by the Conference Centre fell out of my bag. The "impatient" man reached to pick it up, but his movement was slow and the man behind him picked it up instead and glanced at it before handing it back to me. I thanked him, now really on edge.

We'd no sooner gone through to the waiting lounge than our flight was called. So no cup of tea and I'd had no time for anything since my early lunch. I hoped there'd be something on the airplane. The plane we boarded only took about thirty people, but there was space for me to have a seat with no-one beside me for which I was thankful. I was tired out by the stress of the last few hours and wanted a chance to relax. I kept my rucksack with me, tucking it under the seat so that I was aware of it the whole journey and what it contained.

It was a lovely sunny day and the mountains beneath us looked stunning, their bulk traced by rivers, their steep sides massed green by trees. Even now there was a sprinkling of snow on the peaks and the valleys ran between them like veins in cheese. As I stared out of the window I wondered where Misty and her family were. I had no indication from the dreams how far away they were and it was impossible they could be physically close – the miles in between were too huge. But I could still feel them inside.

The two hours went quickly, but then I found there was a further coach and ferry journey to get to Prince Rupert. The airport was built on an island just off the city as the whole area is so mountainous and flat areas are at a premium. Most trading had always been, and still was, done by boat. Only in the last one hundred years had it been connected by railway and road.

True to its name as the city of rainbows it was cloudy when we arrived but not actually raining. Throughout the journey, I'd felt as if someone was staring at me but hadn't wanted to look around in case I drew attention to myself. Assuming it was the man I had held up at the airport, I was rather surprised, and none too happy, when he chose to sit next to me on the coach. I was reading the book on the Queen Charlotte Islands.

"Are you planning to go there, then?" he asked suddenly.

"Why have you been there?"

His face took on a sour expression. "Sure – that's where I got this stiff leg – fell while climbing – so I'm told – I don't remember." Obviously not a man of many words.

"I'm sorry to hear that." I replied politely.

"Yes got bits of metal in it, but I guess I'm lucky. Could have died out there."

"I'm sure you could have," I tried to sound interested.

All of a sudden he smiled and his face lit up, the pain lines smoothed out. "I'm bothering you, aren't I? Sorry. My name's Andrew by the way, Andrew Fraser."

"Hello, Andrew Fraser – and you're not bothering me, really." I shut the book decisively. "I probably won't ever get to the Islands anyway."

"I'm not keen to go back – after the accident." He looked like he was going to say more but contented himself with handing me a business card. "Look – take my card – you never know when you might need a friend. I've also a part share in a plane, so I could always fly you to the Islands."

Was he making up for being impatient at the airport? "Thanks – I'll bear it in mind." I tucked the card in the inside pocket of my jacket. As I did so, I felt the earring I was carrying as a talisman and I though of the birds. Something must have shown in my face.

"Are you alright?" Andrew asked.

"Yes – fine, thanks." I answered hurriedly. "Why shouldn't I be?"

"That I don't know," he looked at me thoughtfully, "and I don't think you're about to tell me, are you – and, of course, why should you?"

"It's nothing." I certainly wasn't about to explain about the birds to a stranger in a strange land.

"Okay – I'll mind my own business. We've arrived anyway."

The coach dropped us off in the centre of Prince Rupert outside a hotel. I went inside to use the telephone to call a cab to take me to the address that Gabriel had given me. I'd given up trying to find an area that my mobile phone worked in. Andrew followed me in, limping stiffly after the restrictions of the journey.

"If you're after a cab why don't we share?"

My inclination was to say "no" but it seemed churlish. "Okay."

He rang the number for a cab above the phone. "They'll be here in five minutes."

We waited in silence along with the man who'd picked up my pass at the airport. I was aware of him glancing at me, but he looked away when I looked back. Andrew looked as if he'd liked to have asked something. I was glad he didn't as I didn't feel in a very confiding mood – I hadn't even given him my name.

Not having a clue where I was going, I showed the address to the cab driver. He then asked Andrew where he wanted dropping off.

"Out towards Port Edward – I'll show you when we get there."

"I'll drop the young lady off first, then."

"Good idea," declared Andrew. "Drive past the Museum, though – she'd like to see that."

We passed a wooden building with beautifully carved totem poles as part of the structure, the overlapping logs giving it a simple grandeur. "That's where you want to go if you want to see some of the heritage of the Queen Charlotte Islands – the history – even some of the totem poles. Worth a visit."

It only took five minutes to reach the street I needed. The main streets were all so wide and the shops and houses almost frontier town to my eyes. So many were built of wood, with clapperboard and corrugated roofs predominating. The houses on the outskirts were similarly built of wood with verandas and a variety and an irregularity that added to their charm. With trees almost completely surrounding the city, huge and numerous, it was the obvious material to use.

Andrew looked surprised when we pulled up outside a house on the outskirts of the town. It was near the end of a street of houses, its side bordered by trees, its veranda decorated with pots of bright flowers and its boarding painted a deep blue.

"Hey, I know this place. Ben and Ella Lawrence live here. She came to see me when – .. ." He fell silent and appeared to have forgotten my existence so I got out of the cab. The cab driver put my bags on the sidewalk and I reached for my money.

"No, leave it," Andrew called from inside the cab. "I'll sort it." He leant out of the window. "I won't get out – the leg – but remember you've got my card. Phone at any time – okay?"

"Thanks, I'll remember." Who knew what lay ahead, when I might need a friend? At that moment I felt very much alone, so I smiled at him but he'd already told the driver to carry on. A strange man, I thought, not one it would be easy to get to know. Maybe he was different before the accident.

I rang the bell of the house and waited. I could hear raised voices that were cut off as footsteps came down the stairs to the door. A young girl opened it, not much above five feet in her presently bare feet, with the beautiful high cheekbones of the native Indian and the soft brown skin that went with it.

"Are you Sara?" she asked. I nodded. "Come on in, then."

She closed the door behind me but not before having a look up the street. She led the way in. Standing in a doorway to the back of the house was a tall, well set young man with a gentleness in his eyes that belied the determined set of his mouth and shoulders. His dark hair was tied back and further emphasised the strong jaw. Beside him the girl looked tiny.

"Hi, I'm Ben Lawrence and this is Ella." He had a slow, sure way of speaking which fitted with his build. "Gabriel's told us all about you. We are to take special care of you it seems."

I smiled and shook the hand he extended, warmed by the firmness of the handshake. "That sounds good to me. Just a cup of tea would do for now, though."

We went through to the kitchen and Ella put the kettle on the stove. There was a lovely old pine table in the middle of the large room and we sat down there.

"Now, first things first. Sorry to get down to business straight away, but we need to know if you still have the photographs and feather safe." I nodded. "That's a relief. Did you have any problems?"

"No more than a few." I smiled. I felt safe in this huge kitchen with the warmth of wood around me. Wood had always affected me that way.

"Tell us." Ben commanded. It was a relief to be able to discuss it all with someone who had some idea what was going on. At least, I assumed he did.

When I'd finished, Ben looked over at Ella. "We'd better get ready to leave straight away."

"Can you tell me what's so special about these photographs, Ben? Gabriel wouldn't discuss it over the phone."

"I do, but I'd rather leave it till he gets here. There might be more to add by then."

"When do you reckon that will be?"

"Within the next half an hour, if the flights all run to schedule. He was leaving Australia last night, our time, to fly to Los Angeles and then on up to Vancouver from there. He wasn't keen going through Vancouver, but there was no choice."

"Anyway come and see the room we've prepared for you," Ella intervened, "then you can freshen up a bit."

She took me up a flight of stairs and into a room with a sloping ceiling on one side, which was, just as the kitchen, lined in wood. I couldn't resist laying my hand on it and she smiled.

"I'll leave you to it. If you're not down we'll let you know when Gabriel gets here."

"Thanks."

I unpacked my wash things, wondering how long they'd be out of the suitcase this time. Feeling guilty about doing it, I hid the photographs and feather behind the cedar bed head.

I looked out through the window into the large garden that stretched at the back of the house, bordered by trees. Its size was a surprise but the biggest surprise was the sight of several aviaries taking up a fair amount of the space. Home from home, I thought. I sat for a while just staring out of the window enjoying the peace, then went to join Ben and Ella downstairs.

They were both sitting at the kitchen table and their discussion suspended when I walked in.

"We weren't sure whether you'd want a rest or not." Ella said quickly to hide the pause my entrance had caused.

"No, I'm too wound up for that and Gabriel should be here soon, shouldn't he?" I asked.

Ben checked his watch, but I felt it was only a gesture; they both knew the time perfectly well and were on edge.

"I couldn't help noticing the aviaries from the window. What birds do you have in them?"

Ella took over the conversation. "Quite a variety usually – anything from little auks to bald eagles. Whatever blows in really. Like you we care for them and return them when we can."

"Will I have a chance to see them, do you think?"

"Maybe later. At the moment we're waiting for Gabriel to ring so Ben can go and pick him up." She looked again at her watch.

"He's late isn't he?"

"Not by much." But the worry showed in her voice. More and more I wondered what I'd got myself into.

Suddenly Ben got up. "Look, I'm going down to the airport anyway. I'll ring if I can." He turned to me, his tone steady and kindly. "Don't worry, now, Sara. I'm sure everything is in hand. When we come back, though, I'd like a talk with you on your own, if you wouldn't mind."

Surprised I replied. "Of course."

Ella and I sat and chatted whilst we waited to hear from Ben or Gabriel. Every so often the conversation would lapse as we both wondered what was going on. Gabriel was now over an hour and a half late, but that could easily be accounted for by traffic problems. Ella brought some books from the shelves in the living room for me to look at, books concerning the care of birds here in Canada. They'd have been fascinating at any other time, but I found myself just flicking through the pages without taking very much in. I would have liked to ask Ella about Paul and Kate, but felt I would only get an evasive reply.

Suddenly I shivered for no reason. Ella was busy in the kitchen so I put my head in my hands and concentrated on the feeling that had made my flesh quiver. It was Misty calling to me and I didn't understand what she was trying to tell me. I sensed an urgency about her and the image of her pulling on my sleeve came into my mind. If Misty was in trouble I had no way of helping her, no means of knowing where she was, but a strong desire to go to her welled up in me. I went into the kitchen to say something to Ella, but couldn't find the words to explain how I felt – instead I made an excuse to go upstairs.

I retrieved the photographs and feather from behind the bed, put it in my bag, and, leaving a note saying I'd gone for a walk, I let myself quietly out of the house. A walk in the damp air might just clear my brain.

The urgency I felt from Mistral continued and I felt helpless. As I reached the bottom of the road and tried to decide whether to go right or left, I heard a car drive slowly past Ben and Ella's house. I turned to go back thinking it was Gabriel here at last. But no one got out of the car. It was parked on the opposite side of the road from Ben and Ella's. Immediately I felt that something was not quite right. I wondered if I was being paranoid again, but a bit of caution would do no harm.

Quickly I chose the road to the left to go down which led back to the main road, but only a short way so that the car would still be in sight but it would be unlikely they could see me. Nothing happened for a while and I began to think that I was imagining things and it was probably just a courting couple or something, when the passenger door opened and a man got out, closing the door quietly behind him. The driver started the engine and drove a little further down the road towards where I was standing. I stood back quickly, knocking my knee on the wall by my side and biting back a curse.

The engine came to a stop and I heard the car door open and close. Hoping it was clear, I ventured a quick peep round the corner, in time to see the driver join his companion. With a nod the driver went down the side of Ben's house towards the back. From this distance I couldn't identify either of them, and for all I knew they could be friends of Ben and Ella, but there was something furtive about their behaviour that precluded this.

The passenger knocked on the door and Ella opened it, but

seemed reluctant to let him in. From where I stood, it looked like he showed her a pass of some sort and then firmly pressed the door so she had to admit him. If they were something to do with the photographs how could I leave Ella alone to face them? Yet, I argued, what would I gain by returning if it was the photographs they wanted – I had them in my shoulder bag so if they couldn't find them in the house, surely they'd just leave. I decided it would be best to wait for Ben and Gabriel to come back

Why didn't Ben and Gabriel come? I checked my watch and they were now nearly two hours overdue. I tried contacting Misty, but couldn't raise her image. Perhaps I was just too tense.

An estate car came down the road slowly, but it went past the house, so couldn't be Ben. It was, though, I realised with surprise, Andrew Fraser. As if by instinct he pulled into the road close to where I was lurking. I had to decide if he was to be trusted, but he had already said that he knew Ben and Ella. I had nowhere else to turn. Throwing caution to the wind I approached his car and climbed into the passenger seat.

A startled Andrew turned to face me. "Well, hello again, Sara. Where did you spring from?"

So he had noticed my name back at the airport. But more than anything at this stage I needed someone who might help and so far he'd shown me nothing to indicate I should mistrust him.

"You know the house I'm staying at – Ben and Ella – you said you knew them?"

"Yes, I did – why?"

"Well – I know we've hardly met, but could I ask you a favour?"

"You can always ask. What is it – are you in some sort of trouble already – I only left you an hour ago," he said in mock exasperation.

"Sort of – well it's more Ella, really. You see, Ben's not there at the moment and these men have gone into the house and I'm not sure if they're – you know – okay."

"And why wouldn't they be 'okay'?"

"I'm possibly getting this all out of proportion – maybe they're just from the gas board."

"And you want me to march up to the door and ask for their credentials, is that it – or, in my case, limp up to the door." He smiled wryly.

"Okay, okay it all sounds far-fetched, I know, but there are reasons."

"What have you got yourself mixed up in, Sara?" He gave me a long appraising look that made me blush.

"I'm really not sure." I said and shivered.

"Well, that's helpful." He drummed his fingers on the steering wheel. "Look – if I do help you out, I shall expect something in return." He must have caught the look on my face. He laughed. "No, no, that's not what I meant – although – come to think of it ..." again I noticed how his smile lit up the otherwise dour face. "If you'd bothered to read the card I gave you – I take it you didn't?" I shook my head. "Well, it clearly states that I'm a journalist and it goes with the territory that I'm nosy."

"Seems an appropriate qualification for a journalist." I replied in a small voice. Involving a journalist suddenly didn't seem such a good idea.

"So is expecting a pound of flesh ... in the way of a story. There just has to be one here and I want first bite."

"That's not up to me. Perhaps it would just be better if I wait for Ben to come back. But – thanks all the same." I opened the car door ready to get out and, as I did, a car pulled up a little way up from the Ben and Ella's and, even at that distance I could recognise Gabriel.

"Quick, can you reach that car that's just pulled up before they get to the door?"

Without a word he started up the engine – only then did I notice that the car was adapted with hand controls. Obviously his leg limited his ability to drive. It certainly showed no sign of it, though as he sped up the road towards the car with Gabriel now getting out of it. He had hardly stopped when I wrenched open the door and the next thing I was being hugged to Gabriel's lean muscular chest. Any other time it would have been bliss, but this was, unfortunately, not the time.

"Quick, Gabriel" – it came out muffled as I was still against his chest – "Ella is in the house with these two men and I don't know who they are or what they want, but they've been there for more than half an hour."

Ben's "Heck, no." coincided with Gabriel's "Now calm down and tell us properly."

I gave them a brief outline of what had happened. The car

was not one Ben recognised.

Andrew had come up by this time having parked his car.

"Who's this?" Gabriel asked abruptly. He wasn't usually rude, so I reckoned he must be very tired or very worried. I introduced Andrew. Ben glanced at him sharply when he heard his name, but said nothing. I could tell that neither of them were at all happy that I'd involved him.

"What have you told him?" Gabriel asked.

Andrew intervened. "Absolutely nothing, but I'm sure she will when she's ready. I'll say goodbye, then. You know where to reach me, Sara."

"Thanks, Andrew. I'm sorry."

"Don't be. See you – I hope."

Gabriel frowned after him and was going to say something but Ben forestalled him.

"I'm going to find what's going on with Ella. You two stay out here – I mean it, Gabriel – it's better if I tackle these guys alone. If I'm not out in ten minutes, you'd best call the police." There was a deep frown on his broad forehead. "I don't like this. How could anyone have found out either of you are here, if that is what they want?"

"I wish I knew. We'll wait in the car until you come out – okay?"

"I think it might be better if you go to the lodge – take the car – we've got the pickup."

"Not until I know what's happened to Ella." Gabriel was firm.

"Okay, but any sign of things going wrong and you go. Understood?"

"Understood. We'll give you ten minutes."

We watched Ben let himself in acting as if nothing was wrong. I found I was holding my breath again. We seemed to be staring intently at the house for hours, my hands rigid in my lap, Gabriel rubbing the bump on his nose, but when I checked my watch I discovered it was exactly seven minutes before the door opened and the two men I had seen enter emerged, one of them limping.

As they headed for their car, I saw the one in profile and realised with shock that it was the man I had seen at the airport and again at the hotel, the one who'd picked up my pass. I thought again of Ben's wide, determined set of shoulder and mouth and was grateful he was on our side, and grateful he had been able to rid the house of those two. It was fairly obvious by now that they weren't from the Gas Board.

Ben signalled for us to come to the house. Although we hadn't seen each other for days, Gabriel and I hadn't exchanged a word all the time we were waiting for Ben. There was so much to say too – maybe too much.

Ella greeted us. "Thank goodness you're both alright." She reached up and gave Gabriel a hug.

"We were a lot more concerned about you," he said as he ruffled her hair. He looked about him. "Looks like they were after the photographs then. They didn't hurt you did they, Ella?"

"No." she replied "Threatened, but didn't actually hurt me. They didn't say much, just searched the place. They soon left when Ben said he'd already called the police." She looked at Ben smiling. "Plus a little extra persuasion." Ella turned to me. "What made you go off like that?"

"I'm really sorry Ella. I just sort of had to – and then I just didn't know what to do when I saw them go into the house."

"Hey, I'm not cross about it – I'm just thankful you did. I'd found your note just before they came and luckily I'd thrown it in the bin. I just told them that the stuff in your room belonged to a relative from Vancouver. They couldn't prove it was yours – no labels – no passport. You don't know how relieved I was about that. Presumably everything, including the photographs are in that bag?"

I nodded and reached in for the package. Gabriel stopped me.

"Leave that now. Ben's right – we should go to the lodge. Go and pack your things as quickly as possible."

As I packed it came to me that the reason I had so fortuitously left the house was Misty and there was no sign of alarm from her now. Had she been warning me and if so, how did she know about the danger?

I packed quickly, thinking that my premonition about how long I'd be there was right – I never even got to sleep in the bed and I was by now, very tired. So much had happened all I could do was go with the tide. With that thought came another – my longing to embark for the peace of the Queen Charlotte Islands and a glimpse of Peale's Peregrine was growing.

CHAPTER NINE

It took us half an hour to reach the lodge. Set up a track which would be hard on an ordinary car but which the pickup tackled with no problem, the lodge was a large cabin surrounded on three sides by cedar trees. The fourth side had a glorious view over a small lake with an island in the middle of it. Alongside the track ran a river, tumbling over large boulders on its way to feed the lake. What a wonderful place to spend a holiday I thought, but I guessed that it was unlikely to be that for any of us.

Ben had arranged for the injured birds they had in to be fed and he'd brought with him in a box one peregrine that needed careful force-feeding. It lifted my heart to see a real live peregrine again and I asked Ben if I could help him feed while Ella sorted us something to eat. It was now near eight in the evening and I was tired and hungry, my internal clock thrown out by the three thousand mile journey.

We went together to a lean-to shed at the back. We got the bird out of the box and she remained passive in Ben's hands. He had been treating her for five days now and she was slow to put on weight.

"There's something on her mind, I reckon. It's a bit worrying as we can find nothing anatomically wrong with her and no infection. That's one of the reasons I was so pleased when Gabriel said he was coming. He'll sort her out."

"Each time I see them I'm startled by their beauty." The bird gazed back at me with her velvet brown eye. "Do you want me to hold her or feed her?"

"Would you mind holding her? I want to check the back of her throat."

I took her from him but as my hands tightened gently round her body, clamping her wings, my mind was pierced by a bright light that made me wince. Ben was watching me closely.

"Are you alright, Sara, or is the light too bright?"

I looked up at him, bewildered, but there was no light, and the one in my mind had dimmed, leaving an after image of shadows left by many wings.

Ben smiled apologetically at me. "Sorry, I just wanted to be sure."

"Sure about what?"

"Did you see the light?"

I nodded. "But I was sure it was inside my head."

"It was. She has the power to do this and I reckon that's what is sapping her strength. I just wanted to know if Gabriel was right about you."

"I'm sorry, Ben, this is going over my head a bit. Do you mind if I sit down?"

"Here, give her to me." Gladly I handed the peregrine back to him. She turned to look at me before he put her back in the box and in her eyes I saw what I had first seen in Misty's eyes. Immediately, as I closed my eyes for a second, I saw Misty and Rift, but no Scrap, and they were sitting relaxed, preening and content. I hoped this was as it was and not wishful thinking on my part. I was feeling the separation from them and still feared for them. How strangely deep the roots of their love had gone.

"Now, give me your hand." Ben commanded. "Close your eyes and relax."

It took me a while to oblige – I was so far out of my depth, relaxation was difficult. With an effort I drained all the tension and tiredness out of my body and suddenly my mind opened up – I saw Ben and behind him, with wings outspread, a huge bald eagle. I had never seen one in the flesh, but this bird seemed massive, its wings so wide and strong. I looked on in awe and then I heard a voice say "Listen", but I had no idea whether it was Ben who had spoken.

In my mind I answered – "I am listening." A jumble of images followed, too fast for me to grasp. "Slow down," I breathed in my head. Immediately the flow slowed and I could see lakes and mountains covered in tall trees, familiar territory I would have thought for a bald eagle. Then I knew I was flying with him and it took my breath away. I had only ever flown with Misty and her flight was more dashing than this – this was a feeling of being in power over the air, commanding it to support the huge wings as he soared with only a slight lift of a feather end, majestic – in charge.

With Misty I felt the joy she took in the wind under her wings, but with this magnificent bird I felt an acceptance of it as his due. The power was stunning, and yet I preferred the light heartedness of Misty. Then he took me to her and there was Rift too and Scrap, and it was the place where I'd turned the peregrine to stone. I knew by their attitude they were waiting for me.

"Come." I heard in my head and I felt a wing waft across my cheek and I opened my eyes in surprise. There was nothing there, only Ben and the breeze from the door.

Ben smiled into my eyes. "Did you see him?" He sighed with relief when I nodded. "Magnificent isn't he? I call him Vigilant because he always seems to be there."

"He's your guiding spirit as Mistral is mine." The realisation filled me with awe – and relief that I was not alone – that he too could 'sense' a bird.

"I healed him as you healed Mistral. But it goes much deeper than that as you know. You're the first person I've been able to share this with other than Ella and Gabriel. Thank the gods you've come. I think we're going to need all the help we can get. Come on let's get back to the others."

Gabriel was helping Ella empty the box of food she'd packed. When we came in Gabriel sat down at the long kitchen table and Ben and I joined him. A welcome steaming jug of coffee sat in the middle of the table and I could hear Ella preparing food in the small kitchen.

"Right, I think it's about time we brought Sara up to date with what's going on."

"That'd be nice," I responded sweetly.

"By the way, Gabriel – you were right." Ben interrupted. "She could sense Vigilant but I sure don't know what she saw. Sara?"

How to describe it? "It was a bit like flying with a barn door, none of Misty's delicacy." I smiled teasingly at Ben. He just smiled back, not offended – he'd seen my face – he knew how impressed I'd really been. "He took me to a place I keep seeing in my dreams."

"Is it anything like the place in the photographs?" Gabriel asked eagerly.

"I think so, but it's hard to tell. Are you going to tell me more about these photographs which have, quite frankly, put me to a lot of trouble?" They fell about laughing. I had to join in – it had sounded rather prim, but at least it helped release some of the tension we all felt.

"For such gross understatement, I'm tempted not to," Gabriel declared. "In fact, would you mind very much if we reversed things and you told me what's happened since I rang you in Vancouver. Then I promise we'll tell you everything we know – which, I hasten to add, is not anywhere near as much as we'd like."

I went through it all – right up to the moment I'd arrived at Prince Rupert, making it clear in my own defence, how I'd come to meet Andrew Fraser.

"I'm sorry if I was rude to him, Sara, but until we know exactly what is going on, we really can't trust anyone, and he did, after all, know you were at the house, which we don't think anyone else did."

"Well, he'd dropped me off there – and he said he knew Ben."

"Ben?" Gabriel turned to him.

"The name sounds kinda familiar, but I don't reckon I know the guy." Ben dismissed it. "Anyway are we any nearer to identifying the photographs or the feather, Gabriel?"

"No, I found out very little back in Australia. Kate knew Paul was onto something – was quite hyped up about it – but he never discussed it with her. But she did mention that Paul'd had a visit from Dr Julian Long. And that was after the date on the microbiology report. She'd heard raised voices, but he'd asked her to leave the room, so couldn't intervene." He turned to me. "That's why I was worried when I heard he'd turned up again, Sara – and that's why I wanted you out of Vancouver. Until we know more about what's happened to Paul – I think we need to avoid the man."

"Fine by me," I declared. "I didn't take to him one little bit. But who is this Paul?"

"Paul works with me at the University." Gabriel explained. "He told Kate he was having some holiday and then going to the conference and he hasn't been heard of since – and that was over ten days ago, now."

"He was supposed to be staying over with us." Ben said. "But we've not had as much as a call from him."

"He may not be a particularly thoughtful guy," Gabriel acknowledged, "but he would have kept in touch with Kate."

Ella came in from the kitchen with bread, cheese and fruit for us all. I realised I was starving.

"He only called her once when he stayed last time." Ella commented. "And they'd not long been married then."

"Let's have a look at the feather and report, Sara." Gabriel suggested. "They might, at least, give us some clues. I checked with the microbiology department and Paul had had a feather tested through them, but they knew no more than that."

"But where did the feather come from, Gabriel?" I asked as I got the envelope out of my bag.

"That we don't know for sure, but the fact that Paul was on his way here and sent me the letter with the feather in it the day he left, knowing I was coming to the conference – well it has to be connected." I handed him the feather. He looked at it carefully. "You're right, Sara, I haven't seen anything quite like this feather before."

Ben had picked up the photographs – after all he was most familiar with the area. "Hey, Gabriel – there's some figures on the back of this one – looks like a map reference to me."

He handed it to Gabriel. "Well, if it is, it's not longitude and latitude, so we'd need to know which map it was taken from."

I gathered my thoughts. "So that's why the photographs are so important. You think they show you where he might have gone and may lead you to where he found the feather?"

"It would make sense." Ben stated.

"Have you told the police he's missing?" I asked.

"Kate's so used to him just going off without letting her know where he is, so she did delay," his tone was defensive, "but she has let them know now. If I hadn't been so worried about her, Sara, I wouldn't have just gone like that, but she'd got herself so worked up and she's only got two months to go – I thought she might miscarry like last time." His blue eyes darkened with the thought of it and I wondered at his relationship with this 'Kate'.

"I didn't really like leaving her yesterday," he went on, "but then I needed to make sure you were alright, Sara."

"Well, thank you for that." I wasn't going to confess how let down I'd felt – not in front of the others.

Ella got up to get a bottle of wine and I helped her get out the glasses to give myself time to think. She was very quiet and I felt there was something about all this she didn't approve of. I remembered the raised voices when I first came to their house and wondered. I'd got myself embroiled in something I was neither happy about nor understood. 'Thanks, Misty' I said in my head. 'We need you' came back.

I couldn't resist asking her quietly – "Have you met Kate, Ella?"

"No, Sara, but Gabriel introduced them – Paul and Kate – so I think he feels responsible in some way."

I wondered how well he'd known her before she met Paul. We sat down at the table and Ella poured the wine.

"The fact that Dr Long is onto this only indicates that Paul's got himself tangled in something a bit dodgy." Gabriel rubbed a hand over his face. "Long's a weak man and has a reputation for flying rather close to the wind where his 'discoveries' are concerned. No one has been able to prove that he has stolen other people's work, but it is strongly rumoured that he has in the past. Now he has a larger professional reputation to protect, we rather fear he may go to greater lengths."

"Are you so sure that the photograph and feather have anything to do with a 'discovery', then, Gabriel? And how did Long get involved?" I asked.

"We can't be sure. Paul may have told someone else about it, maybe to enlist their help with finance."

"But does this have anything to do with the birds – our birds,

Gabriel? That's why I'm here, after all."

Ben replied. "We believe so and your dream seems to sort of confirm it. It's also too much of a coincidence that four people that Gabriel knows have this strange ability to 'hear' birds."

"Four people?" I asked startled.

"As far as we know. With a bit of luck we'll all be meeting soon. They were coming to the conference anyway, but Gabriel's warned them to come straight here. They may be needed."

"Do the birds tie in with Paul – was he one of the 'dreamers'?"

"No." Gabriel answered. "But he knew of Ben, Joe and Callum through me. You know the last few months he's been a bit distant and on edge." Gabriel shook his head baffled. "I wish I'd taken more notice."

"So you think the photograph and the dreams are connected, Gabriel?" I was still trying to work my way through the morass.

"You've been having the dreams for about – what – three months, haven't you Sara?" Gabriel asked. I nodded. "So has Ben. I've been having them a bit longer than that." He ignored the look I gave him. "Now it seems Paul may have made his 'discovery' about the time those dreams started. How much urgency do you feel in these dreams, Sara?"

"It's increasing all the time." I replied

"That's what Ben feels, too. Look, would you and Ben be willing to experiment join forces and see what you can see combined?"

I needed time to think – I'd be opening up my mind to someone else and putting Ben in touch with my family. I'd be taking a risk on their behalf. I put my head in my hands as I thought it through. Instantly Misty, Scrap and Rift were there and I heard the voice I now thought of as Vigilant's. "Trust" – it said.

I lifted my head. "Okay, I'll give it a try."

Gabriel turned to Ella. "Could you try and contact the other two – see if they're in Vancouver yet." Ella got up reluctantly. "Joe may have a mobile phone with him – let's hope there's a signal."

Suddenly an image entered my head – the gentle weather beaten face. I gasped. "Joe – is he the man in the mirror?"

Gabriel nodded, a smile on his face. "You recognised him, Gabriel, but you didn't say anything."

"I reckoned you were traumatised enough as it was and it could wait."

"But have I seen the other one?"

"You spoke to him in Scotland – I was staying with him." Gabriel replied.

"And he also cares for birds if I remember rightly."

Ella came back into the room. "They've been held up in Vancouver, but should be here by first thing tomorrow morning."

"Then we'll just have to wait," replied Gabriel. He turned to Ben. "Could you take Sara into the studio and try and contact Vigilant and the others."

"Sure." Ben replied and led the way. As we went I noticed the look on Ella' face. From the moment I met her, I'd sensed a passion in her, larger than her small frame and it centred on Ben. Fleetingly she feared I could pose a threat to this as I may be able to get closer to him than she could. As if he sensed this he turned to her and smiled reassuringly and lovingly at her. She grinned back as though ashamed of having been caught in such a lack of faith.

Ben and I went into his studio and I was amazed to see a room full of light and an array of paintings that took my breath away. Most of them were of bald eagles and each one had such life in them.

"Vigilant?" I asked. Ben nodded. "But they're wonderful, Ben. Is this how you earn your living."

"Scrape a living may be more accurate."

"They're wonderful." With reluctance I drew my eyes from the paintings. "Do you know where Vigilant is, Ben, because I don't know where Mistral is and I'm getting worried?"

"No, Sara, I don't, but I often don't. He comes and goes as he pleases."

"But do you feel he's close?" I persisted.

"Yes, I guess I do. Do you feel Mistral is?"

"Yes, but I've come thousands of miles, so it doesn't make any sense."

"Why? It might be unusual behaviour for peregrines to fly that far even in migration, but I don't believe we are talking of things which are quite normal, do you?"

I sighed. "I suppose not."

"Come on then – let's see if we can find them."

"Could we start with the mirror do you think?"

"Sure – if you prefer."

I drew Misty's feather from my shoulder bag and stuck it into the frame of the mirror that hung on the one wall of the studio. As I did so, I saw that a tracery of feathers had been carved into the wood of the frame and her feather seemed a continuation of the beautiful work. I smiled at Ben. "Another talent?"

"No, my grandfather made it. He too was Haida."

"He was remarkably talented. It must have been from him that you inherited your artistic skills."

"Amongst others." Ben smiled and as I watched his reflection in the mirror, it seemed to change, to age and darken, and then I was looking at the face I always saw accompanied by the Raven. A gentle smile played at the corners of the mouth, a mouth as determined as Ben's, but sadder and wiser. Ben moved and the image faded. He saw my face and asked what I had seen.

"Your grandfather, I think, but I've seen the face before and always accompanied by a Raven." Ben took me by the shoulders and turned me round to face him.

"How can you have seen him?" he asked, distressed. "I long for him to come to me and he doesn't."

"Perhaps you want it too much, Ben." I rubbed my shoulders where his fingers had dug in. He looked shamefaced and muttered "Sorry."

"That's okay – you just don't know your own strength, Ben. Perhaps your longing to see your grandfather is blocking the way. I may be wrong, it may be someone else I've seen in the mirror, but he is very like you."

"Really?" Ben straightened his broad shoulders. "I was only seven when he died, but I admired him as I have never admired anyone since. It was said he could talk with the birds."

"As you do, Ben." I pointed out gently.

"I do, don't I? So – do you think he'd be proud of me?" His tone was hesitant

I'd turned back to the mirror and caught a glimpse of the face with the Raven again. 'Bring him to me' it seemed to be saying so I turned and took Ben's hand and drew him alongside me in front of the mirror. Keeping hold of his hand I spoke to him.

"Open your heart, not just your mind, Ben. Look for him there." As I spoke I saw the image return and this time there was a bald eagle standing behind the face, alongside the Raven.

"Grandfather." Ben breathed.

The face beamed with a smile of pure pleasure in what he saw and the gentle eyes lit. There was no need for words. Ben's grip tightened on my hand – my poor hand. I felt tears glisten in my eyes for the beauty of the moment that I had somehow helped to bring about – and the pain in my hand. The old eyes took us both in and I felt the warmth of the spirit that walked with the Raven. He said something that I did not understand and then the image faded. Only Vigilant remained. Then he too had gone.

Ben let out a deep sigh. "Wow – thanks, Sara," was all he found to say, but I knew what it had meant.

"What did he say – I didn't understand it?" I asked.

"It translated as 'Be vigilant, my grandson Eagle. The time is near for magic. Follow your guide.'"

"Is it coincidence that he used 'vigilant' do you think."

"No, I think it just confirms that we are right to trust what we are seeing. What it will bring to us – well time, and the birds, will tell."

"Are you frightened by all this, Ben?"

"Yes, but excited too. I used to dream that I'd be able to talk to the birds like Grandfather. And Vigilant is as close to me as a brother."

"And Scrap and Rift are like my own children. And yet I can't protect them."

"We can only do what they seem to be asking us to do, Sara. If you were seeing Grandfather in your dreams then you must have been brought here for a purpose. We must find out why. Are you ready to try to reach Mistral."

"Okay."

We turned back to the mirror. The sensations I experienced when the images returned were stronger than before. Everything was clearer and I felt as if I was seeing through two pairs of eyes. I was flying, sometimes with the light flight of Mistral and then with the heavier flight of Vigilant. It was like being tossed around in the air and made me feel dizzy. As if each was trying to gain supremacy. I pulled away feeling sick.

"This isn't working, Ben. I feel as though I'm being pulled apart. Perhaps we should try finding them one at a time and then connecting."

"Okay by me. You try for Mistral first then."

I closed my eyes briefly to orient myself, then opened them and reached into my heart for Misty. Her image came through more powerfully than it had for days. She wasn't with Scrap and Rift, but there was another peregrine by her side and I recognised it as the one I had seen alongside her on the carved rock – Peale's Peregrine, female by her size. I was distracted for a minute wondering if this was going to be the only sight I would get of this special bird, and the image faded.

I turned to Ben. "She's there but I still don't know where."

"I'll try for Vigilant then." He concentrated on the glass of the mirror and I saw his face clear. Knowing the pleasure I always had on first seeing Mistral I guessed he had found Vigilant. I relaxed my mind trying also to reach him.

At first I could only hear soft pipe music that I assumed came from the living room. Then I felt the impression of water droplets on my face and, looking into the mirror, I saw a waterfall and I stood at its foot. Looking up towards the top of the tumbling water I saw an outcrop of rock on either side of the water. They appeared to have been carved in the same way as the pole in my dream, although not as tall. A bird, the Raven and an Eagle, topped each rock. Someone took my hand and led me through the back of the waterfall. I felt, rather than saw that it was Ben's grandfather, for he didn't turn his head, just drew me gently by the hand. I sensed someone behind me and assumed it was Ben. As he reached out his hand to touch me on the shoulder, I knew it wasn't Ben, but Gabriel. His touch burned my skin, but I didn't turn round.

An insistent ringing brought me back to the studio and my own reflection in the mirror. Disappointed I looked around for Ben. He wasn't in the room. I could hear him talking to Gabriel next door so I turned back to the mirror and took Misty's feather from its edge. I felt a warmth in my heart as I held it lightly in my hand. I put it carefully in my bag that I'd hung on the back of the chair Ben sat at as he painted. The work on the easel was a sketch of Vigilant preparing to launch himself from a cliff out over the sea.

From next door I heard my name being mentioned and, feeling a little guilty, I put my ear to the door. My instincts for self-preservation had been sharpened over the last few days and I needed all the information I could gather to protect my family and myself. I heard Ella say "Okay" and what sounded like the phone going down. That must have been the ringing I'd heard. I wondered how long I'd been at the waterfall.

"We can't risk it, Ben." I heard Gabriel say. "We don't know how powerful these images are. Would you want to be trapped in an image while you watched someone die?"

"I guess not. But just what is our priority. To find out what's happened to Paul or to find what Paul found?"

"I believe that they're both interlinked. Look, if we find where he disappeared we may have both answers, surely."

"Not necessarily. Okay, we may have to go and find the place and any clues, but what if Sara can just – show us what's happened. Have you thought of the dangers of searching, Gabriel?"

"Of course, I have." Gabriel sounded irritated. "Why do you think I came when I heard about Long?"

"Couldn't we just ask her?" Ella pleaded.

"Getting Sara to 'look' for Paul would be far less dangerous than actually taking her there," Ben insisted. "After all she's the only one who seems to have any inkling where it might be. I'm getting nothing back from Vigilant and what I've just seen of her in there – well she sure is further into this than I am."

"Okay, okay, we'll ask her." I heard a chair scrape back and then Gabriel say – "What's that?"

"No-one knows we're here, surely?" I sensed the alarm in Ella's voice.

"They shouldn't," responded Ben grimly. "You stay here and I'll go and sort it out."

This did not seem a good moment to come out so I stayed where I was and thought about what they wanted me to do. I could see the sense in it, but I was still a bit shaky where the images were concerned and doubted my ability to turn it on at will. Despite that, I sat by the easel and relaxed – maybe I could find the answer for them on my own.

There was something nagging at the back of my mind that made it difficult to concentrate. Suddenly I had it. Ben had said his grandfather was a Haida and I remembered where I'd heard that word before – in the book I'd purchased on the Queen Charlotte Islands. So Ben's family must have originated from there. I supposed it wasn't that strange as it was only a hundred miles or so across the waters from Prince Rupert, but it was another cog in the wheel.

I had no time to wonder about it longer. I heard a crash as if a door had been slammed back against a wall and then raised voices. Reckoning this may not be a good time to come out either, I returned quietly to the door for another bout of 'self preservation'. The voices I heard raised the hackles on the back of my neck, the one being Dr Long's, I was sure. There were two other voices that I didn't recognise. I didn't dare risk peeping into the room.

Gabriel was talking quietly and reasonably – and lying through his teeth. "Look we don't have any photograph. If you would just explain what this is all about, maybe we can clear this up."

"Come now, Mr Rogers. We're not here to play games. We're quite ready to offer you a substantial amount for that photograph."

"What – instead of taking it by force as you tried to earlier."

"Now, we did the young lady no harm, did we, my dear?" Long at his smarmiest. I could imagine the disgusted look on Ella' face.

"You forced your way into my house," the anger shone through Ben's words "and threatened my wife, then ransacked the place in front of her. No harm – you have to be joking."

"Okay, Ben." Gabriel spoke softly. "We'd like you to leave now. We have no photograph. Whoever gave you this information must have got their facts wrong. I suggest you go and check with them."

"We have very accurate information, Mr Rogers – such as your visitor from England, whom I don't see at the moment. Where is she?"

"It's none of your business." Ben answered fiercely. Again Gabriel restrained him.

"She's gone to stay overnight with friends for a while." He raised his voice to say this and I knew it was a warning.

"Well you won't mind if we search, will you."

"We damn well do." Ben declared and I heard a chair overturn and Ella call out.

"Try that again and my colleague will break her arm. Now I'll ask again – if you don't wish her hurt – you won't mind if we search, will you?"

"You bastards." I could imagine the agony Ben felt being unable to do anything.

It was difficult to tell how many of the thugs there were, but my prime concern was my own predicament – I had to get out before they searched this room. One of us free would be better than all of us cooped up together while they searched. If they didn't find the photographs I wondered what they'd do. I needed to get help.

The joy of finding Ben had doors opening out onto the veranda! Grabbing my bag, I opened the door to the outside as quietly as possible, holding my breath in the forlorn hope that this would make any difference. The studio looked out across an open area that was studded with bushes and fringed with trees. Fortunately the front, where I had heard the car pull up, was not in view, so anyone left in the car would not see me, I just had to worry about those in the house.

With my heart pounding I made a dash for the nearest bush and waited a few seconds. No shout came from behind me in the lodge, so keeping as low as possible and almost crawling I made my way to the next one. Looking back at the lodge, I could now see the car in the front and there was someone sitting in the driver's seat. He seemed to find the study of his nails more fascinating than anything that might be going on around him – which was a relief – so I made a dash for the trees.

Breathing heavily, I leant against the trunk of a young cedar, the contact giving me courage. I didn't, though, have the faintest idea where I was or in which direction to head. I had seen one or two other lodges on the one mile track which we had come up on the way here so, if I could loop round to meet the track well out of view of Ben's lodge, I might make it to the nearest without being seen and ring for help. Speed was of the essence so I set off at a jog through the trees. I felt a warmth from the protection the trees offered, my footsteps cushioned by the debris beneath the branches, but more light would have been a blessing.

CHAPTER TEN

It must have been ten minutes before I came to the first habitation and it was starting to get dark. There were no lights on in the house, so I assumed no-one was at home and, when I tried the door, it didn't budge. I went round the back to try for a back entrance but as I rounded the corner of the house I heard a vehicle coming down the road from the direction of Ben and Ella' s lodge. I pulled myself into the shadow of the house and peered out. The vehicle was the one that had been parked outside Ben's with the manicurist at the wheel, that I'd seen as I crawled through the bushes. I could just make out the number of occupants in the lessening light. My heart skipped when I saw Ella between the two men in the back. There was no one in the passenger seat in the front, so, if there'd been three in the house and one in the car, even my rudimentary maths made that one missing.

I couldn't now ring the police, either – if they had Ella it could be for no other purpose than as a hostage. I didn't even dare approach the lodge openly in case one of Long's thugs was still there, but I headed back there in case I could think of anything constructive to do. The light from the pencil torch

I carried in my bag was scarcely sufficient to stop me barking my shins as I tripped over roots, so that I arrived at the lodge with my temper roughened as well as my shins.

When I reached the edge of the trees by the lodge I was at a loss to know what to do next. Ben's pickup was still there and there were lights on in the house but I didn't dare approach. Instead I sat at the foot of a cedar and leant against its trunk that sheltered me from being seen from the lodge. I then attempted something I wouldn't have dared if I hadn't been desperate. I tried direct contact with Vigilant.

It was hard concentrating out in the air, feeling vulnerable and not a little confused. The tree again helped, but it was Mistral I reached first. I saw her turn her head towards me and flood my mind with that special love of hers and the relief this brought me relaxed me and at last I was able to 'see' Vigilant, shadowy at first and then with a strength that made me wince. I concentrated hard on an image of Ben and had a response similar to Misty's love but with more reserve. I suppose a magnificent creature, which he truly was, should hold a little something back, but I very much preferred Misty's total commitment.

Thankfully I felt rather than saw an image of Ben reaching out to Vigilant and I knew he had made contact. I concentrated hard on an image of myself with my back against the tree and transmitted this to Vigilant. I heard Mistral chitter as if she had actually seen me which I knew was impossible, but this seemed to spur Vigilant on. It must have worked because a light came on in the studio and I saw a figure standing at the window looking towards the trees. I knew he couldn't see me and I wanted to be sure who it was before I revealed myself.

It was hard to believe that I had contacted another person through a bird who was, as yet, a stranger to me, but it had to be. As I watched he reached for the painting on the easel and switching off the main light put on the one over the easel. He put the painting under the light so that it reflected the image clearly to me and lit some of his face. It was Ben. He took the painting back into the living room and closed the door, but left the light on in the studio. I waited a couple of minutes but he didn't return. Again, pointlessly holding my breath, I made my way cautiously to the veranda doors which led into the studio and let myself in. I listened at the door and could hear a strange voice alongside Ben and Gabriel's so I knew it wasn't safe to go in. Long must have left number three thug behind.

I found pen and paper and wrote a note for Ben, asking what I should do and then found a space at the end of the studio where I could conceal myself and wait for Ben to return. My heart was thumping again – I didn't need it to tell me I did not at all like what was going on – I already knew.

Ben returned in five minutes carrying the painting. He saw my carefully placed note straight away. He looked quickly round the room and relief flooded his face when he saw me.

"Quick, Gabriel's taken him into the kitchen." He said quietly. "We can't just chuck him out – they've got Ella – did you know?" I heard the anguish in his voice.

"I saw the car. I'm so sorry, Ben. What will they do?"

"They've taken her as hostage to our 'good behaviour'."

"Why the thug then?"

"Just to make doubly sure we stay here, I suppose – and to let them know when you come back – they seem to think you have more than the photographs and feather – which they got."

"Oh no – after all that." I didn't like the other bit much either. "They didn't hurt anyone did they?"

"Only threatened to break Ella's arm. The one they've left is carrying a gun – not actually pointing it, but he's made it obvious he's got it. Not that we'd risk anything while they've got Ella and they know it."

"What do you want me to do?"

"I haven't had a chance to tell Gabriel you're here. Did you really manage to contact Vigilant – or is this all a coincidence?"

"No coincidence. I didn't know what else to do. Thank God it worked – I wouldn't like to try it again!"

"You'd better go. Look, can you contact Joe and Callum and let them know what's happened? Here's Joe's cell phone number and our number here. Tell them not to come up to the house. Now Long's got the photograph he'll have plenty on his mind to keep it occupied, but you'd be as well to keep out of sight."

"Don't worry – I will." Even to my ears it sounded heartfelt.

I didn't say out loud what was on my mind – what if they didn't find the lake? It was like looking for a needle in a haystack without the clues we had. And they still had Ella. Perhaps they thought she knew where it was.

"Are you alright for money, Sara?" Ben interrupted my misgivings.

"Yes, I'll be okay. I'll go straight to the airport now and wait for the flight. I don't suppose they're interested in Joe and Callum, are they?"

"They don't know about them. At least not that they can tie in with this."

"Do you want me to tell them just to go home?"

"The conference is still on, so their time won't be wasted, but there's nothing we can do about the photograph now, not while they have Ella. They'd better not hurt her that's all." I gave him a hug – it was like putting my arms round a tree.

"I'll see what I can find out – discreetly, of course."

"Just look after yourself and if you need anything – well – you can contact me on Vigilant's number." I appreciated the attempt.

Gabriel called from the living room, a warning, I felt. Ben went out with another painting to show Gabriel, closing the door behind him but leaving the light on. I crept out onto the veranda and crossed again the now familiar path to the trees.

Progress was slow back to the main road. The moonlight was intermittent, but of some help once I'd left the shelter of the trees. I concentrated on what I'd to do rather than think of Ella and how tired I was. I had to find out where they had taken her, but first I'd need to sort out Joe and Callum. I was looking forward to meeting them – it's always a relief to find you are not on your own, not as odd as you thought. They might have pieces to add to the jigsaw that would enable us to clear up the whole thing and go home, which, at this moment, was all I wanted to do. Feeling sorry for myself being left with everything to tackle on my own, I realised I had not even had time to myself with Gabriel and no idea when I'd see him again. And I still didn't know about Kate's baby.

With these cheerful thoughts I reached the road and risked asking the people at one of the houses if I could use their phone. I said my car had broken down and I needed a cab. They very kindly offered to see if they could repair it, but I told them I had to be in Prince Rupert just as soon as possible and they accepted it. I had a welcome cup of tea while I waited for the cab to arrive and the feeling of being in a normal house, albeit in a foreign country, was very refreshing as was the tea. So far I had found the Canadians I had met really friendly and helpful.

I was unable to contact Joe, so found out the time of the arrival of their plane the next day. They were due in at seven the next morning, which gave me a chance to get some much-needed sleep. I booked in at the hotel nearest the ferry terminal from the airport, (where I had been – was it only a few hours before – it felt more like a week) set the alarm for six and fell immediately asleep.

I was so tired that the dreams I had were misty and indistinct, but I was aware of four peregrines and two other birds. Next morning I had a huge breakfast, making up for all my missed meals, and went over to the airport to await the plane's arrival.

As I watched the people disembark from the plane, I caught sight of a dark skinned man who turned to the rugged, sandy haired man at his side and smiled. As their glances contacted I saw immediately behind my eyes, two birds, a young peregrine and a golden eagle. So that was what I'd dreamed last night. Did the birds send me the dream so I could be sure to recognise the two men I needed so desperately to speak with?

As they walked across the tarmac, Joe looked towards the window at which I stood and smiled. Yet, he couldn't have known I was there – he would be expecting Gabriel or Ben or Ella nor could he have known where they would be standing. But he had picked me out – there was no doubt about it. I waited for them to retrieve their baggage and come out.

Callum was slightly behind Joe, pushing the trolley, as they came out into the building. Again I was reminded of the birds and, as if I had connected through them directly to Joe, he made his way over to where I stood, slightly behind a pillar.

He held out a large hand, oversized for his body, for me to

grasp. "You must be Sara. I am Joe Muscat. Don't be surprised that I know you. We met before remember?"

His hand was warm and comforting and the kindness was there in the blue eyes, paled by the sun – just as it had been when I'd seen him before. "In the mirror." I stated in a hushed voice.

"In the mirror," he repeated not the least bit phased. "Callum says that he hasn't had the pleasure of a previous meeting, though."

He indicated the man who had now joined us and, close to, I could see the sandy golden coloured beard that matched the hair. The hazel eyes contained more reserve than Joe's, but were friendly enough. He smiled, which eased the rugged lines of his face to an attractive boyishness, and held out his hand. I noticed the scars left by deep puncture wounds on the back of his hand and on his wrist and felt the calluses on his palm. My scars were more delicate than these so I assumed this was obviously a man used to dealing with larger birds. Then I remembered the golden eagle and the size of their feet.

"Callum McAllister, Sara." The accent confirmed his Scottish colouring. "We spoke briefly on the telephone, I believe."

"Pleased to meet you – both." I smiled. I really liked the sparkle in Joe's eye, and I thought how aptly each was matched with his bird – the shorter, slightly broader Joe with his boisterous manner and casually smart clothes and the quieter, taller, golden haired Callum. Joe would be in his early forties I reckoned, but Callum probably wasn't yet thirty, yet I sensed an innocent quality in Joe which made him appear younger than the more serious Callum.

"Now, where are we to go?" Joe asked. "And where is Gabriel? I have not seen him for a while." He must have seen the look in my eyes. "There is some trouble – I see it in your face. Tell me – what is wrong?"

"Let's find somewhere for some coffee and I'll try and explain."

We climbed aboard the complimentary coach for the ferry and reached Prince Rupert city half an hour later and found a café. Callum went to get the coffees and while he was gone Joe reached over and took my hand.

"Your little peregrine – he is alright?"

Astonished I replied. "Scrap? As far as I know, but I haven't seen him for ages."

"Do you need to see him?" he asked with a smile. "Surely you only have to look inside, just as I do for Omen."

"Your peregrine." It was a statement rather than a question. "But she is with Scrap, I saw them last night – sorry – dreamt them."

"Ever since he brought her the message in Malta she has pined for him. He has a big heart for one so small." I felt my eyes fill with tears. Scrap had really been there – had flown all that way – alone and still so young. Joe patted my hand "There – I didn't mean to make you more unhappy."

"You didn't, but I do miss them."

"There are three you 'see' I believe – all one family?" I nodded. "You are fortunate indeed. You must also be very special. I feel proud yet humble to be so chosen- you do too, I think."

"And frightened. Why have we been chosen? Will we fail them? Where are they? There are so many questions."

"We can only answer them one at a time. That is why Callum and myself are here. To answer the questions – all four of us together."

"That isn't going to be possible, I'm afraid – not straight away anyway. Look, let's wait until Callum comes back and I'll bring you up to date."

Callum arrived back with the coffees and some toast and pancakes for himself and Joe. I gathered there had been little food on the flight.

"Now, begin, Sara." Joe commanded.

"Has Gabriel told you anything about a photograph and a feather?"

"A special photograph that he believes has something to do with the birds?" Callum asked.

"Yes, well – I'd better try and explain." I went through the story as well as I could with the information I had to hand. "Have either of you had a dream about this place?" They both shook their heads.

"Not as you describe it, Sara." Callum replied. "I've seen a carved crag with Wraith and a lot of other birds on it." I assumed that Wraith was the golden eagle I had 'seen' with Callum.

"Myself also – with Omen." Joe agreed. "But no lake, Sara."

I sighed. "Then I'm the only one. Does that mean it doesn't exist? But I've seen the birds there." I had so hoped Callum or Joe could shed some light on this.

"Come, Sara. We may never know the answer to this riddle. Our hands are tied whilst they have Ella are they not? First we must find her and make them give her back." Joe spoke with such simplicity it made me smile. "That is much better. Now we must have a plan, isn't that so?"

Callum was deep in thought. He raised his head. "If we can find this place before them they'll have to give Ella back – there's no point in them keeping her. As long as Gabriel and Ben keep out of it, they will have kept their part of the bargain."

"I don't think these people are that reasonable, Callum. Long may not be willing to harm Ella, but we know little about the people he's got himself muddled up with to finance this expedition, and we have no idea what lengths they may go to. It's just too risky."

"Then we have to find out through the birds – if they are connected with this. From what you say, Sara, I think it's possible." He smiled self-consciously. "If anyone had told me a year ago that I'd make such a statement – well you know what it's like."

"For me, I have had longer." Joe declared. "I had a bird before Omen two years ago now. It was long before I accepted what he was telling me. I am a well respected businessman – I would lose that if people knew I talked to the birds." Joe let out a peal of laughter that turned several heads in the café. Callum and I smiled – it was good to find others with the same problems.

"If it hadn't been for Gabriel – well – I might have believed my head had been fried!"

"You knew Gabriel two years ago, then, Joe?"

"Certainly, yes. He came on recommendation. I had a sick peregrine and a friend of a friend – you know how it is – he told me this man was visiting my town and he was a healer of the animals and the birds. Me, a hard-headed businessman – well – I needed the proof of my eyes. This bird was special, though, so I thought why not?

"I watched as he held the bird and I saw the eyes of the bird and they looked at me and seemed to become much bigger and

I was held by them. Now I know that he was reaching out to me, but then, I just saw what Gabriel did for that bird. Within two days he was well and I had tried everything. All he did was hold the bird then hand it back to me with the words I didn't understand. 'He has a great need for you.' I found it all rather strange, but I felt, also, a deep affinity with this man who had given me back this bird. We have corresponded ever since. That is how I know about you three. The centre to all this I believe it is Gabriel. We all have our special birds – he hears them all, but doesn't understand their words only their needs."

I remembered Gabriel 'contacting' Mistral and thought Joe just might be right.

"If your experience started two years ago, how can you be sure this has anything to do with what's happening now?" I asked. "Gabriel only mentioned what had been happening over the last few months, when Paul found the feather. Surely the timing makes this impossible."

"I don't know, Sara, but if Gabriel believes it then so do I."

"That doesn't help us plan what we are to do, though." Callum had finished his toast and pancakes by now. "Let's get some more coffee. Your turn, Joe."

When Joe had gone to the counter Callum asked. "What do you think, Sara? We can't all be mad, can we? And I would say that Joe is right when he says he's well respected. His clothes and luggage show a certain affluence." The last statement was a little wistful.

"Do I take it you don't place yourself in the same category – or is it the Scot's nose for money coming out?" I teased. I was surprised that I felt relaxed enough with him for this and was glad when he laughed.

"Now that's a blow below the belt, Sara, particularly with a name like yours."

"I'm only half Scots – the other half is Welsh."

"But you're not saying which half, eh? Probably the one responsible for your colouring. Anyway you're right about the category. I'm a poor starving sculptor myself, so seeing easy money does make me drool a bit."

"We don't know it's easy money, Callum. In fact we know very little. But I trust Gabriel's instincts. It's interesting, though – do you realise we all have something else in common, other than a love for birds. You say you are a sculptor, I'm a jeweller and Ben's a very talented painter. I wonder if Joe's business involves making things."

"Now's your chance to ask him." Joe returned with the coffee.

"Ask what?" he asked.

"I was just commenting to Callum that it's odd that we all have the connection of earning our living in the arts – although 'living' may be a bit of an exaggeration – so we were wondering if you too made things."

"The trade of my fathers was in silversmithing and, yes I continue to practise that trade as well as my dealing in stones, which is a lot more profitable I can tell you." He laughed at his own pomposity, but I was growing to really like Joe.

"Don't you think it strange – you a silversmith, Callum a sculptor and Ben, a painter, and myself a jeweller?"

"Perhaps it is just that we are more intuitive, hence our closeness to the birds."

"Possibly. Joe, could I pick your brains about something?"

"Surely, Sara – pick away!"

"Can you think of any stone that is sort of matt yet shiny black, fairly easy to carve, but still close grained?"

"Only obsidian or jet I can think of, Sara. What stone do you speak of?"

"I don't know – just one I saw," I finished lamely.

"Hah, in a dream I think – no?" I nodded blushing. "Is it important, this stone?"

"I really don't know. I think I'll just use jet." I brought the subject to an end, not really understanding why it was so important to get the right stone for the earring.

After further discussions, it was decided that Callum would return to Vancouver and find out everything he could about whoever may be backing Dr Long and anyone who might have seen Paul. Meanwhile Joe and I would stay here and gather news from this end.

"I will stay with Sara," Joe declared, "and try and keep her out of trouble. I think she has a nose for it." He smiled gently at me as he said it so I couldn't take offence. "Not that it is not a very pretty nose."

Callum checked the time of the next flight and he had three

hours to fill, so we decided to book in at the hotel and see if we could contact the birds together – it was, after all, what we had all come for.

Having booked a cab, I returned to the others and helped them gather their luggage.

"Do you know," Callum declared, "it's eight years since I as much as set foot over the border of Scotland and now I find myself half way round the world and living in aeroplanes." He didn't sound worried by it, more excited, and I envied him.

"Are you alright for cash?" I asked out of Joe's hearing.

"Yes, thanks, Sara. I had a grant to come as the conference directly affects the work I'm doing. Like Gabriel, I'm supposed to be doing a seminar. When his call came from Prince Rupert, I thought I was going to have to miss it, but I should be back in time. Which is perhaps just as well," he looked quizzically at me, "- since one of their previous speakers did a midnight flit the day before yesterday?" Was it only the day before yesterday, surely it was weeks ago?

"Were they very put out?"

"Not as much as when Dr Long refused to do the second lecture he was booked for. That won't do his reputation much good. Seriously, though, Sara – that man is paranoid about his reputation – he wouldn't risk it for just anything – this has to be very important."

"I know, but what can we do – we're involved now, not maybe of our own volition, but – here we are and yet now our hands are tied."

"Just be careful is all I'm saying."

We made our way to the cab. As we climbed in I had a look around, convinced someone was watching us but I couldn't see anyone. It was the start of rush hour on the long, straight streets of Prince Rupert, so perhaps I just wasn't used to so many people.

We booked into the hotel, Joe insisting on paying for both Callum and my rooms. I like to be independent where such matters are concerned but he did it in such a kind gentlemanly way, that I didn't feel offended. We all three went to Joe's room and sat round the table that was placed in front of the window.

"I've only got an hour," said Callum, "Let's hope it's enough."

"How are we going to approach this?" I asked.
"Like Sara, I find the mirror concentrates things for me." Joe declared. "But I don't see how that will help us all at the same time. I have found also meditation helps, as Gabriel taught me."
"He taught me too. What about you Sara?"
"Me too. Doesn't this feel a bit like being trained for a big event – Gabriel pulling the strings." I knew it was hardly fair, but I wanted him there helping – it wasn't just the family I was missing. Deep down I also feared that he might only have come to see me to find out what he could, not from any previous feelings we may have had.
"Come, now, Sara. You are not being kind." Joe stood up and patted me on the shoulder. "I am more comfortable sitting on the floor. I leave you two to settle yourselves and then we will link through the birds."
He sounded so certain I took courage from it. I sat on the floor with my back against the wall. Closing my eyes, the room soon faded and my mind opened up to Misty. I asked her to put me in touch with Vigilant – if we couldn't have Ben, maybe I could bring him in via Vigilant. I recognised his heavier thoughts as he joined Mistral. Then we were joined by Rift and Scrap with his new friend, Omen, and, coming up last, Wraith. They were all there swirling around in my head. I had the feeling of dizziness I had sometimes had in the past, but I knew I couldn't let go. Then it was as if the horizon expanded outwards and I no longer felt restricted. My mind opened up of its own accord.
I saw all the places I'd seen in my dreams, one after the other, but this time accompanied by the other three birds, until I came to the lake, then it was only Misty, Rift and Vigilant. The others had faded. I concentrated hard on the lake, imprinting it on my mind. As I did so two things happened. Omen appeared accompanied by Scrap and then I saw a man standing on the shore of the lake looking upwards. There was a shot and the man at the shore went running back into the trees towards the direction of the shot. I felt a stab of pain and then a deep welling of grief as Omen opened her beak and screamed.
The pain brought me to and I had difficulty focusing. Callum was kneeling beside me calling to me. I couldn't see him properly and realised it was the tears streaming down my face. I

turned quickly to Joe, worried for him – it was Omen who had screamed. His face looked much older and I could see the grief, but his eyes were still closed.

"Quickly, Callum, wake him up."

"No, better he comes to himself gently."

At that Joe opened his eyes. He saw us both staring at him in concern and he managed a smile.

"So now I know how, but I don't know who." His tone was grim.

"Is Omen alright, Joe?" Before the question left my lips, I heard it in my head – Scrap reassuring – his new friend was alright.

"Was that the place in the photograph, Sara?"

"I don't know what you saw, Joe," I cried in despair. "How can I tell?"

He shut his eyes. "Describe it to me," he commanded. I did as I was bid. "It is the place."

"I'm sorry," Callum interposed, "but I never saw that place. I found Wraith and he was with four peregrines and a bald eagle, but they disappeared and I couldn't follow."

"It may be that the place has no significance for you as yet," Joe declared. "For me, it has, but I don't know why it has for Sara. I fear you may be the channel, my dear, and that is why you see further than us."

"I don't understand any of it. Why did Omen scream like that Joe?" I asked

"You didn't see the peregrine that was shot, then, Sara?" I shook my head. "It was Peal, the peregrine that Gabriel healed two years ago. He helped me care for Omen when she first came to me. I lost him many months ago, but could still 'talk' to him. Until suddenly about three weeks ago – then there was nothing. I had never experienced this 'talking' before him, you understand, so I could only guess that I wasn't hearing him because he was dead. Omen left a week after, but I can still talk to her."

"Then the blood I first saw in the lake was his, not Paul's as I thought?"

"How can we know, Sara?" He sounded very tired.

Callum interrupted. "Look, you two, I've got to make tracks. I've got the number here, as our mobiles don't work. Can you be sure to leave a number where I can contact you if you go anywhere else."

"If we're really stuck we'll contact you through Wraith." Callum looked at me sceptically. "Well it worked with Vigilant."

"Okay, but I'll trust to good old fashioned telephone wires if you don't mind."

He turned at the door. "Now, you take care, do you hear. I'll be back as soon as possible. Bye, just now." And he was gone.

CHAPTER ELEVEN

I helped Joe to his feet. "Come, Sara, let's take some time to ourselves. We will change and then we will go exploring. I need the bracing air here in Canada to clear my head. You, I think, need a break from all this 'talking' to the birds. Your mind is tired, is it not?"

"Confused, more than tired."

"Well, a break will cure that too, perhaps. I will meet you downstairs in half an hour."

I took the chance to have a welcome shower and sort out my clothes. I had torn my sweater in the trees by the lodge, but, fortunately, I had a spare one in my capacious shoulder bag. After all I had to keep up a standard with Joe as my escort. When I arrived downstairs I realised I needn't have bothered. There was Joe looking somehow incongruous in jeans and a T-shirt and carrying a sweater. I was sure that, had I been able to see the labels, they would all have been expensive, but he looked every inch the casual tourist.

As we came out of the hotel, I again had that feeling of being watched, but I always felt vulnerable in cities, whereas many of my town friends felt that way in the dark of the countryside.

"Shall we indulge in some window shopping, Sara."

"As long as it's only looking," I cautioned.

"We will see."

Our feet seemed to automatically find their way to the jewellery shops. Joe had an eye for the precious jewellery displayed in the windows, but I preferred the freer designs of the costume jewellery. There was one superb piece with a pippin shaped opal, rich in blue and green, which really caught my eye. I had a passion for opals.

"Perhaps I shall buy that for you," Joe said.

"You will not," I said firmly.

He smiled into my eyes. "I thought that would be your answer. One who flies with Mistral has little need for such earthly splendours, eh?" I knew he was right. They meant more to me than any piece fashioned by man, never mind with how much love. I touched the little feather earring in my pocket.

We did the tourist bit, both of us taken by the long, straight streets and the predominance of flat roofed buildings. We bought some expensive waterproof gear and walking boots for Joe, who had come ill prepared for the colder, wetter climate, and a change of clothes for me as my suitcase was still at the lodge. Then we had lunch in a small restaurant.

The meal gave us time to get to know each other better and the more I was with him the more I felt at home with this Maltese silversmith who spoke such excellent English, despite being partly brought up in Saudi Arabia and having a French mother. We talked of his fight with the authorities to try and get the shooting of small birds banned, and the dangers of this work. And he told me of his wife who had left him, unable to cope with his passion for falcons, instilled in him in Saudi.

We decided to walk back to the hotel a different way. As we passed down a side street, I noticed a shop whose doorway was bordered by a totem pole on either side. Remembering my dream I asked Joe if we could go in and look around. The shop was part Gallery and part gift shop. We started in the Gallery. I came to a halt in front of one of the smaller paintings and turned to Joe.

"That is Vigilant – that's one of Ben's paintings. Isn't he wonderful."

"He has great power."

"Who?" I asked. "Vigilant or Ben."

He put his head on one side. "I would say both, would not you?"

"Yes, I would." I said with feeling. I remembered Ben's feelings about his grandfather and mentioned this to Joe.

"And this is the man you think you see in your 'visionings'?"

I had never thought of them like that but it seemed appropriate. "Yes. I feel he is somehow very important."

As I looked again at the painting, I suddenly started to feel giddy. Joe reached out a hand to steady me.

"Sara, what is wrong?"

"I don't know. I thought I saw his face in the painting." I shrugged my shoulders. "I'm alright now."

"Perhaps we had better go."

"No." My voice was sharper than I had intended. "I must go and look at the carvings."

"Very well, Sara." Joe replied but he kept his hand on my arm as we went to the other side of the shop. I was drawn to the cabinet that contained the jewellery, of little interest to Joe, as it was all costume jewellery. Beautifully crafted in a variety of materials, it had a theme similar to the poles – bold, natural yet geometric designs.

As I leant over to get a better view, I knocked against a miniature chest of drawers that Joe just managed to rescue before it fell to the floor. As he brought it upright one of the drawers opened and the light shone on a shiny, carved black bead. As if mesmerised, my hand reached out for the bead. I couldn't be sure but it looked identical to the one I had seen which should hang from the earring in my bag.

The man in charge, who had the high cheekbones and strong jaw I associated with the native Haida, had heard the commotion and came to find if we needed any help. Joe just looked at me and I nodded.

"The young lady would, I think, like to purchase the bead she has in her hand, if that were at all possible, sir."

The man smiled at me. "She most certainly may. Those are just bits and pieces left over from broken jewellery. In fact, I would be grateful if the young lady would accept it as a gift." A face smiled in my head – grandfather?

"Thank you, I shall accept it with gratitude." He went to place it in a small bag, but I stopped him. "Would you do one more favour for me, please." I reached into my bag and unwrapped the earring. "Could I borrow a pair of pliers to put it straight onto this."

He took the earring from my hand and turned it to the light to get a better look at it. The little feather was wafted in the breeze and it caught at my heart. A little bit of the past sat in his hand and, although I wasn't to know it then, a bit of the future. He examined it closely and looked up at me.

"This is remarkably similar to a piece I have seen before. Where did you come by it?"

"I made it. What is the stone the bead is made from – do you know?"

"Argillite, I believe, you would call it. We Haida use it a lot for our carvings and jewellery. It is found on the Queen Charlottes, and it is the tradition that only Haida descendants may carve it." I caught Joe's eye and then realised I hadn't told him about the Queen Charlotte Islands. The wheel began once more to revolve.

I put the bead on with the pliers and it looked just right. I carefully wrapped it up and placed it back in my bag. Joe attracted the salesman's eye.

"How much is the painting of the bald eagle in your Gallery, sir? I would like to purchase it." I felt great warmth for this man – I knew he wished to compensate the man for the kindness he had shown me. I would have offended him if I had offered him money for the bead – this way he need not lose out. The price of four hundred Canadian dollars didn't faze Joe and the purchase was made. It was small enough to go under his arm and he had a smile of satisfaction on his face all the way back to the hotel

"Thank you, Joe." I gave his arm a hug.

"I assure you the pleasure is all mine. It is a beautiful piece of work."

Back at the hotel, we once again approached the problem that couldn't be put off any longer. I decided to confide in Joe my thoughts on the Queen Charlotte Islands. I like to believe in coincidences, but I also believe they have a significance.

I explained to him about the totem poles I saw in my dream,

the face of Ben's grandfather, who was a native of the Islands, the peregrine I often saw with Mistral and now the bead.

"I may be imagining it – just because I really do want to go to the Islands to see Peale's Peregrine. I've come so far."

"Indeed you have and not just in miles. You have an amazing power, Sara. What I saw this morning, surely, came directly from your mind, through Omen, perhaps, but they were images I haven't seen before and yet I feel them true." He paused. "There is one thing I did not tell you also and that is that Peal, my first bird, was a member of that family a Peale's Peregrine. That is, of course, how he got his name."

I gasped. "How did he come to be in Malta?"

"Maybe like too many birds, through illegal means. He suffered badly in the heat, as so many before him and so he came to me. I recognised him straight away. Like yourself, I have an enormous respect for the peregrine family and so I study them. But I do not like to see them taken from their normal homes. That is why I sent your Scrap back to you when he would have preferred to dally with my Omen, I think."

"I was worried when I felt the heat in the mirror."

"You felt the heat, Sara? You are a lot closer to these birds than you think. Surely you must have some idea where they are."

"I can't always understand the images they send me, Joe. All the time I feel they are so close, but it isn't possible – it's just so far for them."

"These are strange times, Sara, and what we may accept as normal may be about to change."

I made a decision. "Joe, will you come with me to the Queen Charlotte Islands and we can look together for Peale's Peregrine, even if we find nothing else."

"Sara, my dear, that is a journey I would take with all the pleasure of my heart, but would we not be putting Ella's life at risk?"

"But it's only Gabriel and Ben who are sworn to stay where they are. Long could look forever and never find the lake in the photograph. We think we know where it is because, for some reason all their own, the birds are showing us the way. I know we need to find Ella first, but that may take too long. Please, Joe, contact Omen – ask her how long we have got. I have no doubt there is an urgency."

"We still could not take the risk," he answered severely. "Can you imagine trying to explain in a court of law, our actions? We would, for certain, be locked up forever. Everything must appear as if we have only the photograph to follow – you must see this Sara."

"Yes, I do, Joe. I'm sorry. It's just so frustrating."

"I understand. But there is nothing, I suppose, to stop us taking a tourist trip to the Islands later."

"Could we, Joe?" my heart leaped. Then reality bit. "But they'd ask for our passports, surely, and I still don't know if Long and his associates are watching the airport."

"Come, now, Sara. Long is looking for The Lake hoping to gain none of us know what. He has Ben and Gabriel tied down, so they can't beat him to it."

"But he still wanted to know where I was. And Joe, twice today, I've felt we're being watched."

"You are tired, Sara, and frightened too – yes?" I nodded. "So maybe this is just imagination."

"Maybe. If we could only find Ella – we really ought to go to the police, Joe."

"I think not, Sara. If that had been the case then Ben would have asked you to – would he not?"

"I suppose so," I replied doubtfully. "But we ought to tell someone what is going on in case things go wrong."

"And who should this person be. I know no-one I can trust except those who already know what is going on."

I had a sudden thought. "I knew there was another reference to the Islands. Andrew Fraser. He was injured there."

"Who is this Fraser?" Joe asked.

I explained how I had met Andrew and how he'd helped me at Ben's house.

"But Gabriel – he is not sure?"

"He's not sure about anything at the moment. If we had a chance to meet Andrew we might find out more and Gabriel may feel differently about him."

"Then you trust him, Sara?"

I thought for a bit before answering. I tend to judge people by how I feel about them when I first meet them, but I had been mislead in the past. "I think so, Joe, although there is something about him which is strange, but I can't put my finger on it."

"And you say he was injured on these Islands."

"So he said. Perhaps a journalist isn't the person to involve in this."

"Or maybe, the very person we need. Think how much information he would have access to and I would assume he would know the police. How would it be, Sara, if we invited him for supper and I can let you know what I feel about him."

"That sounds okay to me. Shall I give him a ring?"

Joe looked at his watch. "It is now four o'clock. Callum should have something to report by now. Let us wait for Callum to ring us. Then we are free to make arrangements with your Mr Andrew."

"Should we try and see Gabriel and Ben, do you think?"

"We will make plans when we hear from Callum, I think. Now, Sara, I suggest you get some sleep. I will wait to hear from Callum and wake you as soon as there is any news."

"I'd appreciate that, Joe. I'll see you around half five if not before."

"Good. Now sleep well, Sara, and dream of your Mistral."

It was a relief to lie quietly and feel someone else was in charge. Joe would take care of things as far as he was able and there was Callum in Vancouver.

I did dream of Mistral and Rift and Scrap, only this was a dream from before, back in Wales and we were all together, the birds, Bran and me. We were at the cliff and Misty, Rift and Scrap went to sit in a row above the nest site, still, as if carved from rock. Then a mist rolled towards the cliff. Before it engulfed the family two shadowy outlines flew out of the mist and all three rose to meet them. Five birds flew together with such joy and before the mist hid them from my view, I knew I was seeing the whole family, as it should have been. I woke up crying and knew that what I felt was Mistral's grief and that it was for the two shadows. Her mate would not be returning.

Seeking Andrew's help seemed more important now, as the urgency was building up inside me, restrained only by the knowledge of Ella's danger. Oh, if only she were free – I could then choose to continue the search or go back to my peaceful home in Wales, which, when I was there, often appeared peaceful to distraction, but not now.

I had the card that Ella had written their phone numbers on. Perhaps we could ring Ben and Gabriel at the lodge – we didn't, after all, have to say who we were, just arrange a time to meet. I tried to contact Vigilant, but just got some vague images that told me nothing so I bent to retrieve the card from my bag, which was beside the table in my room. As I straightened I hit my head on the side of the table hard enough to make me clutch my hands to my head. As I waited for the pain to recede, still holding the card, I felt the familiar giddiness and sat down waiting for the images to start.

No birds appeared, but I 'heard' the vibrations in my head that I now associated with Vigilant. I was aware of being in a room, dark, except for a bedside light and my head hurt, the sort of throbbing head you get after a hangover. There was a tiny stray of light that shone through a knothole in the shutters onto the dingy carpet, highlighting the aura of long neglect.

As I lay there I heard the revving of engines and had to orient myself a bit to identify it. Only when the sound increased and then faded could I identify it as an aircraft taking off. At that there was a knock at the door and the shock released me and I was back sitting on the edge of the bed in the hotel room.

The knock came again and Joe called out. The pain in my head was receding and I stood up feeling shaky. I went quickly to the door. Joe took one look at my face and steered me to the chair by the window.

"You need some fresh air. I will open the window."

"I'm alright, Joe."

"You are not, Sara. Now, tell me."

I told him what I'd seen. "But I've never seen the place before, Joe, I'm sure. It wasn't a dream. I was awake. I'd already dreamt about Mistral. I was definitely awake."

"What is it you have in your hand?" I was still clutching the card Ella had given me.

I handed it to Joe. "It's Ben's phone numbers – Ella wrote it down for me, because I didn't have it to warn Ben and Gabriel when those men came to the house."

"Good, then we can ring them, can we not? If that other answers we will say we have a wrong number."

"That one's the number at the lodge – we could try that. They may have news of Ella. Have you heard from Callum yet?"

"Just ten minutes ago. He has found the name of the man that is backing this Dr Long. Now – this is the good bit – he has his own plane!"

"Sorry, Joe, why is that good?" My head still felt muzzy.

"That is the means that they will use to find the lake – yes?" I nodded. "And they must file flight plans – yes?" Again I nodded. "So we can find out where they are and where they are going." He sat back happy with himself.

"How does this help us find Ella?"

His face fell. "Well not a lot, I suppose – without searching this man's house, which would not be very possible, I think."

"Very unpossible, I should think. He'd also know better than to keep her there. She could be anywhere – he's obviously got lots of money – he could bribe anyone to hide her. Or they might take her with them, particularly if they think she knows more than she's saying."

"But at least if we know where they are – we will know when they find the lake."

"If they find the lake. I suppose we could go to the police with what we know, now we know who is behind it. Kidnap is a serious crime."

"Perhaps we should ring Gabriel first. She may already be free. He, after all, does not know where we are."

I didn't have a chance to answer as the phone by the bed rang. I reached for it and heard the voice of the receptionist downstairs.

"Ms MacCallum?" she asked.

"Yes," I confirmed

"There is a gentleman wishes to speak to you down in reception."

I was alarmed – no one knew I was here, surely. Joe saw the look on my face.

"What is it, Sara?"

I put my hand over the mouthpiece. "Someone wishes to see me – but no-one should know we are here."

"Then ask for their name," he suggested patiently.

I did as I was bid.

"A Mr Fraser, Ms MacCallum," was the reply.

I hesitated for a minute. "Very well, I'll be down in a minute." I put the receiver down.

"Well?" Joe asked.

"It's Andrew Fraser. How did he know I was here?"

"Well – there is one way to discover the answer. We will go and inspect him."

"Look, Joe – we don't yet know if he is connected with Long in some way. I'd much rather he didn't know about you until I can be sure. Then, if anything goes wrong – well – you'll still be able to act."

"Very well, Sara, if that is what you want. I will go down now and sit in the lounge by the entrance." He put on the brightly striped jacket he had thrown onto the bed when he'd come in. "You can then bring him in there and I'll maybe have a chance to do some eavesdropping." He laughed at himself. "I feel like one of these agent people. Do you not feel this is an exciting adventure, Sara?"

I smiled at him indulgently. "I'm too busy being confused." I didn't add frightened too.

CHAPTER TWELVE

I gave Joe a few minutes to get himself settled in the lounge and then went down to meet Andrew. I would certainly value Joe's opinion of him – I wanted to be sure my instincts about him were right. I liked him – I wanted to be right.

He limped over towards me.

"Andrew, this is a nice surprise, but how did you know I was here?" I shook his outstretched hand.

"Why – were you avoiding me?" I'd forgotten his rather abrasive manner.

"No – but then I hadn't told you where I was either." I replied coldly. I was determined to get an answer out of him. A lot may depend on who knew I was here. "Let's have coffee and we can discuss this sitting down." I pointedly avoided looking at his leg as I said this. I didn't want him to play the martyr and refuse to sit down. I needed Joe to give him the once over.

"Okay by me."

I ordered the coffee and led the way into the lounge. There were a few people in the room but I soon picked out Joe sitting reading a paper. I chose a place so that I would have my back to Joe but he could see Andrew in profile and near enough for him to be able to hear most of what we said.

"Now, Andrew, I'd like a straight answer. How did you know I was here?"

"I'm sorry if my presence offends you."

"Oh, come on, Andrew." I was getting impatient. "You know there's something wrong and your journalist nose is twitching – I understand that, but it doesn't explain how you found me."

"Okay, no need to get so tetchy. You did say you'd keep me in touch, though."

"For goodness sake, Andrew, that was only yesterday. There's nothing happened since." I lied.

"Oh, no? That's not what I've heard. Look, Sara, I know trouble when I see it and at the moment I see it travelling around with you. I just wonder if I can help."

"You can help by answering my question, Andrew." I replied exasperated.

"Okay – it was pure luck. I was at the airport ... meeting someone" I heard the evasion in his tone, "and saw you and two men with you, so I followed you. Only just to make sure you were okay. Okay?"

That would account for the feelings I had of being watched – I was being. It was that that helped me believe him.

"Not really – I don't like being followed, strangely enough," I answered. "But you're here now so you can tell me what this trouble is you've been hearing about."

"And you'll make it worth my while?" His smile took the sting away and I wished he would smile more often. Maybe it gave a glimpse of the Andrew that existed before the accident. I smiled in return but made no promises.

"I'll take that as a yes then, Sara. Well, in my job you get a lot of snippets of information and you have to gather them all together and try and make sense of them." I nodded for him to continue. "Well, I've always had an interest in conservation matters so those pieces usually land on my desk. That's why I was pretty sure I knew the guy who lives in the house I dropped you off at – he looks after birds doesn't he?" I nodded again.

"I've known of him for a few years, in fact his wife visited me in hospital – or so I was told – I was pretty shook up at the time so I don't remember – but his name came up again a week or so back. Seems he was a friend of some chap who's gone missing.

"Anyway, I was asked to cover this conference down in Vancouver which was to do with ecology." I could almost sense Joe stretching his hearing to catch every word. "I did some background reading on the speakers at the conference – it's always as well to be prepared in case you get the chance to ask a revealing question.

"Now there's one chap, pretty high up in his field who got 'my journalist nose twitching'." He smiled over at me. "I knew I'd heard his name somewhere and I did some research. I have a friend who understands all these scientific things and I asked him to check up on a rumour I'd heard that this chap had altered data to suit his own research. I won't bore you with the details, but it turns out the rumour is true, but no-one's willing to do anything about it, whether because such cases are expensive or because he's known to be a vindictive fellow, I don't know. Anyway, I filed this away in the chance I could use it and off I went to the conference."

I kept quiet not wanting to give anything away, but praying Joe could hear it all. There seemed no stopping the previously taciturn Andrew.

"And who should disappear straight after his first lecture, but this very chap I was interested in. Nothing unusual in that you might think. Maybe he'd gone sightseeing. But, I'd been watching him, you see and there was no doubt he was on edge and the speed with which he left the Conference Centre – well, it was suspicious, that's all. No comments so far? Feel free to add anything."

I looked all innocence, at least I hoped that was what it looked like, and asked him to continue.

"Okay, have it your own way, but do stop me if you've heard it all before. Where was I? Oh yes. Well, I couldn't follow him then because there were some facts I needed to check. I was talking to the lady at the conference reception area – Mrs – what's her name."

Without thinking I said "Stewart" and blushed at the look of triumph on Andrew's face. I cursed myself for falling into his trap.

A voice spoke from the side of me – it was Joe.

"Please do excuse me for interrupting, sir, but I feel it would be best if I introduced myself." Andrew stood up and shook Joe's outstretched hand. "I think, Sara," Joe continued "that Mr Fraser has been aware of my presence for some time and I am not a person who would like to be accused of the discourtesy of eavesdropping." He turned to smile at Andrew who shrugged his shoulders.

"Well I'd seen him with you at the airport, Sara, and you have to admit he is quite eye-catching." Joe's guffaw attracted glances from the other people in the lounge.

"Do you know, Sara, I think I like this journalist fellow of yours. Now let us continue this matter of the disappearing lecturer. It is getting very interesting, I think, Sara."

"But you knew I'd been at the Conference Centre, Andrew – so was it just coincidence you were on the same plane as me?"

"Actually I couldn't believe my luck – you might not have noticed that I changed seats so that I could sit by you?" I shook my head – I'd been too wrapped up in my own thoughts. "It really was coincidence, Sara. I used to fly for that company and when I needed to get to Prince Rupert – they offered me a free seat – well I could hardly refuse. I saw you waiting to board and recognised you from the Conference Centre. I happened to be there when you were brushed aside so brusquely by our lecturer, and again when he was asking questions about where you were staying. Mrs Stewart was not happy about it I can tell you."

I shook my head in bewilderment. "It just seems such a coincidence to me. Are you sure you weren't sent to find me?"

Andrew looked hurt, but answered readily. "Will you take my word if I swear I wasn't? Anyway how the hell would I know you were heading towards Prince Rupert – it's one hell of a long way from Vancouver?"

I thought about what he'd said. "Okay, I accept your word, Andrew."

Joe let out a gush of breath. "Well, thank the gods that is over. Now, perhaps, Sara, we can get down to the matter in our hand."

Andrew turned to Joe. "I would be interested to know where you fit in, sir."

"Ah, now, that is not so easy. Would you consider me very rude if I avoided answering that question for now? Please be assured I will tell you what I can when I can."

"Fair enough. I think we can drop the pretences now that we aren't all on the same track. Sara?"

"Okay, I did say I'd give you a story if I could, but just for now, we need some information which you may be able to give us from what you've been saying. We all know we're talking of Dr Julian Long, and we now know the name of the man we think he's working for a Mr Jack Hilton – do you know him?" Andrew nodded. "What we need to know, if possible, is where that particular person keeps his private aeroplane."

"As far as I know, it's here at Prince Rupert. Why?"

"We would be most interested in seeing the flight plans he may have filed today, Mr Fraser. Would this be a possibility?"

"I don't see why not – I still have contacts from when I used to fly – before the accident. But why do you need to know?"

"Let us just say he is looking for something and we wish to know if he finds it."

"This 'something' is central to all this, isn't it?"

"It is, indeed, Mr Fraser, but we are not at liberty to reveal this thing, not I hasten to add, because we do not want to repay your kindness in sharing your information with us. It is simply that we do not know."

It was Andrew's turn to look bewildered. He turned to me. "So where do you fit in all this, Sara?"

"That's an even longer story for which we definitely don't have time. You mentioned that Ben Lawrence's wife visited you in hospital, Andrew, but you don't remember her?"

"There are a lot of things I don't remember since the accident."

"Well, she's involved in this as well." I went on to tell him as much as I thought he needed to know in order to enlist his help.

"Hey, I don't like the sound of that. That seems extreme even for Long – although not for Mr precious Hilton, I suppose."

"What sort of lengths do you think he will go to then?" I asked alarmed.

"Don't worry, Sara. I don't think Ella is any real danger, particularly if Ben keeps his end of the bargain." But I could hear the doubt in his voice.

"Should we go and see them, do you think – Ben and Gabriel?"

"Well we certainly need to see if anything has changed." He thought for a moment. "Whoever Hilton has left there is unlikely to know my voice. Perhaps I could ring?"

"It's worth a try. What do you think, Joe?"

"It may be better if we arrange that I go to the house – it is just possible, is it not, Mr Fraser, that the man inside may know your face?"

"Possible, I suppose."

"Then I will be the one to go."

"What if something goes wrong, Joe? We need you here, not stuck in the lodge with Ben and Gabriel."

"We have to take that risk, Sara, and if I say that I have a bird that is injured, surely nothing can be suspicious about that."

"Joe, could I have a word, please? Sorry, Andrew, won't be a moment."

I took Joe to one side. "I could try and contact Ben through Vigilant, Joe – after all he came through just now. Wouldn't that be safer than anyone getting suspicious?"

"Very well, Sara. We will await you down here. You go to your room and I'll make some excuse to Andrew. If it fails to work, then I think it will be necessary for me to go there, Sara. Ella has to be our first thought, does she not?"

"I know, Joe, but this may be safer all round. I'll be as quick as I can."

I went straight to my room leaving poor Joe to make something up to convince Andrew. I felt hurried which didn't help me relax, so I used the mirror, hoping Ben's grandfather would appear. Instead I saw Vigilant almost straight away, as if he had been waiting and was eager to hear me. I gave him an image of me in the room of the hotel and then I tried to project the image of Ben and Ella together. Vigilant's vibrations came through muddled and I tried again. This time I felt a clarity in the vibrations but I could only 'see' an image of Ella. Then I felt my head start to pump again and I was in the dark room. I reached out for Ben, but only felt a blackness and the pain.

As I came to a realisation dawned. The image I had of the

darkened room was from Ella. She had found a way of communicating with Vigilant, how I didn't know, unless, of course, she'd been able to all along. So – if we could find this room, perhaps we would find Ella. My initial elation was followed by caution. What if I'd misinterpreted the whole thing? What if I wasn't even in touch with Vigilant – it had worked before but was this the same? If it was then I knew one thing for certain. Ella was being kept at an airfield somewhere. There was sense in this, after all Hilton had to keep his plane somewhere. According to Andrew it was at Prince Rupert.

I hurried downstairs. Joe and Andrew appeared to be getting on well. I heard Joe's guffaw of laughter and it was good to see Andrew looking relaxed.

"Hey, you two, where's my drink then?" Joe was on his feet straight away.

"Sara, what will you have?"

"I'll come with you and see what they've got." I said and headed towards the bar.

"So?" Joe asked when we were out of earshot.

"I think I know where Ella is, Joe." I was feeling excited but kept my tone low. "I can't be sure, but you know when I had that bump on the head and saw the dark room – well I saw it again just now when I contacted Vigilant."

"And you believe this room is where Ella is? But I did not know she 'talked' to Vigilant."

"Neither did I, so I could be wrong. But what if I'm not, Joe – we could find her and than Gabriel and Ben would be free."

"Except for the person at the house. You are forgetting, I think, Sara, that he has a gun."

"I'm not forgetting, Joe – but surely we must try and find Ella."

"Yes, Sara, of course. How, though do we explain this knowledge of yours to Mr Fraser?"

I groaned. "Well we can't tell him the truth – not a journalist. But we could say we had had some information – couldn't we – from an anonymous source?"

"A tip-off?" Joe smiled at his use of the word.

"A tip-off." I agreed.

"You go back to Mr Fraser and I will bring your drink."

I returned to Andrew and found he had grown tense again.

"Sara, something is going on between you and Mr Muscat and I'm not sure I like being excluded. I thought you needed my help – how can I help when you keep things from me?"

"They're not things you need to know, Andrew, honestly."

"I'd sure like to be the judge of that, thank you," he replied curtly.

"Look, please just accept that there are things that are not mine to share. Just because you are a journalist doesn't mean you have to have all the facts, surely."

"From where I'm standing I do."

I was getting impatient with him. "Well, at the moment you're sitting, not standing, so you can either take it or leave it." I held my breath – hoping his 'nose' would be stronger than his pique.

"Okay, I don't have much choice do I?" But he still did not look happy. "If there comes a time when I really need to know, then I expect you to tell me, Sara, is that quite clear?"

"Quite."

Joe arrived with my orange juice (I needed a clear head – this was no time for vodka) and a coffee for Andrew. He had a bottle of water for himself. He sensed the tense atmosphere and cocked one eyebrow at me – I just shrugged.

"Now, Mr Fraser, has Sara told you that we have had some information which could help us locate Mrs Lawrence?"

"No, she has told me nothing, as usual."

"Come, now, Mr Fraser, this is no time for disagreements. Would you not agree that while Mrs Lawrence is in danger we should join our forces, not fight amongst ourselves?" Joe gave his most charming smile.

"I suppose so. So what's this information you have?"

"Not much, I'm afraid, but you may be able to throw some light upon it, knowing the area. When you said that Hilton's plane it is at Prince Rupert airfield – could it be anywhere else, do you think?"

"It may be – I don't know that much about his movements."

"Only the information is that she is being held near to an airfield and I can't see them risking a busy airport, can you?"

"Well, there are parts around the field that aren't that frequented.

"Are there any houses nearby?" I asked.

"Tell you what, why don't we go and have a look."
"Surely we can't just snoop around an airport?"
"You can, if you know the right people – which I do." Andrew replied smugly. "Providing, of course it's made worth my while."
"If it is money you require," Joe said stiffly, "then of course you must name your price."
Andrew had the grace to look shame-faced. "No, Mr Muscat, thank you, but it isn't your money I want – just a story."
"Oh, I think we can guarantee you that, don't you, Sara?"
"Well, I'm sure Ella will have a thing or two to say to you if we can find her." I wouldn't be drawn further than that.
"Right, let's go then." Andrew rose stiffly to his feet. I saw the grimace of pain as he straightened the injured leg. I could hardly wonder if he was a bit sharp – after all I was holding out on him, offering him little in return for his help.

CHAPTER THIRTEEN

We waited in Andrew's car while he found the person at the airfield he needed to talk to. I told Joe the sort of place we were looking for – somewhere not well cared for with shutters at the windows and near what may be a hangar. I felt a knot of nervousness in my stomach. We were about to try and make one of my 'visionings' into truth and I wasn't sure whether I wanted to or not. I wanted to find Ella, obviously, but if what I 'saw' proved true, then life was not likely ever to be the same again for me. Joe sensed my unease and squeezed my hand.

"What will be, will be, Sara. There will be no going back – no?"

"No, Joe and that's what scares me."

"I understand – but remember Mistral – would you be without her now?" I shook my head. "Nor would I part with my Omen."

"What omen?" Andrew had returned to the car without us hearing him.

"Just a part of my family belief." Joe was quicker than me. I was still searching in my addled brain for an answer.

"Right," Andrew sounded doubtful. "Well it's all arranged. There's no planes due for half an hour, so we can go to the far end of the airfield where the buildings are not in use. But we must report back when we've finished."

"Thanks, Andrew."

We parked near the perimeter fence and got out.

"Now, where do you reckon we should start?"

Joe turned to me. "Sara? After all it was to you that the information was given." I blessed him for the subtlety of it.

"There was something about a house or a bungalow, so perhaps we could look for that."

"There's an old bungalow over in the far corner – not been lived in for a while, I reckon. Do you want to start there?"

"Sounds as good as anywhere to me."

"Look, Sara, if you'd rather stay in the car, we can go ahead without you. After all, if you're right, there just could be some trouble."

"I'm aware of that, thank you, Andrew, but I need to be there."

"Okay, but the least sign of trouble and I want you out, is that clear?" I looked him in the eyes and he blushed. He was genuinely worried about what happened to me and it embarrassed him. Maybe I had, after all, got under that prickly skin of his.

"That's alright by me," I replied cheerfully. "I never have had much of an affinity with violence."

"Me, I have not neither," agreed Joe. "Perhaps I will stay in the car," he teased. "Perhaps we should, after all, go for the police."

"Let's play it by ear," Andrew compromised, not wanting to miss a story or the excitement.

"Or nose." I commented under my breath. Andrew heard me and gave me a wry smile. I smiled in return and a truce was formed.

I'd brought my camera with me as a pretext for us being there. There were no trees to disguise our approach, but we felt an open appearance was best, so we walked casually. Just past a hangar I could see the bungalow now, and we were approaching it from the back. The bungalow was just outside the perimeter fence, so we couldn't approach it from this side.

We retraced our footsteps to the car, not hurrying. We had to return to the main gates to get onto the road that would take us to the bungalow.

"You think that's the one, Sara?" Andrew asked.

"It fits the description" I replied. I leant back against the seat and closed my eyes. Joe was in the front with Andrew, which gave me a chance to try and reach Ella. No sooner had I shut my eyes and opened my mind to Vigilant than he was there, living up to his name, but more powerful this time. I pictured Ella in my mind, but I only got a jumble of images back. "Slow down" I breathed and then realised I'd said it out loud.

"But I'm hardly doing twenty," Andrew commented. "This road is too rough for anything else." Joe turned to look at me. I mouthed the word Vigilant and he nodded his head in understanding. I would have valued his help, but knew he could do nothing while he sat alongside Andrew – it took too much concentration.

"We're nearly there, " Andrew said, "so I'll park here. If it is the right house, we don't want to announce ourselves before we're ready."

He pulled into the side of the road. "Sara, why don't you stay here? Mr Muscat and I can find out if there's anyone there."

"No," I said firmly. "I'm in this too – so I'm coming."

"Okay, but try and stay out of trouble."

"Yes, sir," I replied with a light heartedness I was far from feeling. The layout of the bungalow was right – we seemed to have hit the jackpot first time, but I would need to see more to be sure.

Joe spoke. "Why don't I knock at the door and tell anyone who may answer that I'm lost. I look like a tourist, do I not?" He still had his T-shirt and jeans on, so I gave him my camera to complete the picture.

"Perfect," I proclaimed. "While you're doing that I'll just have a look round the back."

"Hey, that should be my job," Andrew protested.

"Your job, Mr Fraser, is to make sure I do not too get kidnapped, is that not so, Sara?"

"Indeed it is, Joe."

"Okay, have it your own way, but do try and keep out of sight, Sara."

Fortunately the area around the bungalow was overgrown with tall grass and bushes, so it was no problem getting to the back without being seen. I heard Joe knock at the front door, but couldn't hear any movements within the house. There was a tumble down fence – and the shutters. My heart pounded when I saw the knothole and I felt my knees weaken. I'd had deja-vue before and that was weird enough, but this was weirder still – but I just felt it had to be the same place. I returned to the front of the house. Joe and Andrew were discussing the best way to break in as the door was locked.

Joe looked at me and I nodded. Andrew intercepted the look. "What is it with you two? You're still holding back." He looked at our blank faces and shrugged. "Well, Miss Know-all, is this the right place or not?"

"Yes, I'm pretty sure it is."

"Okay – so we're going in then?"

"Most definitely," Joe confirmed. "Perhaps it would be better round the back."

"If we can get the shutters off, we may be able to get in through one of the windows." I led the way round the back.

Joe held back a bit and asked quietly, "Which window?"

"The one with the knot hole I told you about." He just nodded and joined Andrew.

"I suppose removing shutters can't be classed as breaking and entering."

"Surely you've had to do such things before in your journalistic career?" I asked teasingly.

"Hardly – not with my leg," was the gruff reply. "We could just unscrew the hinges, I suppose. Anyone got a Swiss army knife?"

"Looking at the state of rust – I think a little pulling in the right place may bring these shutters off. Shall we try this one first, Mr Fraser?" Joe indicated the one with the knotholes.

"Okay, but could we drop the Mr bit – just Andrew will do."

"That is kind and I am Joe."

I looked on with impatience whilst they got these strangely timed formalities over with. I was eager to get in and away as quickly as possible, someone may come back at any time.

It took little effort to remove the shutters, and Joe was able to peer into the room through the grimy window. "Sara, she is there," he said in a hushed and awed voice. "She is there."

I leant against the wall to steady myself. I had fluctuated between certainty and doubt, sometimes convinced I was right and then cursing myself for a fool. So I was no fool – at least not over this – I had the right house and we had only to get Ella out and I could go home. Joe had forced the catch on the window and looked further in.

"Is she alright?" I asked as I levered myself away from the wall. Andrew caught my eye.

"That was very accurate information you had. Seems like an insider to me."

"Something like that. Anyway let's get her out. I'm the smallest – I'll climb through first and see if she's okay."

"She looks to be asleep." Joe informed us. "Perhaps they have her drugged, do you think?"

I groaned. "More than likely which is going to make it difficult to get her out. I'll try and wake her. Joe, can you follow me in and see if you can find another way out."

"Certainly, Sara. Perhaps Andrew can keep watch out here in case anyone should return." That way he wouldn't have to try and climb through the window – another example of Joe's kindness.

I wormed my way through the window and approached the bed. The room was just as I had seen it – the lamp still on. Ella looked pale but she was breathing evenly and I could see nothing else wrong with her. I shook her gently by the shoulder and called her name. She muttered something but didn't wake up. This was going to be difficult. I went to the window.

"You'd better bring the car up, Andrew. I can't wake her." He went off round the side towards the car.

Joe joined me in the room. "She sleeps deeply, yes?"

"I'll try some cold water – there's some by her bed." Joe offered me his handkerchief and I dipped it in the water. I applied it gently to Ella's forehead. Again she stirred but didn't wake up. Joe went to find a door that we could open to get her out.

In desperation I felt myself delving into my mind for Vigilant – could he reach her. Instead I found Misty and she chittered in warning, but it was too loud for me to distinguish what it was about. Then I felt Vigilant's vibrations add to hers. I put my hands to my head trying to make sense of them. Joe came back into the room.

"Sara, what is wrong? Mistral?"

"Yes and Vigilant. They're upset about something but I don't know what, but I think we should hurry."

"Come, then – let us get Ella out. The back door is now open, but where is Andrew with the car? I do not hear it."

"Don't forget his leg holds him up, Joe."

"I do not forget that, but even with it he should be here by now."

We tried putting Ella on her feet and seeing if we could support her between us, but she was such a dead weight we decided to carry her in a blanket, Joe at her head and me at her feet. We carried her into the overgrown garden at the back, had a rest and then carried her to the front of the house. We laid her gently on the grass and waited for the sound of Andrew's car. A bend in the road prevented us seeing the part of the road where we'd left the car.

"You wait with Ella, Joe, I'm going to see what's happened to Andrew. We need to get moving." I was feeling really on edge.

As I got round the bend in the road I could see Andrew limping down the road towards me and I wondered what was wrong with the car. Then I realised it was nothing to do with the car – behind Andrew walked another man and even from here I could see the gun in his hand. I didn't know what to do – the man had already seen me, so flight was out of the question. I decided to walk away from the front of the house away from Joe and Ella. In warning to Joe I shouted at Andrew.

"What the hell's going on?"

"Just shut it," came from the man carrying the gun pointed at Andrew's back, "and move away from the house where I can see you."

"But what's this all about? If we're trespassing, I'm sorry, but surely that's no reason to point a gun at someone. We aren't burglars or anything."

"Good try, Miss, but I saw you from the hangar. Now, we'll all go into the house and then we'll see what I'm to do with you."

I saw shame in Andrew's face and that made me angry, very angry. Then I realised it wasn't just my anger – it was filling my head and it hurt. I closed my eyes and it seemed to focus into the centre of my head. When I opened my eyes I knew why. High in the sky I saw a huge dark shadow that sped towards us and I knew that I was seeing Vigilant for the first time and it was an awesome sight. I knew too, what he intended and I tried to guide him, tried to show him what to do. I had to stall for time – keep the man in the open.

"Now wait just a minute," I protested. I stepped towards them and drew Andrew by the arm to my side so that we stood facing the man, between him and Ella and Joe. Under my breath I whispered to Andrew. "Be ready."

"No talking you two." The man felt threatened facing us both. He knew nothing about the shadow heading now straight for his exposed back. Concentrating I tried to guide Vigilant to take an oblique angle so that, if the gun went off, it wouldn't hit any of us. I had to lean hard against Andrew to steady myself as I felt the old feeling of flying with Vigilant take over. It meant I could keep my eyes closed but know when the moment of impact was going to take place.

At the last minute I shouted "Duck" (although it might have been more accurate to say "bald eagle", but we'll let that pass) and pulled on Andrew's arm. I felt the jar as Vigilant hit the man knocking the arm that held the gun so hard that the gun fell from his fingers. Then I was released back into my own mind and Vigilant was soaring off to take his place on a telegraph post, where he quietly, and proudly, preened himself.

Andrew had been quick off the mark, thanks to my warning. After a "What the hell?" he'd picked up the gun and had it pointed at the man. The man was obviously in shock, not even noticing the blood dripping onto the road from the gash Vigilant had opened in his arm.

Joe hurried forward. "Are you both alright?"

I nodded and reached out a hand to him. "Did you see him – wasn't he magnificent?"

"I assume you mean the bird," came Andrew's acerbic reply. "But did you see the speed with which I reached the gun?" The light-heartedness was a result of the release from tension, but it suited him. "To weightier issues – what are we going to do with this fellow? When we've decided that then I want some answers. I'll not be put off this time either, Sara."

Of course, he had the right to those answers, but would he believe them when he heard them? I doubted it.

"We should hand him over to the police." Joe declared.

"But they'd ask all sorts of questions and we're free now, Joe. Gabriel and Ben are free – let's keep it like that for now. We need to keep this chap out of action for a while, though. Any suggestions, Andrew?"

"Why not lock him in the house and then send someone to free him when the coast is clear?"

We agreed on this. Andrew brought up the car whilst Joe kept the gun pointed rather uncertainly at our captive. Andrew found some cord to incapacitate him after roughly bandaging his arm, to prevent him bleeding on his car. We then placed Ella in the flat boot of the estate and made her as comfortable as possible.

There was a coat of Andrew's in the back and I asked if I could borrow it. He looked puzzled but agreed. Vigilant was still on the post, looking more alert now. The yellow of his eye seemed to shine out at me in satisfaction, only the black outline preventing the colour being lost in the white of his magnificent head. His beak was truly the largest beak I had ever seen and the size of his yellow feet was equally awe inspiring, and I had seen the size of the strong, wide wings, so knew how heavy he was likely to be. But, determined not to be deterred, I wrapped the coat around my arm and called to him. I would never have attempted this with a bird so large if I hadn't been able to "talk" to him. I knew it would be the greatest honour if he came, but the need to put our relationship on a more solid, physical footing was strong enough to try – that way what had happened wouldn't seem so strange.

I placed my arm on the gatepost of the house to take the weight that I knew would be great and opened my mind to him, pouring my gratitude into it and my admiration. It must have been the admiration that did it. As I watched he glided down from the post towards me and landed with a gentleness that astounded me. Eye to eye we stood a while, whilst I drank in the beauty of him, then I told him we were going with Ella to Ben. He threw an image of Mistral into my mind and took off on his great wings.

I felt shaky with the emotion of the encounter, and found Joe at my side. I turned to face him and was warmed by the look of such pride in his eyes.

"You are highly honoured, Sara, – yes?"

"Oh yes, Joe." My heart was singing.

Andrew stood by the car with his mouth open. "Did I really

see what I just saw?"

"Such was your privilege." Joe uttered pompously.

I handed Andrew his coat. "Thanks – I don't think he's harmed it." He took it from me unconsciously, still in a daze.

"Come, Andrew," Joe commanded, "it is time we should go."

We took the chance to question our captive about who was paying him and what drug he had been feeding Ella. It was with relief we found they were only sleeping pills so it wouldn't be long before she was back to normal. Deprived of his gun, he proved quite amenable and eager to tell us what he could, including a number on which we could reach Hilton. He apparently hadn't been very keen to take on the task of keeping Ella drugged, but was more afraid of failing his employer.

The wait for the ferry across to the mainland seemed interminable, but it gave us a chance to get a snack and come up with a strategy before arriving at the lodge. Vigilant would be ahead of us. I felt pretty sure he would pass the news onto Ben, but I wanted to be sure.

Once we'd cleared Prince Rupert I asked, "Andrew, do you mind if I close my eyes for a bit, I'm a bit tired?"

"No, go ahead. You've had a busy time. I'll wake you when I need directions."

His attitude towards me had changed. He was more civil and there was none of the prickles. I rather missed them.

Settling down, I reached for Vigilant and told him I wanted to speak to Ben. His thoughts were jumbled as they were so often. I concentrated on myself in the car and travelling to the lodge, but Vigilant seemed preoccupied and I only got misty images back from him. I enjoyed sitting there with my eyes closed, though. Then all of sudden I shot bolt upright. Misty had come through to me, but so strongly and with so much joy, I was jolted. I knew she was close. I felt Joe's hand on my shoulder and realised how far we had come together in the short time since we met, because I also felt Omen in my head and she was calling to Joe. In the distance I sensed Scrap and Rift. They were in the place of the rocks.

Andrew looked at me in the rear view mirror. "Sara, are you alright?"

"Never better," I answered readily.

"Sara," he spoke quietly, "I remember Ella now – you know

– when she came to visit me in hospital. It's part of that time I've blocked out, but, seeing you with that bird has reminded me – it had something to do with birds, but I just can't remember what. Do you think she'd be offended if I asked her when she wakes up?"

"I shouldn't think so. You told me you'd had a bump on the head. Concussion can do funny things." I spoke from experience. Concussion was the commonest symptom I had in the birds that came to me. "You must have given your head quite a crack."

"I really don't remember. I lie awake at night sometimes, worrying about the things I can't remember. Surely it should have come back by now?"

"Well, recognising Ella is a step in the right direction."

"Yes, it is, isn't it?" He sounded more cheerful. "Did I really see you with a bald eagle on your arm – or am I still suffering from concussion?"

I laughed. "No, he really was there."

"It's one of the most spectacular things I've seen, do you know that, Sara?" He sounded embarrassed, so I chuckled to lighten things for him.

Then I realised where we were. "We're nearly there, Andrew, it's the next turn on the left."

He turned off the road and we came to a halt. "Now what do we do."

"Let me off just a few yards short of the lodge and I'll find my way in."

"But how will you get in without being seen?"

"Look, I've been there, don't forget, I'm the only one who knows the layout. Please, Andrew, trust me, I know what I'm doing."

"Your record so far might not back that up, but, okay, we'll give you five minutes, no longer, Sara, is that quite clear?"

"Give or take a minute or two."

We drove on and Andrew let me out just short of the final turning to Ben and Ella's lodge. I crept into the trees and stood for a while near the back of the house, looking for the lights. It was already dusk – another day nearly gone. Looking towards the house I saw, standing on the roof, the outline of a bird that could only be Vigilant. So he had come here. My heart lifted.

Then I saw a shadow land by his side and my heart pounded.

I knew from the feeling in my being and the joy in my mind that it was Misty. It was all I could do not to call out loud. I dared not attract attention to myself. Her eyes searched the growing dark. I knew they saw ten times better than my own, but when had we needed sight to guide us. I opened my mind and she came like an arrow to the tree where I stood. I cared little that I had no glove to protect my hand, but I never needed it – her touch was as light as it could be, just a gentle pressure to keep her steady as we stared at each other. I rubbed her chest while I asked her how Scrap and Rift were, how she came to be there and all the other puzzles in my mind.

She hopped onto my left shoulder and rubbed her head against mine. It felt so good to be in her company again, I almost forgot why I was there. Then a light went on in Ben's studio. I relaxed – Vigilant had done his work after all. Then I saw that it was Gabriel, not Ben. I couldn't see his face, but I recognised his outline. He seemed to look directly over to where I was and then turned abruptly back into the living room.

I was disappointed, maybe he hadn't understood, but Mistral preened my hair happily and once more made me content. I relaxed back against the tree and waited. It could only have been a few minutes and I saw Vigilant fly off in the direction of the car with Ella in it. I waited again but nothing happened. I closed my eyes and tried to see what Vigilant was seeing, but instead I saw an image of Gabriel, smiling and relaxed and it could only have come from Mistral. Or so I thought, until I felt a touch on my right shoulder. I knew the touch and the smell, but kept my eyes shut for a moment longer, savouring the feeling I'd longed for.

Mistral left my shoulder and I opened my eyes and stared straight into Gabriel's. There was no need for words. Carefully he folded me to him and I laid my head on his shoulder. Only then did the tears I had hidden for so long well up inside me and I wept, safe and secure in his arms, as if my heart would break – half with joy at finding myself so enclosed and half from relief. He held me until the worst was over, then, brushing the tears away with his thumb, he put his arm round my shoulder and led me to the lodge. We had said nothing because nothing needed saying. Tears are great healers and healers have great shoulders to cry on!

CHAPTER FOURTEEN

We arrived in the living room in time to see Ben carrying Ella in and Andrew limping in behind him. I looked around for the thug left behind with Ben and Gabriel but there was no sign of him. A faint knocking noise, though, was coming from the cupboard under the stairs.

Joe came in last and at the sight of him Gabriel hurried forward and shook him vigorously by the hand. Joe turned to look at me.

"I have kept her safe for you, have I not?"

"Or was it the other way round?" Gabriel asked, but Joe's grin took no offence. "Where's Callum?"

"In Vancouver. He has been doing the investigator bit for us." Joe answered.

I heard Ella mutter as she stirred in Ben's arms as he laid her on the sofa. "I'll kill them if they've harmed her."

"I'm sure it was only sleeping pills, Ben," I reassured him. "She'll probably wake up with only a headache." Remembering what it had felt like in the image I didn't envy her.

Gabriel turned to Andrew. "I must apologise if I was rude when we first met." He held out his hand. "Thank you for bringing them home."

"He did more than that, Gabriel. None of this would have been possible without him." I was quick to come to Andrew's defence – I'd seen the look on his face when Gabriel and I had come in hand in hand. He'd seen me as perhaps more than just a good story and it hurt me to hurt him.

Ella was waking up. She still looked very pale and sleepy.

"Where's Vigilant?" she asked drowsily

"Outside, sweetheart," Ben answered.

"Oh, Ben, I had the strangest dream. Where's Sara?"

I stepped forward. "I'm here Ella."

"Oh, good, I thought you'd left me in that dreadful place, but you've come back for me."

"I think she's a bit confused, Sara." Ben looked worried, but I understood. Just as I had seen her, Ella had seen me, whether through Vigilant or not, and believed I was with her in the room, which explained why the pain had seemed so strong to me.

"Come on, sweetheart, let's get you to bed, you'll feel better in the morning."

"Right – who's eaten?" Gabriel asked.

"None of us." I replied.

"Omelettes okay?"

"Anything to fill the stomach." Joe replied.

"Can you give us a hand, Sara?" Gabriel asked. We went through to the kitchen and Gabriel closed the door.

"I don't know how much you've told Andrew about all this, Sara, so I thought I'd better be careful what I say in front of him."

I whisked the eggs as we talked. It was good to do normal things again. "He only knows what he's picked up himself – he was already onto Long. I think we should tell him everything, though, Gabriel. He may not believe it but I think he'll be a useful ally all the same." Gabriel was about to open his mouth to protest. "We'd never have found Ella without his help."

"You like him, don't you?"

"Yes and he's not had it easy. His leg gives him a lot of pain but he never mentions it."

"Just how much do you like him, Sara?" He turned me towards him, the whisk still in my hand dripping egg on the floor. “This much, perhaps?” He leant forward and kissed me gently on the lips. I closed my eyes and immediately Misty was there, chittering. “Shut up, Misty.” I muttered. Gabriel burst into laughter.

“You're a born romantic, Sara. You stand there with your whisk dripping egg all over the clean floor muttering threats.”

“Oh, give me another chance, Gabriel. I promise I'll do better.” This time he removed the whisk before putting his arms gently around me and his lips very firmly against mine. I just melted. I'd so longed to feel his kiss again and the strong lean body which pressed itself against mine. So I returned his kiss without reserve – well, with fervour really – but still aware Misty was there. How I wished the others weren't. Any more passion would just have to wait and I'd already waited nearly three years – oh well, patience is a virtue and all that.

I surfaced breathlessly to smell the butter burning in the frying pan. Gabriel leant over towards the stove and removed the pan without taking his other arm from around me.

“So, what is the answer to my question?” he asked, one irritating, quizzical eyebrow raised.

“Which one?”

“What do you mean, which one?”

“The one you asked with your body or the verbal one?”

“Okay, how about both?”

“No and yes.” I replied

“Sara ...” his tone was exasperated “Can't you answer a straight question – or do I have to be a bird. Shall I ask Mistral?”

“Can you?”

“I'm learning – she's been with us all day. Ben tried talking to her through Vigilant but he seemed to have other things on his mind.”

“He certainly did.” The memory flooded back. “I doubt we'd be here now without him, and we'd never have found Ella. I'll let Joe tell you about Vigilant's rescue.”

“Are you avoiding answering my question, Sara?”

I was saved from answering by Big Ben. “What are you trying to do – burn the place down – it stinks in here.” We must both have looked guilty because Ben burst out laughing. “You guys look like two teenagers caught out. Look I'll take over – you go and organise some drinks Gabriel. Sara can help me in here."

Gabriel went into the living room. Ben cleaned out the pan and returned it to the heat with more butter.

"How's Ella?" I asked.

"Oh, Sara, I can't thank you enough for bringing her back. I guess you don't know how much you love someone till you think you may not see them again. It's been hell."

"Well, I couldn't have done it without Vigilant. He not only showed me where she was, he helped us rescue her." I didn't mention that he'd flown down to me. I remembered how I had felt when Mistral talked to Gabriel. "I'll tell you all about it over supper."

It was a cheerful meal with the release from the tension of the last few days. We made enough for Long's employee and he joined us readily at the table. When it came time to discuss things, though, he was returned to the cupboard. It was interesting how amenable he had become since being separated from his gun.

During the meal there had been a peremptory tap on the window, and, with Ben's ready agreement, I let Misty in. We had, after all, been parted for ages and it was good to have her company again. When we were all sitting in the living room, she came to sit on my shoulder and, for a moment, it was like being back in Wales in less complicated times, before we had some unknown task to undertake.

Andrew was staring at Misty, sitting quietly on my shoulder. "How many birds do you have, Sara?" he asked.

"I don't actually have any, Andrew. Mistral lives with me when she chooses and goes off when she doesn't."

"She looks pretty settled now. Why is she staring at me like that, though?"

I looked at Misty on my shoulder and she was staring at Andrew intently as if trying to get into his mind. Instead she threw an image into mine. I closed my eyes for a minute, but the picture was very hazy, as though she herself was not seeing it clearly. It was of a face that looked like Andrew's, but it was very still. I shook my head clear of the image and realised Andrew was watching me.

I laughed to cover the moment. "Must be your irresistible charm, Andrew."

"No." Andrew suddenly shouted, putting his hands over his face. Everyone in the room went quiet. Joe, who was sitting next to him, placed his hand on Andrew's arm.

"Andrew, please, what is the matter?"

Andrew turned to Ben. "I must see your wife." And he half rose as though to go to her. Joe still had his hand on his arm and pulled him back onto the sofa.

"Please, Andrew, Ella is not well enough yet. Let her sleep."

Andrew looked around apologetically. "I'm sorry. I wasn't thinking straight. I'm, sorry – only I suddenly had all these images in my head." He pressed the palms of his hands against his forehead. "I think I'm beginning to remember again and it's all so confusing."

I came to his rescue. "Ben, do you remember when Ella visited Andrew in hospital?"

Ben looked blank for a moment. "Of course – that's why your name was familiar. Yes, yes she did. You'd had a bad fall and serious concussion. They were worried about you – you kept muttering about birds. That's why Ella was called in. Helen, who works at the hospital, asked if she'd come and see if she could make any sense of what you were saying. It was obviously bothering you a lot and they thought Ella's knowledge of birds would help clear it up."

"And did it?" Andrew asked eagerly.

"No, I don't reckon it did – do you?" Ben saw Andrew's face. "But I'll certainly ask her if it's that important – but not until she's slept off the effect of those tablets."

Gabriel abruptly changed the conversation. "We have yet to decide what to do about our friend in the cupboard. What do you think, Joe?"

"Me, I would go to the police and let them sort it out. Maybe they would not be able to tie in Dr Long with these two that have caused trouble, but they cannot deny the kidnap of Ella."

"Ben?" Gabriel asked.

"I don't know. Now we've got Ella back safely, we've still got a bit of time before Long gets to know we're free to move once more. Should we use the time to carry on looking for Paul or let it rest and see what Long turns up?"

"We've all come a long way just to turn round and go home. How do you feel, Sara?"

I found it difficult to gather my thoughts because Misty was still sending images, only this time of the carved rock face and it made concentration difficult, particularly as the faint image of Andrew was also there.

"Sara?" Gabriel asked again.

"Would you mind if I had a word with Andrew alone, Gabriel?"

"Feel free," he replied rather coldly.

"Use my studio," Ben volunteered. I smiled my gratitude and wondered if he too was getting messages.

Andrew followed me readily enough. I went through the outside doors to the veranda and, putting Misty on the rail, sat down on the steps that led down to the garden area. Andrew sat beside me.

"Sorry about my outburst, Sara," Andrew began but I stopped him.

"It's not about that Andrew. I did promise you an explanation at some point, but I need to know whether you want to continue to be involved in this. If the decision is to go to the police, then you'll have a story anyway about the kidnap – and your part in the rescue, of course. But I'm sure you're aware there's more at stake here than that."

"Yes, and I'd like to know when I'm going to be let in on things."

"That has to be everyone's decision, Andrew. And it's possible they may not want to involve you further. But do you want to continue with us?"

"If you'd asked me that a coupe of hours ago, I'd have said yes definitely ..."

"What's changed then, Andrew?"

"Come on, Sara – I don't need to spell it out. You must have known how I felt about you."

I looked him in the eyes, although he tried to avoid the contact. "Andrew, since I've known you, which has only been a few days after all, you've been as prickly as a hedgehog. No, I didn't know, not until I saw the look in your eyes when I came in with Gabriel, and I'm sorry. But you gave me no indication."

He sighed. "Would it have made any difference if I had?"

"Not between Gabriel and me, no – we've known each other for many years. But I might have hesitated to involve you

– I assumed it was your journalistic 'nose' which was leading you."

"I admit I was curious." He stopped as if searching for words. "I wasn't always this prickly, Sara."

"I can see that when you smile." My reward was one of those smiles. I couldn't deny that in different circumstances things may have been different between Andrew and me. "I assume the accident was responsible."

"It's the feeling of not being in control – there's a chunk of your life missing and there's nothing you can do to get it back."

"Except perhaps to return to the place where it all happened." I suggested.

"I've thought about it, Sara, but there's something always stops me. Something in my head says – 'you must not return alone'."

"Why did you add – alone – then, Andrew? Would you go if you weren't alone?"

"I don't know – it's just how it is in my head."

"Have you thought what it would be like to have total recall of everything that happened? So often the brain protects itself by blotting out what it can't face."

"But it's still as if an important part of my life is missing."

"Is that why it's so important for you to speak to Ella – you think she can shed some light on that time?"

"I suppose so. It was that bird of yours, Sara, she made me feel – I don't know – just staring at me like that."

"She meant no harm, Andrew."

"I know, I know. But it was like she got inside my head. I just felt I had to do something .... crazy, hey?"

"If only you knew," I muttered under my breath.

"What's all this leading to, Sara?"

"I want to ask you a favour, but I don't want to put you in a situation you may not like."

"What's changed all of a sudden?"

"Ouch."

"Sorry. Go on, ask."

"Would you fly me to the Queen Charlotte Islands, Andrew – if the others don't want to come."

"What's so special about the Islands, Sara?" he asked

suspiciously.

"Nothing, Andrew." I replied evasively. "I just want the chance to see Peal's Peregrine – after all I've not had much of a holiday so far."

"No you haven't have you." He thought hard a moment. "Okay, I'll take you. I've got to face it sometime."

I smiled with relief and felt Misty stir on the rail as she threw an image of Scrap, Rift and Omen into my mind, circling in the air above the carved rock. Were my instincts about the Islands right, then – is that where they all were – and why?

"If you feel you can't, Andrew, I can always get a charter flight or," I couldn't resist testing Misty, "not go at all." Misty started to chitter and I knew I'd been right.

"I'll do it, Sara." Andrew declared firmly.

"What will you do?" I hadn't heard Gabriel come through the veranda doors.

Andrew answered off the cuff. "Take her flying."

"Hardly a novelty, then," Gabriel commented.

"What do you mean?"

"You haven't told him you have a Pilot's Licence, then, Sara?"

"Lapsed years ago, Gabriel. I can't seem to find the money or the time since you left." I was cross with him for interrupting and I'd have preferred to tell Andrew myself that I used to fly, in the easy years when I didn't have the responsibility of a hundred birds a year to care for.

"You've had enough time, now, Sara. We need to take a vote on what we're going to do."

"Okay, we're coming." I left Mistral outside and said good-night to her. She looked me in the eye and I knew she wouldn't be there in the morning, but the images were reassuring – she wouldn't be far away.

We entered the living room and took our seats as before. Gabriel seemed to be in charge.

"We need to decide whether to continue looking for Paul, now we know it could be dangerous." Gabriel looked at me. "Sara?"

I was devastated to be the one he turned to first. I knew the birds wouldn't let me stop until I'd joined them. I had to go on, but with the others – I didn't know. I did know that I didn't want to go alone.

"I don't know, Gabriel – I never met Paul – how can I judge?"

"Do you want to continue, Sara?" Gabriel was firm.

Joe, bless him, came to my rescue. "How can she answer that, Gabriel – you know the position she is in. Like myself she has come half way round the world for what may prove a dream – you brought her – never forget that."

Gabriel put his head in his hands. I longed to touch him, but didn't dare. The face he turned towards us looked older, the sapphire blue eyes darker once more.

"Joe – you're right, and you above all others know why we're here. You all know me as a healer, except Andrew here, but none of you know what healing involves. You three, Sara, Joe and Ben, you know what physical healing is, but not what spiritual healing means – the drain on ones inner soul. Over the years I stopped listening to the inner problems that manifested themselves in the outward symptom. I couldn't solve, only alleviate them so I ignored them." We all stared at him, not understanding.

"Then I came to you, Joe and your peregrine, and he told me tales I didn't want to hear, so I told him to tell you instead. Ben, do you remember the first bald eagle you had in – two years ago – he told me the same tale – so I told him the same. Only you weren't ready to hear him, despite your grandfather's teaching.

"Then there was Callum, only that was only four months ago, and his eagle told the same tales. This time I understood them better, but still I told him to tell Callum – still I didn't want to know."

I knew instinctively it was my turn.

"Sara," he turned to me and took my hand. "For you I have no excuse. All those years ago when I first knew you – when I first loved you." My heart pounded. "They wanted to tell you the tales I wouldn't listen to, tales of horror and death, of the great change which they feared. But I wouldn't let them trouble you, fearful what you would do." He let go of my hand and looked away. "Then I left you and Mistral found you. She knew you'd care enough to try and make a difference, so she entrusted her family to you, and I've brought you and them half way round the world, because I refused to listen. And because I wouldn't listen, I no longer understand. Sara, I don't know what to do," he cried out in despair and put his hands once more over his face.

I knelt in front of him, devastated by his outburst, and took his hands gently away from his face and held them in my own. There was a silence in the room. I leaned forward and kissed him on the brow. He looked up at me, searching my eyes.

With absolute certainty I said "I know what they want, Gabriel – we only have to go with them."

Keeping one of Gabriel's hands in mine I reached my other to Joe and he came and took it and pulled me to my feet, then reached his free hand for Ben. Ben took Gabriel's other hand and pulled him to his feet. We stood in silence while I called on Mistral, Scrap, Rift, Omen, Vigilant and Wraith. They came through to me all of them with such power I swayed. I felt Andrew put his arms on my shoulders to steady me and I leant against him, glad of the support. Tempering the power, I transferred the images into the minds of the others – the lake – the rock face – and lastly the image of Ben's grandfather and the Raven. I felt the caress of the old man's gentle smile and then everything went dark.

CHAPTER FIFTEEN

I was aware of being gently laid on a bed and a blanket placed over me. I smiled up into Joe's face and he leant down and kissed my forehead. "Sleep well, my little one. You have done all you can – we will do the rest." With that I fell asleep.

It was just after dawn when I woke, starving. I went through the living room to the kitchen. Andrew lay asleep on the sofa and I stopped for a moment to study the lines of his face gentled by sleep, so different from the waking pain lines usually showing.

I made coffee and it was as though the smell filtrated the whole house, drawing everyone out of bed. Within minutes Ben was there, tousle haired and beautifully bare-chested managing to look even taller and broader in pyjama bottoms and bare feet.

"How's Ella?" I asked, averting my eyes from all that muscle.

"Still sleeping," he replied. "More to the point how are you? You gave us quite a shock last night. Thank God Andrew was holding onto you. That's some power you have, Sara. Talking of Andrew, I think it may be as well if you have a chat with him

– he's a bit in shock."

"A bit is an understatement," came from the doorway.

"Morning, Andrew," I responded and poured another coffee. "Toast?" I asked.

"Yes, please," came almost simultaneously from them both.

It was peaceful doing the ordinary things of preparing breakfast. I rarely bothered at home. They both sat at the kitchen table whilst I made the toast and it was hard to believe the traumas we'd been through the last few days and the ones yet to come.

Ben took breakfast to the cupboard, along with the gun.

When he was out of earshot Andrew turned to me. "Sara, just what have I got myself mixed up in?"

"Probably the story of the year, Andrew, but we may just sue." I replied light heartedly. I felt a load had been lifted off my shoulders and I could face the day, knowing I wasn't alone.

The smile I saw on his face at this news surprised me. I looked closer and realised that the whole face had changed.

"Andrew, you've lost your prickles," I said in surprise.

He rubbed his hand over his jaw. "I don't think so. I wonder if I could borrow a shaver?"

"What happened?" I asked not to be put off by his flippancy.

He looked at me with admiration in his eyes that I found acutely embarrassing.

"Basically – you did, Sara."

"As far as I remember I passed out – and – presumably in the gallant arms of one Andrew Fraser?"

He looked smug. "Indeed you did. I just can't resist a damsel in distress."

"Andrew, I'm finding this hard to take in at this time of the morning. Something has happened to you – for God's sake – tell me what it is?"

"What what is?" Ben had returned from his errand of mercy. I had forgotten what joy it was living alone with no one to interrupt important conversations.

"I'm trying to find out what happened last night." I explained patiently.

"Last night, last night," Ben muttered while looking at the ceiling. "No, can't remember anything special happening – perhaps just the one small thing."

I threw a buttered piece of toast at him and it missed, landing on the floor – butter side up – that had to be a good sign.

"Okay, I give in, anything but the toast. Sorry, Sara." He saw the frustration on my face, but couldn't resist one more jibe. "Well if the main protagonist passes out..."

Andrew supplied the information I wanted. "It seems, Sara, that we can now beat Dr Long at his own game."

"Pardon?"

"Be patient with me, Sara. Unlike you lot, talking with birds is not the thing I was brought up to accept. What I do now accept is that I'm needed to take you all to the area where I had my accident."

"But, Andrew, how can that help?"

"Don't you have any idea what happened last night, Sara?" Ben asked.

"Only that I hoped I joined you altogether with the images I've been having for so long. I was only trying to be helpful."

"Tell her, Andrew."

"You joined me too, Sara, whether because I was holding you up at the time, I don't know, but I suddenly saw something I haven't seen for months because I'd been blocking it out. It has to do with the place where I had my accident. I actually saw it, Sara."

"But weren't you afraid, Andrew?"

He looked shamefaced. "Yes, but it all seems to fit together now. We've been up half the night whilst you've been snoring," this really was a new Andrew "and we've agreed that we need to go to the Queen Charlotte Islands."

At the sound of that name my heart constricted. "Then it really is there?"

"We believe so – but what makes you think so, Sara?" Ben asked

"I wasn't sure until I found the bead, but your grandfather helped, Ben."

"How?" he asked.

"You told me he was a Haida – they're natives of the Islands aren't they?" Ben nodded. "Then there were the totem poles in my dream and the bead, then Joe's peregrine came from there. The coincidence of Andrew being injured there didn't fall into place until we'd found the bead."

"So you knew all along I was involved?" Andrew asked.

"Hardly – it didn't seem to fit in and we don't even know now if we're right. At the moment we're only talking about dreams."

"Not just dreams, though," Ben interposed. "I've had a word with Ella this morning and guess who went with her to the hospital to try and sort Andrew out? Yup – Paul. He was over here staying with us. And –," Ben continued excitedly "he rang Ella a few weeks back, casual like and asked if she knew if that bloke she'd seen at the hospital had recovered his memory. She just thought he was being neighbourly."

"You think Paul got the photos and feathers from Andrew?" I asked, surprised.

Ben nodded. "We'll have to let Gabriel know. Shame you never got to see the photographs, Andrew."

"But..." Andrew began but was interrupted by Joe arriving for breakfast. He came and gave me a fatherly kiss on the cheek, then held me at arm's length looking at me.

"How are we, this morning, Sara? It is good to see the colour once more back in your cheeks."

"I'm fine, thanks, Joe, but I seem to have missed out on all the fun."

"Not fun, Sara, just the business matters. You gave us the problem to solve, now we will. Where is Gabriel?"

"I don't think he's up yet," I replied.

"Well, he is not in his bed, Sara. Ben, have you seen him?"

"No – I've not been up long, but Sara's the first I heard stirring. Then the smell of coffee became irresistible."

Andrew stood up. "Well, I've got work to do. I'll ring when I have any news." He looked at his watch. "It's nearly half seven so there'll be someone at the airport. Make sure you're all ready to move fast – okay?"

"Okay." Ben confirmed.

Andrew ruffled my hair as he passed and I could have sworn his limp was less noticeable. I wondered if he knew what he was taking on.

When he'd gone I turned to Joe. "Shouldn't we look for Gabriel?"

"He will surely return when he is ready to, Sara. He has a lot on his mind."

"I don't really understand it all, Joe."

"We none of us do, Sara, which is why we must continue the journey is it not? Last night I saw your Mistral with my Omen and Scrap. They are getting impatient."

"I feel it with Vigilant too." Ben rose from the table. "Now, if you'll excuse me I'll just get that rogue to ring his boss and let him know everything is just fine. Joe, will you help me?"

Joe's eyes sparkled. "I may hold the gun?"

Ben grinned "Okay, but do try and look as if you mean it." Joe narrowed his eyes experimentally and Ben and I fell about laughing. He really wasn't very convincing.

"It is good that you laugh, though not necessarily that you laugh at me. I am not the gangster type – no?"

"No," we both agreed but this just made Joe smile happily.

I got up from the table to wash the breakfast things, but Joe took them out of my hands.

"Go, Sara. Get yourself some fresh air while we sort out this – thug."

I got my coat from the bedroom and went out into the air, fresh with an overnight fall of rain, but mild to the face. It was no good looking for Mistral. I did, though want to find Gabriel. His outburst last night was so out of character that I was quite concerned for him – he was normally one of the calmest and sure of people I knew.

My stomach turned over when I thought of his words last night. He'd said in front of the others that he had loved me all those years ago, so there was still hope. I hugged this to me and my step was light.

I headed down through the trees to the river that ran alongside the lodge on its way to the lake. The river was swollen by the rain and still ran brown. There was a path that ran close to the bank between the trees and the river. I decided to head downstream for a bit. It gave me a sense of calm and continuity to see the surge of the swell as it flowed.

As I turned onto the path I tripped over a hidden root and would have fallen headlong if a strong arm hadn't grabbed me from behind and pulled me back to safety. I rested for a while with my back supported against Gabriel's chest and felt my heart beat as his other arm came round to encircle me. He held me tight, which was as well as my legs had gone weak as my spirit soared at his touch.

He breathed into my hair. "Sara, is it too late to try and make amends?"

I was too choked to reply. I just didn't want him to ever let go. But then I felt his arms slacken which put me in a difficult position, as I wasn't sure my emoting knees could yet support my weight.

"Gabriel," I croaked.

"It is too late, isn't it?" It will be for me if you let me go, I thought. "I've seen how you are with Andrew. I understand that – he's done far more for you than I have. All I've done is bring you a load of trouble – but I never meant to, Sara, believe me."

By this time he'd completely let go of me and it became necessary for me to sit down abruptly to avoid falling, very ungracefully, flat on my face. I couldn't suppress a giggle, which had the benefit of returning my legs to normal. I reached my hand up to him and he pulled me to my feet, grinning shamefacedly.

"Come on, Gabriel – let's walk a bit." I reached and put my arm round his waist so his arm came naturally around my shoulders. We walked for a bit in silence as I gathered my thoughts.

"I can't say I wasn't hurt all those years ago, Gabriel – I was. You just upped and left, leaving me bewildered."

"I know – I'm really sorry, but I was going through a bit of a crisis and didn't want to involve you. You were so wrapped up in the birds, Sara, and you showed no interest when I was offered the job in Australia. I knew you'd never leave the birds, so it seemed less painful just to go – make a clean break."

"But you never even wrote." It still seemed unjust to me.

"Neither did you, Sara," he replied quietly.

"How could I, Gabriel, you'd left me, remember?"

He stood silent for a minute. "Yes – I know I did and I can see it'll be difficult to trust me again. Look, I know I probably don't have a right to ask – I have no claim on you, Sara, but would you think about staying here and letting us take care of this?"

"I certainly wouldn't! My family are out there, Gabriel – I'd be failing them – and myself, let alone the others."

I often seemed to exasperate Gabriel and this was another of those occasions. "But if we found what they obviously want us to without you – how would that be letting them down?"

"How can you ask that, Gabriel? It's already obvious that all the birds are talking through me – how can you know you don't need me? What if we've got it all wrong? What if it's not the right place? I need to be there, Gabriel."

"Okay, okay, Sara, calm down – it's just that Callum's discovered that Long and his pal, Hilton, have already found their way to the Queen Charlotte Islands so it probably is the right place. They've got the photographs, after all and god knows what other information from Paul. Don't you think I feel guilty enough involving you in this without risking what could be your life?"

"It's my decision, Gabriel." I didn't like that bit about my life, though. "I just don't see that I have a choice except to see it through to the end. And, after all, we do have the birds to help and if you'd seen Vigilant yesterday you'd realise that that's no small thing."

"Okay – I know you're right, but that doesn't mean I have to like it."

"And all because I'm a woman?" I asked.

"Oh you're that alright and a pig-headed one at that."

"Well, as long as we understand each other." I replied sweetly. "Come on we'd better be getting back."

We arrived at the lodge to find Ella up and about but looking very pale. Andrew had arranged a flight for ten, so everyone was dashing about packing – Ben in charge. He was relieved to see Gabriel.

"We were wondering where the hell you were. Callum's been in touch. He arrived last thing last night, so he's meeting us at the airport." He filled Gabriel in on what Ella had remembered. "He was over here staying with us – you remember?"

"I certainly do." Gabriel replied. "And that fits in with when Kate first saw the feathers. So maybe Andrew is the lynch pin here."

"It certainly seems to fit." Ben replied. "Ella has a terrible headache still so she's decided not to come with us – she's going to stay at her mother's."

"Well, at least that's one female with some sense," was Gabriel's unnecessary reply.

"Andrew's arranged for our lodger to stay with friends of his until we return. He's given them instructions to go straight to the police if anything happens."

I checked that Mistral's feather was safe in my pocket along with the little earring. They'd become talismans on the journey and I didn't feel safe without them.

Gabriel had one more try. "Sara, why don't you go with Ella? Joe, persuade her it would be safer."

Joe looked at me. "Gabriel – you are not being fair. She knows it would be safer but has no choice, just as I do not, not if I wish to help my Omen. Leave her be – we may yet have need of her." I smiled my thanks at Joe.

A car pulled up outside and Ben went to see who it was. Two men came in and Ben took them to the cupboard. It was a relief to see someone taking over some of the responsibility. Andrew's friends looked as though they knew how to handle any trouble. We were yet to see if we could.

CHAPTER SIXTEEN

We dropped Ella off at her mother's, and then we went to the airport. Andrew met us in the car park and took us to the aeroplane we were to fly to the Islands in while Gabriel went to find Callum. The plane was a twin-engined, eight seater of which Andrew was the pilot as well as the part owner. Although he wasn't allowed to do commercial work, we weren't actually paying and he was able to fly competently as most of the controls are hand controls, so his leg was not a drawback. I was reminded of the flying instructor that had taken me for my final flying test. Although crippled with arthritis and needing sticks to walk with – he was as competent a pilot as any I had flown with. He found a freedom he didn't have while on the ground.

We had just loaded all the gear we would need on the Islands when Gabriel joined us with Callum, who was looking a little tired after all his jet setting. He smiled at us resignedly before adding his luggage to the pile and shook hands with Andrew. We then all climbed aboard in silence as if aware that we were now committed and there'd be no going back.

Andrew asked if I would like to sit alongside him and

familiarise myself with flying again. It was a chance not to be missed, despite the look in Gabriel's eyes.

It was a lovely sensation to be flying in a small plane again. I had never been at the controls of a twin engined plane, but, once we were airborne, Andrew took me through the instruments and it wasn't much different from flying a single engined plane, only you had two engines to keep an eye on. The journey was a quiet one; everyone seemed to be preoccupied, thinking our own thoughts. None of us knew what lay ahead and if they were like me they were feeling pretty anxious. It was good to have the distraction of occasionally taking over the controls from Andrew and watching for occasional glimpses of whales and the coastline.

We were due to land at Sandspit, which was the main airfield on the Islands. Then we planned to make the journey by seaplane to as near the spot Andrew was picked up from after his accident as possible. The rest would have to be on foot. Andrew flew over the area at one and a half thousand feet before going on to Sandspit, so that we could get a feel of the geography of the place. It all looked covered in trees, but the logging roads and felling were evident in places. The prospect, though, of finding the lake amongst the myriad of rocky inlets was going to be difficult

I glanced sideways at Andrew as we neared the spot and saw with misgiving the sweat pouring off him and his hands begin to shake. Had he, after all, taken on too much? I immediately put my hands on the controls – this was no time, nor height for anything to go wrong. My stomach clenched as I felt the rigidity of the controls in Andrew's hands. I kept my eyes on the artificial horizon dial and checked the heading. I'd been keeping a vague eye on the direction we were going, but I didn't relish trying to find my way to Sandspit – nor was I familiar with the airfield joining procedures here in Canada.

"Andrew," I said as quietly and calmly as possible, " just let go of the controls – please."

The others had by now become aware something was wrong. Andrew's whole body seemed to be shaking. Gabriel was sitting behind me and he reached out his hand and placed it on Andrew's shoulder.

"Andrew, do as Sara says. She knows what to do – just let

go and take some deep breaths." He turned to me. "Sara, I'm going to change places with Joe – will that affect the plane?"

"I'll be ready – just be quick."

"Okay."

I was too busy trying to keep that horizon level to notice what was going on. Misty was coming through but I had to block her out in order to keep my eye on the artificial horizon, but I caught an image of Ben's grandfather with a grim look on his face, which didn't help my state of mind.

After a while I heard a sigh from Andrew beside me and risked a glance. Gabriel had his one hand on the back of Andrew's neck and the other across his forehead and his eyes were closed. Slowly the shaking stopped and Andrew took two deep breaths and seemed to steady. Gabriel removed his hands and put one on my shoulder.

"Okay, Sara?" I nodded and wondered at the heat from the imprint of his hand on my skin.

"Andrew are you ready to take over again?" he asked.

"Yes. Sara, give me back control." I let go with relief and he shot me a look of gratitude.

"I don't have any definite idea where we are, Andrew, but we should be heading northeast towards Sandspit."

His mouth was set in a grim line and my heart went out to him. He'd known this journey was going to be difficult but he hadn't backed out. None of us could have realised how hard it was going to be on him. The rest of the journey passed in silence, just as before but heavier.

We landed without further mishap at the airport and completed the formalities. Andrew had booked a cab to take us to the seaplane at Queen Charlotte City. It all took time as there was another ferry ride to the mainland of Graham Island, the northerly island, just as there had been at Prince Rupert. The seaplane Andrew had arranged was waiting for us, loaded with tents and other essential gear and a pilot who would bring the plane back when we called for it on the radio Andrew had brought. He'd not been idle. We loaded the remainder of our luggage into the plane. Andrew's prickles were back which I found sad, but I couldn't blame him, he felt he had let us all down and he couldn't accept that.

I put my arm through his and drew him a little away from

the others. "It wasn't your fault, Andrew. You weren't to know it would affect you so badly – none of us could."

"God, it was awful, Sara. I just had no control – it was as though I was – oh I don't know – I was so afraid – I just don't understand." He shook his head as though trying to rid it of images he'd rather not see.

"I don't think any of us do – but you do still want to carry on, don't you, Andrew?"

"That'll have to be up to the others, I think." He lowered his prickles for a bit. "You were brilliant, Sara – really. What would have happened if you hadn't been sitting there?"

"There's no point thinking about that now, Andrew. Come on let's join the others."

Gabriel was watching us as we rejoined the group waiting to board the seaplane and Andrew went straight up to him.

"Thanks for what you did back there," he said somewhat gruffly. "I don't know what it was but it sure as heck worked."

"Well it was Sara that really saved our bacon." Gabriel took the opportunity to put his arm round my shoulders and steer me towards the back seat of the seaplane away from Andrew. I turned and saw the hurt look on Andrew's face.

"Gabriel what's the matter with you? He couldn't help what happened."

"He put all our lives in danger, Sara."

"He didn't do it deliberately and you forget that it's his plane he's flown us over in and...."

"Okay – you don't have to keep defending him." He turned his head away.

Joe climbed in alongside Gabriel. "This is no time for the fighting between ourselves. We know not what lies ahead but we face it better if we face it together." I had never seen Joe so stern and it only confirmed he was as nervous as the rest of us, though he tried to hide it under a layer of good humour.

Ben and Callum climbed into the seats in front of us and Andrew sat alongside the pilot. I was thankful that nothing had been said about Andrew not coming with us. We set off on what we hoped was the last part of our long journey.

We kept to the east of the island heading towards the Gwaii Haanas National Park, where Andrew had been climbing before his accident. There were a myriad of islands below us mostly forested, but our eyes were drawn to the long, thin profile of Moresby Island that stretched its jagged leg into the Pacific Ocean. The climate here was similar to our own though slightly warmer which accounted for the huge areas of cedar forest – much of it a thousand years old that coated the ground. The pilot pointed out an area of shingle where once stood one of the Haida villages, now sadly decayed. It was noticeable from the air how precarious a foothold the native Haida had on this land, the forest at their backs and the sea at their front with only a narrow strip dividing the two. It probably did much to account for their myths and beliefs.

All the time we were travelling we kept our eyes skinned for Hilton's plane. We only knew they were on the Islands not where they were. Considering the Islands' small size it would only have taken a matter of a couple hours at the most to fly from top to bottom, but they would need to search the mass of inlets and that would delay them. We all just prayed that we were right about where we were heading and get there first. We wanted to avoid a confrontation at all costs.

We arrived as close as we could get to the point from which it would all be on foot. Transferring our things by canoe to the shore took a little while and gave us a chance to look around at the landscape we were about to invade. Where they could be seen above the tall cedars, the ragged peaks of the mountains beyond were misted with clouds of damp air rising from the trees and casting the nearer ones into stark shadows. The sun burst through intermittently bringing a lightening to the air and the view around us. The lower branches of the trees that grew out of the rocks sprouting from the sea were bare from the continuous spray of the tumbling surf.

From our low viewpoint it looked all very daunting and we'd already seen the difficulty of the terrain from the air, so I, for one, was thankful to have Andrew with us who knew his way around, particularly as we had been warned about the black bears which roam the forest. We had all been issued with bells and whistles to avoid surprising any bears and giving them a chance to get out of our way. If surprised they had been known to attack.

I realised with sadness that I would normally have been

excited at the prospect of exploring the wildlife in such a wild area, excited at the possibility of seeing a Peale's Peregrine, but I was too worried to make this an expedition of pleasure. It would also be necessary to carry the emergency supplies and although these were divided between us according to strength, (of which I pleaded little), I didn't relish the idea of carrying them very far through the damp, rugged terrain.

Whilst Gabriel and Andrew drank their coffee, Joe, Ben, Callum and I took the chance to contact the birds. Once we were in the forest there would be little chance of seeing them if they were there, as the trees stretched tall into the sky. I sensed they were all there, but I felt Mistral and Vigilant were becoming restless again.

We still had several miles of difficult walking to go and we wanted to be there well before dark so we didn't stay long at our lunch. I was thankful for the walking I had done with Mistral, but wondered about Joe and Andrew. Callum had the look of the rugged outdoors on him and Ben's skin glowed with fitness over the muscles, but Joe was probably the oldest there and Andrew's leg was sure to hold him up. I determined to keep an eye on them both – we didn't want to arrive wherever we were going in a state of exhaustion.

Little was said on the journey once we had brought Callum up to date on what was going on. Callum told us how he had got on at the seminar and how easy it had been to extract information about Dr Long, as they were still puzzled and not a little upset by his strange behaviour. In his own quiet way I was sure that Callum would have little trouble extracting information anyway, particularly with the female sex. It was hardly the appropriate time to be wondering why he wasn't married, but the thought did just flash across my curious mind. Gabriel had given him the chance to stay in Prince Rupert, but like Joe, Ben and me we went where our birds led. Callum stayed with us.

Gabriel was very withdrawn during the trek and I knew he was as anxious as the rest of us as to what lay ahead. Gabriel felt he'd led us all to this point and whatever the outcome may be, he was responsible. I was surprised at the heat of his hand as he helped me scramble over the rocks in our path. He too was aware of the weakness in our party and we had more stops than we might otherwise have done and I was glad of the delay. Although I longed to see the family again, I was beginning to have doubts about what lay ahead and my part in it. I didn't want to fail any of them and, if my images were stronger than the others, then a lot of responsibility would lie with me.

A drizzly rain had started which made the going difficult where we broke out of the trees. We found a small outcrop to shelter under to have a break and a cup of coffee. Whilst we sat there looking out at the towering trees and the landscape in front of us, its details misted by the drizzle, Ben told us a little more of his people. Andrew had been right about the place birds had in the Haida beliefs. Their lineage was divided between Eagles and Ravens and descent was through the female line and no Raven could marry an Eagle and vice versa. All Native American Indians lived their lives close to the creatures around them. They treated them with great respect as they represented life to them, and the Haida were no exception. Living as an island race, as they had done for anything up to ten thousand years, they had developed a mythology all their own, based on what they saw all around them.

Haida Land is supported on a pole that rests on the breast of a supernatural being and this pole extends through the firmament into the sky world above, just like a huge cedar tree. Its roots penetrate into the underworld, its trunk extends through the earth and its branches spread into the firmament. Power flows through this pole and accounts for the importance of the carved pole on their houses. The skies are believed to be like a giant plank house through which the sun enters in the morning and leaves by the back door at night, and the stars are light coming through the roof of the celestial house. Harmony between these worlds was important, as any disharmony would reflect into the human world and cause natural disasters.

The chief of all sea creatures was the killer whale; the bear of all land mammals and the eagle of all sky beings and these were represented on the carved poles at the entrance to the Haida houses. They considered that all creatures had souls and they wore masks to represent their personalities at ceremonials. But the birds, in the form of the Raven, formed the important part of their mythology for it was this bird that created the Queen Charlotte Islands out of a black pebble.

Once the land had been inhabited by supernatural beings, the Raven released the Haida people from a clamshell that he dug out of the ground. In the search for food he was accompanied by Eagle and so these two birds became so important. Ben told it all so vividly that I could almost feel these beings all around me and felt, rather than saw, Ben's grandfather.

Ben brought us up to date on the recent history of the Islands and spoke with pride of the fight the Haida Indians had had with the loggers. Against great odds, and with little violence, they had won a victory which resulted in the great rain forested area, now known as the Gwaii Haanas National Park, where we sat at that moment, being declared a Nature Reserve where no logging could take place. I warmed to a people who could achieve so much against the power of money – and who also held birds in such esteem.

There was just enough in the thermos for another cup of coffee each, but for any further cups we would need to use the stove or light a fire. It was as well that we didn't light a fire on this occasion. Callum suddenly said, "hush" and we all fell silent. There was no doubting it – there was a plane overhead. Andrew went outside to see if he could identify it but the drizzly mist prevented him seeing anything.

"Come on, let's get moving." Andrew hurried us to pack everything away.

"You reckon that was Long?" Ben asked.

"I can't be sure, but then we can't take the chance, can we?"

Gabriel was still very silent and I would have liked the comfort of feeling at ease with him, but I didn't. It was Andrew, despite the hindrance of his leg, who kept us all going, pointing out things as we went along which took our minds off the drudge of the difficult walking. The huge cedars, anything up to seven feet in diameter, were spectacular but there were areas where the logs left by the fall of ancient trees made the going rough. The canopy was so dense in parts that little light penetrated. There was a strange otherworldly silence beneath the trees.

I had a blister on one heel from the wet coming through my walking boots where I'd trodden in boggy patches. I could see Joe was having the same problem by the slight limp he'd developed. I went to make sure he was alright and was rewarded by his sparkling smile.

"Blisters?" I asked.

"I have always believed that the good things of life do not come without pain, and this is good is it not?" He spread his arms to indicate the trees around us.

"Yes," I agreed. It was good. Under other circumstances I would have enjoyed being surrounded by so much beauty that breathed of the past, but I was anxious. Joe seemed to be treating it as one big adventure and I envied him this ability.

I caught up with Andrew. "How far now, Andrew?"

"Only about another two kilometres, Sara. Can you manage that?"

"If you can, I certainly can. You've set quite a pace considering."

"Considering this bloody leg, you mean. Well, I've never let it stop me keeping fit. I even believed at one time that I'd be able to climb again, but it's too restricting." He was quiet a moment. "Sara, there's something you ought to know. I didn't want to say anything before because I know how much this expedition means to everyone..."

"Go on, Andrew." I felt a lurch in my stomach at what he might be about to tell me.

"Well, the place I'm taking you to is the place I was found."

"So?"

"When I was in hospital they reckoned I had hit my head before I smashed my leg, maybe by several hours."

I absorbed the information. "You mean ..." I began, my voice high pitched to my ears.

"Keep your voice down, Sara. I don't want the others to know yet, not till we get there. If it's the right place, nothing's lost and they don't need to know."

"But," I tried in a lower pitch, "that means we could be miles out. And we don't even know exactly what we're looking for – so we could be looking for hours. God, Andrew, you should have said before."

"I did try this morning, but the moment passed."

We walked for a while whilst I thought about it. I could still see the image of the lake, so we had as much as Long there, unless he'd discovered something we didn't know. We also had the birds. If what we all felt was true then the birds would still be able to lead us to the place they wanted us to go. Up to now we'd been assuming that the places were the same, what if there was no connection between the lake and the image of the carved rock face? What if what Andrew had seen had nothing to do with the lake and therefore nothing to do with Paul? Only the birds and the dreams told us different.

"I'm sorry, Sara – you think I've brought you out here on a wild goose chase, don't you?" His terminology could have been better.

"I just don't know. But we're committed now so there's no help for it. Don't, for god's sake, say anything to the others. We still have the birds."

"I can't have the same faith in them as you do, Sara. This is well out of my experience. But I'd be grateful not to say anything to the others till necessary. I don't seem to be Gabriel's favourite person right now." He misinterpreted the expression on my face. "I'm not criticising, Sara, he has a right to be angry – don't you think I know I could have killed you all."

I just couldn't discuss what I thought was the reason for Gabriel's antagonism, so I avoided it and tried some encouragement. "That's nonsense, Andrew. Without you we wouldn't even be here."

"And now you rather wish you weren't, don't you?"

"No ... I mean it. We've got to solve this one way or another and this was just the obvious route to try first."

Feeling depressed that we may not after all be close to the end of our journey, I went and joined Joe, avoiding Gabriel in case he noticed the worry in my face. "Joe – do you feel the birds near?"

"Yes, I do, Sara, but you – you are worried about something. Will you share it with me?"

"Not for now, Joe, if you don't mind. It's not really to do with the birds."

"Perhaps then it is to do with the heart, Sara? I have been watching." He stopped for a while to get his breath. "We all heard Gabriel, Sara, when he said he loved you, yet he is not sure you return this love – is that not so?"

"I just don't know, Joe. He will hardly speak to me."

"You have given him little encouragement, I think." Joe was firm. "Sara, now he needs you more than he will ask – do you not understand this? How you have this power with the birds and yet you cannot see into his heart – well." He shook his head. "And you – you love him – no? Yet still you give more time to Andrew."

"Andrew needs me too, Joe."

"Then you will have to choose, Sara." And he limped on.

Had it been possible I would have turned my back on it all and taken the first flight back to Wales and some sort of normality. I suddenly felt very alone. Everyone else was striding towards this 'place' and only I, and, of course, Andrew knew it probably was not the right one.

CHAPTER SEVENTEEN

The rest of the journey I travelled at the back, despite the fear of the occasional black bear. Perfume attracted them, apparently, but, as all I could smell on myself was sweat, (or should I say 'glow'), I hoped that that didn't count and that they'd be more afraid of me than I was of them. Every so often Gabriel turned to make sure I was still following but never smiled. I trudged on cheered every now and again by Misty, who seemed to sense my lowness of spirit. She sent encouraging images into my head, urging me on so that I felt we were, after all, travelling in the right direction.

We came to the foot of the mountains where the trees thinned out and a river tumbled through the rocks. We followed Andrew down the river for about a quarter of a mile until we came to a clearing, almost circular with the river forming the outer rim. Here we stopped for a breather.

Andrew had a good look round and then caught my eye. I went up to speak to him and he drew me away from the others. I could feel Gabriel's eyes on us.

"This is the place marked on the map where they found me, Sara. It doesn't look very hopeful, does it?"

"Let's have a look at the map, Andrew." He spread it wider between his hands. It was the first chance I'd had to examine the terrain in two-dimensional form. Andrew pointed out where we were.

"Look there's a small lake there, Andrew – do you remember anything about that?"

"I'm not sure. I guess it may have been where I was heading. I've examined a lot of the lakes on the Islands, but I wouldn't risk landing a seaplane on that so walking would be the only option. Why – is it helpful?" I could hear the hope in his voice.

"It could be the lake I keep seeing, but I'd need to see it at the right angle – as if I was flying."

"What do you think we should do, Sara? Should I tell the others or just head for this lake?"

"You'll have to tell the others, Andrew. Maybe the people who picked you up got it wrong."

"I don't think so. They had to bring in a helicopter. So this clearing would fit the bill."

"But how far did they have to carry you to the helicopter?"

"I don't know."

Gabriel came to join us. "Well?" he asked coldly.

Andrew looked up from the map. "This is where I was picked up from – it's marked here on the map – see?"

Gabriel looked at the map and then looked around him. "Doesn't look very likely for the place we are looking for, does it?" He gestured for the others to join us. "Looks like Andrew's brought us to a dead end. What do you think, Ben?"

"This is the place?" Ben asked Andrew.

"This is where they brought the helicopter. They had to carry me some way, but I don't know where from. I'm sorry – I was so sure it'd be the right spot."

He looked so shamefaced I took over. "Look, Gabriel, there's a lake here on the map. It's worth having a look at – it's about the right shape."

"But it's a mile away – did they have to carry you a mile over this terrain, Andrew?"

"I don't know, I was unconscious at the time." His tone was defensive. "Look, there's something else you need to know. It's just possible that I fell because I was concussed, not that it happened at the same time."

"You mean you could have been wandering around with concussion for hours?" Gabriel asked incredulously. Andrew nodded. "Then why the hell did you bring us here?"

"The carved rock face – Sara showed me – it was so real – I just felt it had to be here. I did see it and I haven't been able to since the accident – it had to be here."

"Well, look about you – it obviously isn't."

We all felt a sense of disappointment, but Gabriel most of all – after all he still felt responsible for bringing us here. I laid my hand on his arm, but he shook it off and walked away towards the river.

Joe had seen the gesture and the look on my face. "Come, Sara, he is just very worried, as we all are. It feels strange here – no?" I nodded. "This is the time we need the birds, Sara."

"I don't know any more, Joe. I just feel so drained."

Suddenly I felt a strange sensation as though a wind was winding itself around my body and I was spinning round in its arms and yet I wasn't moving. I could hear music and chanting and I saw fire in the middle of the clearing. I shook my head to clear it and it was gone.

"Sara, you have gone very white – what is it?" Joe placed his hand on my arm to steady me. "You are shivering. Perhaps we should light a fire here while we decide what next it is we do."

"No, Joe – we must get moving. There is something here I'm not sure about." To confirm this I heard Misty chitter in my head. I wished she could just lead us to the place, but either she couldn't or it was not part of the plan that seemed to be behind all this. Or maybe she did not know where we were, could only sense that we were close, if indeed we were. Life at this stage was just a little too complicated.

"I'll fetch Gabriel." Ben volunteered. "We need to decide where we go from here – there is a strangeness here."

I was thankful someone else sensed it. "No – I'll go."

I walked over to the bank where Gabriel sat. He didn't look up, but I knew by the set of his shoulders, that he wasn't happy about the situation. I sat down beside him and searched for what to say.

"Gabriel ..." He turned his head away. I tried again. "Gabriel, please. Andrew brought us here because he felt it was right – that it all fitted. We can't stop now. The birds won't let us.

But we need to pull together not apart."

"But I feel apart, Sara – don't you understand?" There was a weariness in his tone. He turned to look at me then and the deep blue was back in his eyes and my heart tightened with love. "You're always trying to defend Andrew."

"Because you're always trying to put him down – which isn't like you, Gabriel." I replied gently.

"Don't you think I have cause, Sara?"

"But he couldn't help the thing in the aeroplane and he didn't know this wasn't where we would find what we all seem to be seeking without knowing what."

"You've just proved my point, Sara – and missed it."

"What do you mean?" I asked bewildered.

He stood up and pulled me to my feet. "We'd better get on – there's only a few hours before dark." He let go of me as soon as I was balanced. I would have liked him to hold on to me longer – to wrap me in his arms where I could feel safe and forget all the uncertainty. But no such idea was obviously on his mind and I wondered again about the changeableness in his moods.

We returned to the others. I felt very vulnerable again in the middle of the circle as though I was standing on sacred ground and longed to move on.

"Where do you think we should head Gabriel?" Callum asked, eager too to be off. "We've reached a dead end here, but we all seem to be in agreement that we should carry on."

"Look, let's discuss this in the shelter of the trees." I shivered again. "There's something ghostly about this place."

We all picked up our supplies and headed for the corner of the circle away from the one we'd entered by and sat down at the base of one of the largest cedar trees on the edge of the forested area. I felt better with the huge bulk of the trunk of the cedar behind my back, but had no idea where the feeling of vulnerability came from. Perhaps I was still scared of the bears – or perhaps Gabriel had got under my skin.

"I reckon we should head for the lake." Ben declared. "If it is, by some chance, the one in the photograph we may well learn something. What do you think, Gabriel?"

"It's worth a try. Let's take a look at the map." He laid it out at our feet so we could all see it. "There's a way round here that leads to the east side of the lake that's not so steep. Otherwise we'll need to climb round this bluff towards the west and come on it from slightly above. That may well be quicker."

"Can we do that instead, Gabriel?" I asked. "After all, that's the view we have of it from the air."

"It'll be harder walking," Andrew pointed out.

"If it's too hard for you, you could always wait here," Gabriel suggested unkindly.

Andrew flushed with anger. "I've come this far, I'm sure I can manage the rest. But have you thought about Sara and Joe?"

Gabriel turned to us. "Well?"

"Now I am rested I am ready." Joe declared.

"And you're not leaving me behind for the bears." They all laughed – but I was quite serious. Much as I would love to see a bear in the wild, I would prefer it to be in safer surroundings.

Just then Callum, whose hearing seemed to be sharper than ours, said "hush" and we all strained to hear what he'd heard. I half expected it to be a bear crashing through the undergrowth, but it wasn't a natural sound – it was the sound of an engine. "What is it?" I asked.

"Sounds like a plane to me," Callum replied. "Can anyone see anything?"

Andrew was the first to spot it. "There, a seaplane." He pointed towards the way we'd come.

"Long do you think?" Callum asked.

"Better stay under the trees in case." Andrew advised.

The plane circled for a bit, then headed back the way it had come.

We made preparations to leave. Our path took us mostly amongst the trees, but we stopped from time to time to listen for the plane.

After about twenty minutes we rounded the bluff and there, laid out at our feet was the lake, partly hidden by the trees. We were at the easternmost tip and the angle wasn't quite right so we continued following the curve of the lake towards the west but still climbing. The ground was carpeted by moss and ferns where it wasn't rocky outcrop.

Suddenly Andrew slipped on a patch of moss, made damp and slippery by the tiny stream that ran over the rock it covered. He couldn't save himself and half fell and half rolled down the hillside until he was out of sight. We were all too shocked for a moment to move and then Ben was off down the slope following the course Andrew had taken but more carefully.

He called up from below. "Andrew's fine, but I might need help getting him back up. He's given his leg a bit of a battering."

"I'll go'" Callum volunteered and, taking off his rucksack, followed Ben down the hillside. They reappeared in a few minutes with Andrew supported between them. He was looking pale and his mouth was in a grim line again. They placed him carefully with his back against a tree and his bad leg straight out in front of him. Andrew thanked them and put his head back against the trunk and took some deep breaths.

I went over and took his hand. "Are you alright, Andrew?"

He nodded, unable to speak for a bit. I got up to ask Gabriel if he could help, but Andrew drew on my hand. "Sara," it came out breathlessly "give me a chance to get my breath back." I sat down beside him.

"Look, Sara, I've really clouted my leg and I'm likely to hold you up, but I really don't want that to stop any of you guys. I've brought you here and, despite the sceptics, I'm sure this is the right place. Little bits of it keep coming back, that's how I came to lose my footing." He winced as he moved his leg a bit to turn to the way he was facing before he fell. "See that peak there?" I followed the line of his finger. "Well there was definitely a figure on the top of it the last time I saw it. That was why I chose to do that climb not the one I'd intended – to find that figure. So that's the way you need to go, Sara, I'm sure of it."

"But none of us are climbers, Andrew. We can't reach that peak."

"You don't need to. Oh, damn this head of mine – and now this leg. If I could just follow the course, I'm sure I'd be able to find what you're looking for, but despite that jolt just now it's all still hazy. It must have been pure luck you getting through to me last night."

Joe had come over. "It is not good, Andrew?"

"No, Joe, not good."

"Joe, could Gabriel help?" I asked.

"With the pain maybe, but not if the bones are broken."

"I don't think there's anything broken," Andrew said hastily.

"It's just badly bruised, but it was getting worse before I fell – this is just the final straw."

"Yet you continued then, Andrew – is that not so?"

"Yes, Joe, but it's going to get more difficult from now on."

"I'll go and see what Gabriel can do." I got up and left Andrew with Joe. Gabriel, Ben and Callum were discussing something but they broke off when I arrived.

"We were just discussing where to go from here, Sara," Ben informed me. "Does the lake look familiar to you at all?"

"Not really from this angle. I just get the feeling that I saw it from the other side."

"Why?" Gabriel asked.

"I don't know – yes, yes I do. Gabriel, don't you remember – the photograph was taken with the trees making shadows on the water. It didn't feel like dawn, not in the dream, so it has to be the setting sun. We're heading west, aren't we, so the area we want would be below us hidden by the trees."

"Sara's right, Gabriel," Ben declared. He needn't have sounded so surprised, I thought.

"Then let's go down there." Callum rose ready to tackle it – I envied him his energy.

I forestalled him. "Gabriel – is there anything you can do for Andrew? He's really knocked his bad leg."

"We'll just have to go on without him."

"That's no reason not to try and help him. He knows he can't come on with us, but can't you do anything to ease the pain."

Gabriel wouldn't meet my eyes. "I don't know. It's not necessarily anything that can be turned on at will. Besides it leaves me very drained and I can't risk that now. We've got to get down to the lake and it's only about three hours until dark."

I got angry at his evasion. "You just don't want to help him, do you Gabriel? You've never liked him from the start. Well he's shown a lot more backbone than you have these last few hours." I stormed off feeling very hurt. In all the time I'd known Gabriel, he'd never have turned down anyone in need. Had he changed so much?

To distract my feelings of confusion, I went and sat apart from the others and stared at the peak Andrew had shown me. I was surprised to hear Gabriel talking to Andrew. "We need to go down to the lake, but you'd better wait here and rest that leg. Will you wait with him, please, Joe?"

"That will be my pleasure," Joe answered gravely, but with a sparkle in his eyes. – I think he was pleased to be excused the trek down to the lake and back. I wished I could have been excused it but knew I had to be there.

It took us ten minutes to reach the lakeside. We really needed to have tackled it from the other side to be sure if it was right. Yet the rocks I sat on were familiar. I shut my eyes, relaxed my mind and reached for Misty, trying to see again the image in my dream.

Suddenly I felt myself whisked skywards and I was flying over the lake again, only this time I was looking down on the lakeside and I could see the four of us down there where I had seen the body erupt from the water. The shock of seeing myself caused me to open my eyes and I was once more earth bound. Quickly I looked skyward and saw an anchor shaped shadow disappear towards Andrew's peak.

I was sure that it had been Rift that I saw, Rift I had flown with, still lacking the grace of her mother's flight – Rift I'd have liked to have touched to show my love. I shut my eyes and was once more flying with her up towards the peak, passing over a river, which tumbled into a waterfall then up into the mountain.

"Are you okay?" Gabriel asked and broke the thread.

I nodded and turned to Ben and Callum. "Anything?" I asked. They both shook their heads. "Perhaps we should have had Joe here after all. He believes it was here that his peregrine Peal was killed."

"Then it is the right place?" Gabriel asked.

"I don't know, I just feel this is the place in the dream."

"So what now?" Ben asked.

"Follow the birds, Ben," I replied. "What else is there to do? Can you contact Vigilant, Ben and Wraith, Callum?"

"We can but try."

I walked away from them further down the shore with Gabriel and then we saw the egg shaped stone in the water. We stared at it a moment.

"I don't like this, Sara."

"You don't like it – how do you think I feel? God, Gabriel, you've only seen this on a photograph." I couldn't go on as

I'd started to shake. It seemed so weird to be standing here. I thought back to the first time I'd seen that photograph – half way round the world from here. I couldn't believe so much had happened in so short a space of time.

I let my mind wander and it was immediately filled with Vigilant. I looked over towards Ben and could see he had made contact. We made our way back to them.

"They're both there, Sara, and very close," Callum exclaimed.

"Can you tell what direction they're coming from, Callum?" I asked.

"Not really," he replied.

Ben was more certain. "Over there, I reckon," and he swung his arm out towards the peak. "Is that where Mistral is?"

I nodded. "It's also the direction that whoever I saw running from the shore took when he ran towards the shot – and," I added loudly, as Gabriel had already turned away, "the direction Andrew said we should go in."

"Then that's where we had better head for." Gabriel threw back over his shoulder as he led the way back up the slope to Joe and Andrew.

When we reached them Gabriel went straight to kneel down beside Andrew. He moved his hands gently down Andrew's leg and I saw Andrew wince with pain. Gabriel held his hands on the leg for perhaps two minutes and then Andrew sighed and the tension left his body. Gabriel then laid his one hand on Andrew's brow whilst still holding his hand over the leg. Sweat poured off Gabriel. I wanted to reach out a hand to him. As if he felt the desire he called to me.

"Sara, come and help. Put your hands as I have mine." I did as he said and closed my eyes in concentration. I could feel pain in my head and then it cleared and instead I could see the peak with the figure on top and then a fast rocky river that tumbled into a waterfall that dropped many feet; then a face so like Ben's grandfather and finally the carved rock face with no living birds on it.

I could feel my fingers tingling where they touched Gabriel's and a warmth deep in my heart. Then I felt Gabriel take his hands away and I came to. Andrew had his eyes closed but his mouth had relaxed.

"You haven't broken anything, Andrew, but you've bruised it badly." Gabriel had stood up and was wiping the sweat from his forehead with the back of his hand. "Try walking on it – you shouldn't feel any pain. Don't worry, it'll hold your weight."

Andrew stood up helped by Ben and took a tentative step forward. His face, tensed against the expectation of pain, relaxed.

"However did you do that, Gabriel? I can't feel a thing, not even the pain I have most of the time. God, it's like a miracle."

Gabriel smiled. "I only channelled your own defences. From now on you should be able to be pain free for a lot of the time. Just learn to relax if it becomes painful again."

"Thanks, Gabriel." Andrew's voice was gruff.

"My pleasure, Andrew." I couldn't believe the change. I must have been standing there with my mouth open because Gabriel winked at me, then turned to the others.

"Andrew, Joe – to bring you up to date. It seems you brought us to the right lake after all, Andrew." Andrew looked relieved. "But the answers, we believe lie up in the hills."

Andrew caught my eye and looked towards the peak. I nodded.

"So, that's where we're going, if that's okay with everyone?" Gabriel asked. "By rights you should rest that leg, Andrew, but we may still need you. Do you think you can make it?"

"I'd like to give it a try."

"Okay – let's go, then."

Ben shouldered the burden of Andrew's rucksack along with his own. Thank God for strong shoulders I thought. Out of us all it was Ben who was the calmest and I wondered if he was feeling his roots, here in the land of his grandfather. As I thought this I saw again that face so like Ben's and it smiled.

This time Gabriel led the way and the dark mood had lifted. He still looked pale, but now he was relaxed and I very much preferred him this way. Maybe we were nearing the end and he sensed it. I only knew that Misty and the family were coming through stronger. I projected an image of where we were in the hope that Mistral would find us. I scanned the sky as we went but there was no sign of the outline I loved so much.

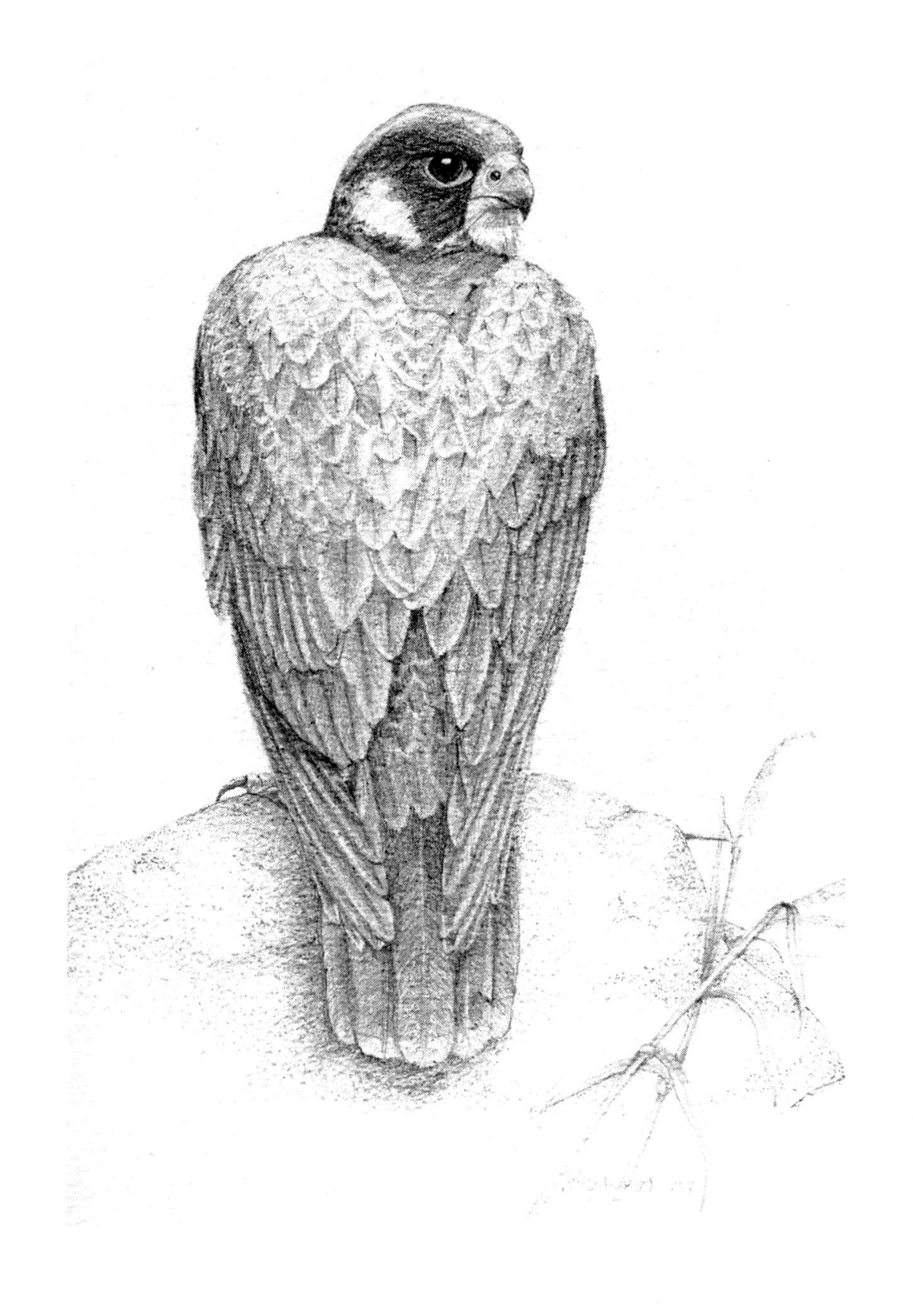

CHAPTER EIGHTEEN

We aimed straight for the peak on Andrew's instructions. He was finding the going difficult, but there was no pain in his face just the stiffness in his leg. I walked for a while beside Gabriel and he turned and threw a mischievous smile at me.

"What's that for?" I asked.

"What?"

"That smile."

"I'll tell you sometime."

"You'll tell me now."

"Or...?" he asked.

But I couldn't answer. We had been following a river for some time clambering up the large boulders that formed its banks. Gabriel, Ben and I were ahead of the others so we three rounded the corner first.

There ahead of us was the waterfall – there was no doubt. I had seen it only an hour ago, when I'd helped Gabriel with Andrew and I had seen it in my dream with Ben's grandfather, but nothing had prepared me for the way I would feel when seeing in the flesh what I had only seen in the 'visionings'. It was awe mixed with real fear and a great longing to run away, and a great longing to run to it. It had been different on the lakeshore – there had been the photograph to prove it – this was just dreams.

But there was no doubt – I recognised the tumbling water that cascaded between the tall pillars of rock which had looked like carved birds, before gushing down the mountainside through the wet boulders – no mists of visionings now, but hard, rocky reality.

Gabriel was looking at me. "Is it the same waterfall, Sara?" I nodded, still overcome.

"Shall we wait for the others to catch up?"

I shook my head vigorously, still in the spell the dream had woven around me.

"It was only you and I, Gabriel, led by Ben's grandfather ... in the dream. Whether that's significant, I don't know – I just feel it is."

"Then I'll go back and ask them to wait." And he was gone before I could say anything.

Ben said nothing as he and I slowly approached the fall and craned our necks back to stare up into the water high above us. Some of the spray touched our faces and, despite the cold, it's touch was gentle, like a blessing. Gabriel came back.

"The others have agreed to wait, but they'll only give us an hour as it's nearly dusk. Ben, can you keep an eye on things out here?"

"Sure." But I sensed the deep disappointment in his tone and felt for him.

I was still looking at the falling water and saw something that would cheer him. "You'll have good company – look – Vigilant's here."

There high above us was Vigilant standing proud and still on the tall outcrop of rock where I had seen him before. He raised one cry to Ben but stayed where he was. Ben stared at him with awe. Then a shadow fell across our faces, flew over our heads and took its place on the opposite side of the waterfall. It was the Raven.

I felt for Misty and she was there, reassuring. Involuntarily my hand tightened around the feather that I carried in my pocket and I felt the hook of the little earring dig into my finger.

I reached my other hand to Ben. He grasped it firmly and understood what I needed. Together we reached our minds for his Haida grandfather.

Then he was there and my mind was flooded with light and I knew we only had to go forward. Reluctantly Ben let go of my hand and, carefully feeling my way with my feet, never taking my eyes from the misty figure I saw before us, I walked through the curtain of water. I hardly felt the sharp needles of the powerful spray, only the warmth of Gabriel's hand on my shoulder. The water dripped from my hair into my eyes, but still I could see that figure. I knew that if I closed my eyes he would still be there, but I needed to watch my feet.

It was dark behind the waterfall, but our path was lit by the figure of light. It got darker still as we followed up a passageway cut from the damp, dripping rock. It was wet underfoot and I was grateful for Gabriel's steadying hand and the warm jacket I had on.

The journey seemed to go on and on steadily climbing upwards and I was already tired. I would have turned back if the messages in my head hadn't insisted I go on. I called to Mistral and heard her chitter just as we emerged into the light. The path we were on ran round a circular enclosure of rock and we were on the top of it. I drew my breath in sharply when I looked down the thirty feet to the floor below with nothing to hang on to. Gabriel was behind me so I leant against him as I steadied myself. He held me close as he too looked down over the edge. We only had a moment to realise what we were looking at before I noticed the figure ahead of us was still moving away from us, becoming dimmer and we couldn't risk losing him.

We kept carefully to the path as we followed, fearful of the drop. Suddenly the figure ahead disappeared from view. We reached the point we had last seen him and saw the dim misty outline of him down a passage that led steeply downward. He turned to make sure we were following and smiled with that gentleness I remembered, but all his features were becoming blurred. We hastened after him, but had to take it carefully as the path was slippery from the water dripping through the rock roof above us.

Then we turned left into the circular enclosure of rock and were in the light. All sign of Ben's grandfather had faded with the brightness. Behind me the archway we had just emerged from was carved from a huge cedar tree whose branches laid a sheltering arm over the ground and swept outward to the rock, partly obliterating what we had travelled so far to see – the place of the Carved Rock. A Raven flew over the circular arena, swung in a circle around it and was gone. Our eyes followed the curve of its flight and lighted on the figures I had seen only in dreams. "So is beauty made from beauty to live forever." I could almost believe the words had been spoken aloud and, as though this was a signal I felt an explosion in my head of noise and clutched my hands to my ears as though to block out the sound.

"Look" Gabriel pointed skyward. High above circled five shadows. Then three shapes detached themselves from the circle and plummeted earthward. At the height of the arena they swept up and, as the Raven had done, swung in a circle above our heads. Then they returned to the two shadows high in the sky. I stood silently calling to them – Mistral, Scrap and Rift – but they weren't ready to come down. Still my heart sang to see them again – to know them safe, to know them here with me, confirming this was where I was meant to be.

I turned to tell Gabriel, but he had his back to me. I looked in the direction he faced and froze. Coming towards us was a figure, not unlike Ben's Haida grandfather, the same high cheekbones and piercing eyes but with dark eyebrows drawn together. There was no gentleness in his face and a rifle pointed directly at Gabriel. I remembered the Haida's fearsome reputation as warriors and stood very still. Gabriel pushed me to the back of him. The figure stopped twenty feet from us and spoke.

"Are you the ones that come to plunder this place?"

"No," Gabriel replied with a calm I was far from feeling. "We were summoned by the Raven."

"Then you will show me."

All this time I had been staring at the man's face and there was something I couldn't place. Then I saw Rift in my mind the last time I had seen her at home and the thing she had placed in my hand for safekeeping. One earring only swung from one side of the Haida's severe face and it was the same as I held in my pocket. I caught a glimpse of the shadow of Ben's grandfather over the Indian's shoulder and he was smiling. Reaching into my pocket I stepped out from behind Gabriel. He placed a hand on my arm to stop me but I walked towards the man until I was between Gabriel and the rifle.

Ten feet away from him I stopped and stretched out my left hand towards him palm up. The hand shook but I ignored it and looked him straight in the eyes.

"The Raven has sent you this gift."

The shaking spread to my whole body as the gun continued to point straight at my stomach and he continued to stare directly into my eyes.

Then a shadow passed between us and I felt a stab of pain in the palm of my hand – the Raven had taken the earring in his strong beak, leaving my palm bleeding. He flew with it to the top of a totem pole in the centre of the rock arena. There at the top he sat while the earring swung from side to side from his beak. How was I to get it back? Then I remembered the dream and, as if in answer, my eyes were drawn upwards and I was staggered by the speed with which Mistral dropped in a stoop directly at the Raven. With breathtaking accuracy she snatched the earring from the Raven and dropped it once more into my still outstretched right hand. I closed my fist over it.

Misty landed on the outstretched arms at the top of the wooden pole, carved like a pair of outstretched wings, to the right of the Raven. Once settled she threw her love and encouragement into my mind and I thanked her.

A satisfied and beautiful smile crossed the severe features in front of me as he stared at Misty and the face changed completely. He placed the gun at his feet and held out his hand. I took a step forward and placed the earring in his palm. As our hands touched briefly I had a vision of Vigilant, strong and clear. I looked up into his eyes. The surprise must have shown because he gave a great laugh that echoed from the rock face.

"My ancestors are Eagle just as they are Raven."

"Then Vigilant comes from you?" I asked, surprised.

"From who else? My name is Kaisun, after the village my ancestors came from."

One last shaft of late sunlight caught the tall pole illuminating the two birds which became three as I looked. Rift had joined her mother. There was no sign of Vigilant, nor Scrap,

Omen or Wraith.

Kaisun turned to Gabriel. "Are you he that heals?" he asked. Gabriel nodded. "Then come."

He led us back towards the archway from which we had emerged. Although the light was poor, masked by the arms of the cedar tree, I could distinguish the beautiful carvings around the doorway. I touched one as I followed Kaisun through the opening, and felt my fingers tingle at the contact. We turned to the left as we passed the steep passage by which we had descended. This brought us out through a concealed door into another, smaller enclosed area, this one surrounded by tall, thin wooden poles about two inches apart. My heart pounded as I realised this was an aviary. I could see the outline of birds perched high ready for the fall of night. What I wouldn't give for such large and lofty aviaries.

"Forgive my greeting to you, but the last who came shot the Ancient One." Kaisun said as he led us to a building built of cedar planks in the corner of the enclosure. "She needs your help – if you can heal as we have been told. Come."

There was a small building attached to the back of the house, also built of cedar planks. Kaisun opened the door and beckoned us in. On a small platform in the corner lay a bird such as I had never laid eyes on before. It was hard to tell how big the wings were as they were only partly extended from her sides, supporting her weight, but her body was large.

It was the eyes that took my attention. They were like no other bird's eyes that I had encountered. As Kaisun shone the lamp on her she raised her head that was smooth, almost reptilian in its roundness, and growing out of a long neck. She uttered a throaty cry in greeting which displayed a small tooth-like ridge along her beak, but she made no other movement. The eyes, which were yellow, lacked the sparkle of life that a healthy bird would show.

In a hushed tone Gabriel asked. "What bird is this?"

"You will know all later. Now, you heal her – please."

I looked into Kaisun's face and realised how much this meant to him.

Gabriel turned to face him. "Kaisun, you must understand that it isn't as simple as that. Even from here I can see she is very near the end. What is wrong with her?"

"I told you – he shot her."

"Remember the feather, Gabriel."

"I remember. Kaisun, I can't guarantee to heal her. I can only try."

"Then you try – please."

"Sara, I'll need your help."

"Me? But I'm no healer."

"I may need you to talk to the birds. Don't you see – this is what they brought us for – you and me, Joe, Ben and Callum? This is no ordinary bird."

He was right. I went quietly to lay my hand on the bird and then closed my eyes and contacted Misty. I got them all and had to let go so confused were the signals. I tried again and some order had been instilled. Vigilant came through the strongest and I felt his sense of pride in the Ancient One, but also hurt, anger and bewilderment. Then Misty took over and I felt her love that had brought me so far and her great need.

"It's up to us now, Gabriel." I left the bird and went up to him and took his hands in mine. "Let's hope we don't fail them."

He looked into my eyes and his seemed to deepen to a deep midnight blue and they held me just as Misty's had. "Together?"

"Together." I confirmed.

Kaisun held a hurricane lamp so that we could get a better view of her. We could see where the shot had entered her chest. It had passed through at an angle but left an enormous gash which was not healing and from which pus oozed evilly. She must have been shot at close range to inflict a wound like this. The skin had healed in parts but was still suppurating in the centre of the wound. I could smell herbs on her and knew Kaisun had done what he could for her. I wondered why he hadn't taken her down to the City and then dismissed the idea. If she was what he claimed – the Ancient One – he couldn't risk the publicity. She would be taken from him and made a showpiece for the world.

I put these thoughts from me and concentrated on staying with the birds. Gabriel had his hands on her body and his eyes closed in concentration. I laid one of my hands on each of his and listened. Suddenly I didn't recognise the voice in my head – it was not of any of the birds I had come to know. It spoke to me of times Long Ago, through countless generations, when its kind quartered the skies above Forest, Lake and Sea. Nowhere was there a sign of humankind – no Fire, no Dwellings. There were creatures below it that I didn't recognise, creatures it preyed upon with Honour, taking wherever possible the Weak and the Sick. I felt a sense of Harmony and a feeling that Life would continue thus Forever.

The imagery was weakening and I had to concentrate harder. Then Time was compressed and I felt the need of the voice to complete the Telling quickly. I saw fields of Ice. I saw images of Death, starving skeletons of birds that had no food, because Humankind had arrived on its World and taken its prey. I saw the Land beneath me change, the Forests disappear, the Moor land burnt, the Hillsides drained and the Valleys flooded. I saw Death from poisoning, Death from shooting, Death from smothering in cramped cages, Death from clinging black filth. I saw Despair and, as I was drawn to the future, I saw Raven black Darkness.

The other birds joined in and they drowned out the weakening voice. Their voices were a scream of anger in my mind so strong that for an instant I blacked out and took my hands from the Ancient One.

At that moment I heard a moan escape from Gabriel and he raised his head. I felt his despair.

"I can only bring her some relief. She has not long, Kaisun."

My heart bled for this wasted life that had survived through to this time only to be brought so low by a man's whim. I thought of all the countless others who had destroyed for their own misguided pleasure and I thought of Mistral's son. I knew the anger would remain with me always.

I turned to Kaisun, afraid how he would react now we had failed him and saw the great sorrow and resignation on his face as he bent to caress the Ancient One. He cradled her for a moment against his chest and then led the way out of the hut. We followed him, Gabriel carrying the lantern.

The light was starting to fade rapidly and I suddenly remembered the others. When I looked at my watch I realised less than an hour had elapsed since we left them – it had seemed so much longer. But then how long does it take for a species to die?

"Kaisun – we didn't come alone – there are others."

He nodded gravely. "I know and they wait outside the water curtain do they not? Do you wish that they should enter here or wait for the one who follows?"

"I don't understand you, Kaisun."

"Come I shall lead the way."

Gabriel had said nothing and was looking pale and withdrawn. I knew he felt the failure to cure the Ancient One deeply – he had come so far for this. I wished I could take the pain away, but couldn't find the words. Instead I hugged him and then took his hand to follow Kaisun.

We returned to Kaisun's home and picked up the other lantern. Gabriel spoke for the first time.

"Kaisun, my heart weeps that I didn't have the power. She wants release from the pain of living and I cannot draw her back."

"It was meant as it happened. Your journey was delayed beyond her endurance."

Kaisun and I went to find the others, leaving Gabriel the time he needed to strengthen himself. We left the house by the right hand door rather than the one to its left that was more ornate. We followed a path to the right that led through a deep narrow ravine to the front of the waterfall. So there was a back and front door to the arena, one guarded by Kaisun, the other by the curtain of water.

We reached a platform at about half the height of the waterfall and looked down. We had made very little sound and there was still enough light to see the group below us at the foot of the waterfall. They stood around looking restless and indecisive. The thought of entering the waterfall without Ben's grandfather as a guide must have been daunting for them and, although there was a chance he would come to guide Ben, I knew he was not sure enough of himself yet to trust in it. It was Joe who became aware we were there. Since Scrap and Omen had become close he seemed to have a heightened awareness of me. He opened his mouth to speak but shut it at the sight of Kaisun. It was only then that I noticed that Kaisun had brought the rifle.

"It's alright, Joe," I hurried to reassure him. I turned to Kaisun. "These are our friends." Then I noticed the look in

Kaisun's eyes and they were staring straight at Andrew.

Andrew went very pale and I could see him trying to control the shaking of his hands.

In a voice that seemed to echo round the rocks, Kaisun spoke directly to Andrew.

"It was told you must never return – yet I see you here."

It was clear that the message had been driven home so well that Andrew had hidden it – until now. But he remembered it well at this moment, and had felt its threat when he had flown over the area with us.

I intervened. "He brought the Healer and us all to this place."

"For that then I welcome him." He smiled and I felt he had known that Andrew would be one of our party, but had enjoyed that little moment of power.

Kaisun turned to Ben.

"Your grandfather has been calling you for many years. At last you have come."

He turned to Callum.

"You are granted the privileges of the Eagle, Spirit of Strength, kin to us. Welcome."

Then he turned to Joe and his expression softened.

"You and I have lost a good brother. He was sent to seek for another Ancient One, but brought back other news. Of a Brother in Spirit." He looked at me. "And a Sister."

He could see that neither of us had understood him.

"Come we will discuss this in more comfort – come."

We followed Kaisun back along the path, Andrew limping reluctantly at the rear. This time we entered the house by the door that opened in the middle of a wide carved pole, not tall like the others I had seen, but as beautifully carved. The door itself was more ornate than the one to the left that we had left the house by. This gesture did us great honour in the Haida tradition as the ornate door is the ceremonial entrance to the house.

"But surely you realised that you couldn't keep this place hidden for long?" I asked.

Kaisun smiled. "It has been hidden for many thousand years. You know this. You are a Toucher of Spirits. You heard what she had to say, as I did. But in answer to your question – yes we knew time was running out. We believed it had when the one you call Andrew came here." He smiled. "Yet he has taken until now to guide you here. The Spirits led him – they know when the time is right."

"Then you wanted him to return? You wanted the place to be found?" Ben asked. Seeing him alongside Kaisun the resemblance was strong. I wondered if they were related through Grandfather.

"That's not how I remember it, " Andrew muttered.

"This has been a secret part of the Islands for many years, but it could not stay that way for long. Your loggers are taking the growth of thousands of years. They believe themselves Lords of the Forest, when only the Tree can be the Lord of the Forest, just as the Birds are the true Lords of the Air. Your tourists are everywhere. It has only been necessary to guard this Place of Lost Spirits since the White Man came to these Islands. I am the seventh Guardian and you," he turned to Ben, "Grandson of Eagle, would have been the eighth when the time came."

"But what would he have been guarding, Kaisun?" I asked. "The Ancient One you speak of?"

"If she could but live – but if I speak to you of the Story of the Birds Carved from Rock – does this not mean something to you?"

"I have seen them in dreams, Kaisun, but I do not know if they are real."

"They are real, Toucher of Spirits. They have been carved over many, many years. They are a record of all living birds from when we first came to these Islands. They record, too, the deaths of these birds, never to return. They are a warning to all who behold them of the greed of all our kind, but more to the White Man who takes from the Earth that which he has no right to, for which he shows no respect." Kaisun was becoming angry. Then he took a deep breath to calm himself.

"In a dream I was shown your coming and that of another – a man of greed, a plunderer, who believes he has the right to take life. That man is now no more, and yet the shadow has not been lifted. That one took the Ancient One from us, and yet I feel there is another who will take more."

"Who is the Ancient One?" Callum asked.

"Ask the Toucher of Spirits – she will tell you."
"I only know what she showed me." I described to them the story she told. "Kaisun can tell you better, but I believe she earned her name as being the nearest to a living 'fossil' than we are ever likely to see again."
"Will we be able to see her?" Andrew asked – for him it was more a matter of journalistic interest than the awe it was for those of us steeped in the avian world.
"You will have that honour. She was the last of the first bird drawn on the rock many thousand years ago by our ancestors. There have only been a pair left for over twenty years and they were not successful in their breeding. We have been obliged to keep them in a cage to prevent what did in the end happen. The Ancient One was lonely when her mate died so I gave her more freedom and that is how she came to be shot."
I helped Kaisun prepare a meal with the supplies we had brought with us. At least we would not have to spend a night under canvas as Kaisun had invited us to share his home. Over supper we discussed the problem of Long and Hilton. We were sure they had not given up. Kaisun was interested in them.
Ben filled in the details. "They have some photographs and a feather that Andrew found which will maybe lead them here in the end. I guess we only got here sooner because we had the help of the birds."
Kaisun smiled at him "And you listened to them – at last."
Ben blushed and then asked. "Have you seen a friend of ours – Paul – it was partly to find him we came? He's the one that took the photos and feather in the first place."
"No – fortunately – you are the first to arrive. This feather – you think it is from the Ancient One?"
Gabriel answered. "We didn't recognise it – we'd never seen its like, but having seen her – yes it was her feather."
"So she attempted her own salvation – she sent her feathers as well as searchers." There was great sadness and great pride in his tone. "But now we must prepare for the others coming – those who do not come with love in their hearts."
"That would sure fit the description of Hilton, I'd say," Ben confirmed.
"At dawn I will show you the Rock, then we will prepare. He

will not approach at night. I will warn Vigilant – you – Toucher of Spirits – will warn your falcon."

"Her name is Mistral, Kaisun and mine is Sara. It's a little shorter than Toucher of Spirits – though not as honourable." I added hastily. Kaisun smiled.

Joe had been quiet during the meal. I had noticed he talked little whilst eating, preferring to enjoy the food. But now he could wait no longer.

"Kaisun, sir, you said by the waterfall – about the loss of a brother. Am I right to think you spoke of the one I called Peal – that he really did come from here?"

"That is the bird. I feel it, that he is dead. He too was shot on that day, trying to protect her. He was one of the Chosen Ones who sought across the world for another First and Last One, who brought back the sadness of the birds everywhere. He left when we knew that time was running out. But this time when he returned he brought back the Hope that there were those who would not let these things happen – Brothers of the Spirit. He spoke to you did he not?" Joe nodded.

"And to you, Touch ...Sara."

"I only saw him in a dream, Kaisun – when he was shot."

"You saw him many times more than that, Sara – and he lives yet in the two young you raised."

"Mistral's mate!" I exclaimed. "So that's why we were brought here. But she never told me."

Joe could keep quiet no longer. "Then my Peal lives on in little Scrap – it is why he was sent to me. Oh, Sara, that makes me so very happy – for I think my Omen and your Scrap are as a pair for life." I felt my eyes fill with tears for the joy this brought Joe. He deserved better than to have his Brother in Spirit shot from the skies.

I asked Andrew to help to clear the dishes while Kaisun discussed with the others what to do when Long inevitably got here.

"This is going to make some story for you, Andrew, if we get back in one piece."

"Do you know, Sara, I don't find that just such a priority at the moment. I'm still not sure what I'm mixed up in, but I do know it's special. If I write about it, I'll make sure that's clear."

I smiled at him. "You've changed, Andrew."

"Yes I really reckon I have. I feel as if a huge load has been lifted off my shoulders. And you've all helped a lot there."

"Just do the story justice if Kaisun lets you print it."

We returned to the others. I asked Kaisun if I might go and say goodnight to Misty.

"Tell her to be ready, Toucher of Spirits, we need all their help."

There was a glorious full moon shining, lighting the rocks as I entered the arena. The odd cloud dimmed its brilliance from time to time but I was able to see enough by its intermittent light to make out the shadows on the pole. I didn't need to see her to know Misty was there – she had been in my mind since I heard about Peal. I didn't know how much of the sorrow I felt was hers or mine, but it mattered little – we both mourned him and the coming end of a friend and a creature whose like we would never see again, but which had brought us half way round the world.

I sat at the foot of the pole looking towards the moon and threw my mind open to them all. The response was sleepy, but they understood the warning – they would watch. Vigilant had already been warned. I heard a sound behind me but didn't turn round – it was so peaceful sitting on the ground lit only by the ghostly light of the moon. I knew before he knelt down behind me and placed his hands on my shoulders that it was Gabriel. We remained like that for several minutes, both soaking in the strange atmosphere of this Special Place.

"We've come a long way, Sara," Gabriel spoke eventually. "But it's not over yet. Without bloodshed we may have difficulty keeping Hilton from desecrating this place."

"I don't think even Long could harm this place, Gabriel. He'll probably want to publicise it, though." I looked about me at the vague outlines of the carving hardly visible in the moonlight. "But if it acts as a warning to the world about what we lose every moment through our own greed – will it not have served its purpose?"

"You have more faith in human nature than I do. The Haida people have protected this place for so many years – Kaisun knows it can't last and the experience of the last few years has brought that home to him. But he will do what he has to in order to protect it."

"What are the plans for tomorrow, Gabriel?" I asked.

He drew me to my feet. "Kaisun has one or two things up his sleeve – but we'll mostly have to play it by ear. I'd rather you kept out of harms way, though, Sara."

"Not that again. If the birds are involved then I am – you know that."

"It doesn't mean I have to like it. Just as I didn't like it when I thought you were dead set on Andrew."

"And what makes you so sure I'm not?"

"Andrew."

"You mean you asked him?" I asked horrified.

"Well, indirectly."

"What the hell do you mean by that?"

"Well I cheated a bit – when I got you to help me with Andrew's leg. As your hands touched mine I just asked the question, first of Andrew, then of you."

I remembered the feeling of warmth in my heart – it was there still. "And what reply did you have from Andrew?" I couldn't resist asking.

"That would hardly be ethical for me to reveal."

I turned round to thump him, but instead found myself held in a bear hug jamming my arms to my side and driving the air out of my body. I heard Misty chitter. The grip slackened enough for me to catch a quick breath and for Gabriel to place his mouth over mine, which instantly stopped that means of gaining air, which by now I desperately needed. I struggled and he released me – too suddenly so that I lurched forward. He caught me by the arms and held me at arm's length.

"I'm sorry, Sara, but can you imagine what it's been like all this time being with you constantly, but hardly being able to touch you? And then when I do, I get scolded by that bird of yours."

"She's not scolding, Gabriel, just encouraging."

"Then she won't mind if I carry on where I left off?"

"I doubt it – if I don't why should she?"

"And you really don't?"

"Have you thought it might have been as difficult for me to have you so close and not reach out for you – or is it only men who are allowed to feel that way?"

To prove my point, this time I reached for him and pulled his head down to mine. I clasped my hands around the back of his neck and murmured the word "together" before pressing my lips to his. He reached down and drew my body against his.

The longing I'd suppressed for so long just seemed to well up inside me, the need I had of him and the joy to know he wanted me as I did him. I was sure now – sure of the way I felt – that I never wanted him to let go – that I wanted to stay secure in his arms forever. Forever, though, was temporarily foreshortened to a few seconds as we heard the cedar door opening and Ben come through. He smiled to see us close.

"Sorry to interrupt." he declared without even a trace of remorse. "I just wanted to ask Sara a favour."

"Well she's granted mine, so feel free." Gabriel offered.

Ben chuckled, and then turned to me. Hesitatingly he began in his slow manner – "I don't know how to ask this, Sara – I can sense my grandfather is here, but I can't 'see' him. Can you, Sara?"

"Not just at the minute, Ben – my mind was on other things, but yes – he is here."

"Do you think he's ashamed of me and that's why I can't see him?"

"No!" The sound echoed in my head and I knew the words came from grandfather. "Why would he be? You are just looking with the wrong eyes. Ask the Raven."

We both looked up towards the top of the pole in the centre of the Special Place where the Raven stood staring down at us. I took Ben's hand and gazed steadily back at the Raven until I felt the familiar feeling of detachment and heard grandfather's voice in my head.

"Bring him to me – let him see."

Slowly I drew Ben towards the pole until we stood directly in front of it. The Raven dropped onto Ben's shoulder and I felt the tension leave him and he breathed the word "Grandfather."

As I looked the carvings on the pole merged into one blurred image and, curling into a mist, spread outwards until the figure of grandfather was there standing before us, as tall as the pole with his arms outspread. Hanging from his shoulders was a cloak made up of the feathers of many different birds that dropped from his outstretched arms like wings. I watched, spellbound as he approached Ben, and, carefully removing the cloak of feathers he placed it around his shoulders where it hung for a moment before evaporating into mist, leaving the Raven still sitting on Ben's shoulders.

"Wear it with pride and humility, Grandson, and never forget the duty and respect we owe all creatures."

He touched Ben lightly on the forehead and smiled a smile full of love before turning the smile on me where it settled in my heart. Then once more all that was in front of us was the pole with the Raven standing proud on top, just as if nothing had happened. But I knew by the set of Ben's shoulders and the dazed smile on his face that he had seen what I had.

He drew me to him in a huge hug, forgetting the strength contained within his great muscles. For the second time within an hour my delicate ribcage took a battering and I began to doubt the advantage of having so much male strength around, attractive though they were. I was to think about this conclusion the next day and change my mind.

"Thanks, Sara."

"It was nothing to do with me," I declared when I'd got my breath back. "Just remember – he'll always be there for you when you need his help – just reach out for him."

"I will – you can be sure of that."

Gabriel joined us and I linked arms with them both as we returned to Kaisun's house. Ben was now looking more confident – but I was still uncertain about tomorrow. All my life I had avoided violence, believing it answered very little, but tomorrow – well tomorrow would come soon enough.

CHAPTER NINETEEN

It seemed that every time I shut my eyes that night, my brain was pounded by images. Some of these were the same visions that I had seen before, but they were all a lot clearer. I could see the lake as I'd seen it earlier that day, but still from the same angle as the dream. And I saw again the death of Peal as Mistral must have seen it.

I dreamt again of the spinning circle of faces with Rift in the middle and awoke with the terrible sensation of falling. I must have called out, for Gabriel came over to my makeshift bed and held me while the shaking stopped. We lay together the rest of the night, content for now just to share the warmth of our bodies and not the need.

Dawn came too soon. It was cold and misty outside, but Kaisun got us all up and fed, ready to face what the day would bring. We were all very quiet, aware of a feeling of destiny, of not really being in charge.

"First I will take you to see the Birds Carved from Rock. It is fitting that you may be the last to see it as it is. Then we plan for battle for Vigilant tells me they are not far away."

The rising sun flooded a ghostly yellow light over one side

of the huge rock arena, but we needed a lantern to see the details on the area shaded by the cedar tree. Each part of the day would illuminate a different part of the circle. The light shone first on the earliest carvings, started thousands of years ago. These were just lightly engraved lines which had recently been painted to give them life and which had been protected by the overhang of rock. It was like reading a book as each species unfolded, revealing its form, a book that seemed to go on forever. Kaisun pointed out the image of the Ancient One at the very beginning of time.

As we went round we saw solid black paint on a large number of the carvings and guessed this indicated the demise of all these birds.

Gradually as the years went by the carvings became more detailed and three dimensional with a simplicity and beauty that took my breath away. I saw Callum run his hands gently over the surface and a contented smile lit his face – he recognised the beauty of the craft. Many of them still had pigments colouring them and I assumed it was part of Kaisun's role to keep them thus sparkling with life. This only emphasised the solemn images of the dead ones painted in black and they ran into many hundreds.

Above the section of carvings I'd seen in my dreams, at the very top, I could see the outline of the three, Mistral, Scrap and Rift. I called them down to me as I hadn't touched the two youngsters for so long. They flew to the lower branches of the cedar tree where I could reach up and talk to each in turn.

Mistral flew onto my shoulder and stood there, preening my hair. Kaisun was watching us, a smile on his face. Rift flew over to him, sat on his shoulder and tweaked playfully at the earring I had made. He put up his hand to stroke her chest.

"So, Peal's Little One, this is your gift and now you will take it away."

"The feather belongs to her brother who was shot." I explained.

"Then it is doubly precious, Peal's Little One, and I thank you for the gift with all my heart, for I have in each ear a feather from father and son."

Satisfied that she had made her point Rift returned to the cedar tree. Then Kaisun called us altogether.

"From your faces I see the Special Place pleases you. Now it needs your help. Are you willing to protect it?"

There wasn't a person there who did not recognise the uniqueness of this place. Here was a chance to make a difference in the world of indifference. We all nodded.

"Then it is necessary to prepare. Sara and Joe, will you ask your birds to watch the pass up here from the lake. We must know when they reach the ridge before the start of the climb to the waterfall. After, please, we need gathered small rocks and branches of trees."

Joe took my hand and we contacted the birds together. It was becoming so that any message given to Scrap was automatically passed on to Omen, which made things a great deal easier for us. We then went in search of the rocks and branches Kaisun required with very little idea what he wanted them for, but confident he knew what he was doing. We didn't talk much and I enjoyed the peaceful companionship surrounded by the trees, rocks and the sharp mountain air.

We'd got quite a pile together when I heard Mistral in my head. They'd reached the bluff. I hurried to Kaisun.

"Then we have about half an hour before they arrive. May the ancestors be with us."

Kaisun told me to keep one of the birds watching the progress of Long's party and get the others back here. This was a bit of a challenge, as I'd never had to instruct the birds individually, just whoever happened to be in my head at the time. I concentrated on Scrap and told him to stay there, but I felt confusion from the others. Mistral understood before Rift and I was rewarded by seeing the two anchor shapes soaring in the sky towards us.

They landed by the pile of rocks and branches we'd collected. Kaisun asked Joe to help him carry branches into the arena and then addressed me.

"Will you see if you can show them the way to carry the rocks, Sara?" I looked at him flabbergasted – so that was why he wanted us to collect them – avian catapults. Well condors dropped their bones from great heights to smash them open, but I assumed Kaisun intended to reverse the process, drop the rocks to break the bones.

"I'll try Kaisun, but I doubt if they'll understand. They are not great nest builders at the best of times."

"Please try, Toucher of Spirits." He threw in the name as a challenge.

It was easier than I thought – Rift seeing it as some new kind of game. Getting her to drop them where I wanted took a little longer and a couple of bumps on the head. Mistral was more serious about it, sensing my concern, and more accurate, thank goodness.

I didn't have time to see what the others were doing. They were working at the top of the waterfall which they reached from the path which Gabriel and I had arrived on last evening which skirted for a while round the rock arena. Kaisun split his time between the arena and the waterfall until he was satisfied we'd all done everything we could. He was ready now to deploy his forces.

He called us all into the arena and I could see that a wooden plank had been placed on top of the branches Joe and I had collected.

"They will be here very soon," Kaisun declared. "We must be ready. The Brothers in Spirit know where they are needed. The one named Andrew, the Guide – you will wait here. You know how to use the radio?" Andrew nodded. "We may have need of it. You, Healer, I wish to keep an eye on all here and help where you are needed." Gabriel, too, nodded.

Kaisun turned to me. "You will come with me, Toucher of Spirits."

Gabriel obviously knew where Kaisun was going. "Kaisun, are you sure – it could be dangerous?"

"I will guard her, Healer." He picked up his gun. "We have need of her."

Gabriel came up to me and put both his hands on my shoulders. "Take great care of yourself, Sara – we have a lot of unfinished business." He kissed me gently on the brow. "Remember, I love you – all."

Warmed by his words, I followed Kaisun down the path towards the waterfall. He stopped on the platform where we'd looked down on the others last night, so we would have a clear view down to the foot of the waterfall and down the track that led up to it.

"Call down the one you call Mistral." Kaisun commanded.

Mistral came straight away and settled on my shoulder.

"We will let the Spirits guide us today, Toucher of Spirits. Perhaps we can touch their hearts and they will go away."

I said nothing. Kaisun did not know Long and Hilton, but I doubted they would be touched by anything other than the promise of money or glory. Although we were in a very much stronger position strategically, we only had the one gun. We did not know if Long and Hilton would have guns but we had to assume they would. I kept well clear of Kaisun's right arm, in case his faith in human nature was misplaced, as I suspected, and warned Mistral to be ready to get herself out of trouble – she had seen what a gun could do – I hoped she understood.

"Look." Kaisun pointed to the top of the waterfall.

It was a moving sight. Where the Raven and Vigilant had stood when we first arrived stood Ben on the left side and Callum on the right nearest us. Both had one arm outstretched, supported by a forked branch. On Ben's arm sat Vigilant and on Callum's, Wraith. It was the first proper sight I'd had of Wraith and, although slightly dwarfed by Vigilant he had a majesty about the warm golden head that stood out well at the top of the waterfall. The shape of his head was sleeker than Vigilant, the beak darker and not so prominent – a creature with a strong beauty which makes your heart catch in your throat.

They looked so very impressive from the angle we viewed them but from the foot of the waterfall they would have looked truly massive. Glancing at Ben I thought I saw the shadow of the cloak of many feathers that sat well on his broad shoulders, and felt his grandfather's protection over him.

It was just possible to make out a plank that went from one side of the waterfall to the other. In the middle was a carved pole similar to the pole in the middle of the arena. Standing in front of this was Joe, on his shoulder sat Omen and Scrap sat on top of the pole.

I caught my breath in admiration. "They look wonderful, Kaisun – but aren't they a bit vulnerable."

"There is protection for all the Brothers in Spirit – you will see. I have made plans for many days now."

We heard the low murmur of voices from the track below us, but they were not yet in sight. This was it, then, they really were coming. I sent warnings to the others, but felt only a patient waiting. Perhaps I was the only nervous one – Kaisun stood there calmly enough, the rifle casually over his arm pointing down the path.

Then they rounded the corner – five of them, heavily laden with pickaxes and spades. At their head, carrying very little was the man I took to be Hilton. The man behind him I didn't recognise but the one behind him I did and I felt a shiver run through my body. The one I'd glimpsed in the mirror, the gloating one. Even from here I could sense the belligerent air that was reinforced by the fact that he had a rifle in his one hand, while he balanced himself with the other. So far only the one gun was visible, a hunter's gun. At the rear came a very tired and nervous Dr Long.

They were concentrating on where they placed their feet and had not even noticed the waterfall yet. Kaisun took the moment and I understood why he chose to stand where he did. As his words rang out they sprang from rock to rock so that, for a moment the people below could not tell where the sound was coming from.

"This is a Sacred Place. Why are you here?"

It would have been comical watching their blank faces as they tried to trace the sound if it hadn't been such a solemn moment. Their eyes settled first on the figures, steady and rock-like that waited at the top of the waterfall. I felt great pride in my Brothers that they did not flinch when the one with the gun raised his rifle and I heard the safety catch click back. Kaisun raised his voice and, at the same time rammed home the bolt on his rifle so that the sound echoed round the rocks once more. This time they saw him and Hilton put a hand on the barrel of the gun that pointed at the top of the waterfall. I had my first view of his face below the hunting cap he was wearing. The cheeks were slightly puffy with good living and the eyes, too close together, had a restless quality about them that seemed to infect his whole body, as though he was never really satisfied with anything. It must have been this that drove his ruthlessness on.

"What do you want here?" Kaisun asked again the rifle still pointed at the group.

The one I presumed was Hilton was the first to recover. "We

mean no harm to this place. We are explorers, we only wish to pass this way in peace."

"This place leads nowhere. This is where your journey ends. Turn back now and do not return."

"What right do you have to forbid us entry here?" Hilton sounded indignant, unused, I assumed, to being refused anything.

"The right conferred by my ancestors – and this." He hefted the gun in his hands.

"If we lay down our gun, will you not lay down yours so that we may discuss this?"

"I have nothing to say to you. Only go."

Suddenly I heard a cry in my head and realised it had also been uttered out loud. Vigilant dropped like a huge arrow towards the group, skimmed over their heads and with a twist tore with his great talons at a branch which overhung the rocks on the other side of the river. Just as he hit it a shot rang out and ricocheted from the rock above our heads. I felt the anger in Mistral and she was off down the slope towards the same clump of trees, to sweep up at the last minute and perch in the top of a tree. Another shot rang out and hit the post just a foot above Joe's head, and six inches below Scrap. He shot off from the pole and Omen followed him. This set all the birds in flight, whilst Kaisun and I were still trying to work out where the shot had come from.

Ben shouted. "In the trees on the opposite side of the bank – more of them." He was rewarded by the sound of a bullet whistling over his head. Now, when I should have been most frightened, I felt an icy calm, instilled by the anger that overcame me. I contacted all the falcons and instructed them all to find the rocks to cast and bombard the group below the waterfall, but to keep ever on the move, out of rifle shot.

Kaisun had chosen his place well – there was a crevice behind the platform which gave us shelter but which allowed us still to see out. I had little time to concentrate on what was happening as I tried to keep the birds co-ordinated.

As the rocks cascaded from the air, it forced the group below us to take cover. A lot of the stones were more accurate than the others and I realised that Ben and Callum had a supply by them, but it was the stones that came from the sky that put the greatest fear into the five below us. We had no idea how many there were in the trees, but it was clear from the next shots that rang out that the birds were their target. The birds, though, had followed my instructions and kept moving. Fortunately they didn't give the hidden one time to take proper aim, otherwise Callum, Ben and Joe would have been easy targets, or so I thought, until I noticed that they each had a hollowed out piece of wood behind which they were protected except for their heads.

I saw the gloating one take the chance of a slight lull to reach for the gun he'd dropped in the first onslaught. A shot rang out from Kaisun and the gun went skidding off the rocks into the water. Immediately another shot hit the rock above our heads. This time it was too much for Vigilant. He attacked the clump of trees again with greater force and penetrated some way into the undergrowth. We heard a yell and then another shot, this time from a handgun. I felt pain in my mind and I knew Vigilant had been hurt. So did Kaisun. I reached a hand for him.

"Keep the Little Ones at their task, Toucher of Spirits. It is our only chance."

As I felt the pain from Vigilant I suddenly felt another anger welling up in me. My eyes were drawn to the pole above Joe's head and there, perched insecurely, but determined stood the Ancient One. With a pride inherited down the years she stared at the group below her. She seemed to summon all her strength ready to fly down to help her Brother in need, but at that moment a shot rang out from the bank, just as a shout was wrenched from the throat of Dr Long. But he was too late to stop the fateful shot. She had known her end was near but her courage had taken her through to the end. Her struggle was over and her lifeless body fell slowly into the water behind Joe and I saw Callum reach down towards her.

Then high above I heard the deep croak of the Raven and suddenly the sky was dark with many of his kind, tumbling and rolling as they flew over, skimming the top of the trees. A great shadow of their many black wings hit the faces of the group at the waterfall and they looked up in awe and terror.

"Stop your firing."

The command came from Hilton. The shots no longer rang

out from the trees and a figure emerged holding a blood soaked handkerchief to a torn cheek, and threw down his gun, a rifle and a handgun. Still Vigilant didn't come out from the trees.

The one across the bank waded across the river to join the others. Six of them stood below us, Hilton and Long still trying to maintain some vestige of authority, but clearly shocked by what'd happened in the last ten minutes.

Long shouted up at Kaisun. "The shooting was not done at my bidding. I only wanted ..."

"And yet you brought these others with you. They are your responsibility, just as the Eagle and the Ancient One was mine. It is now we who will dictate terms and you will answer for the blood you have shed of two Spirit Brothers."

Kaisun handed me the gun. "I must go down to them, Toucher of Spirits. Honour demands it." He showed me what to do with the gun should it be necessary. "You will aim it at the chief man." I took him to mean Hilton.

I'd handled guns before but only as a curiosity and never, never to point at anyone. Then I remembered the Ancient One and, taking my courage from her, hardened myself and the nerves that made my hands shake. I now had our only gun. Fortunately the birds had settled and I did not have the distraction of trying to guide them.

Kaisun went down the steep path to the side of the waterfall.

"You see I have no weapon," he said when he reached them, "so we meet on equal terms."

"Not quite," Hilton declared and whipped a handgun out of nowhere and grabbing Kaisun pointed it directly at his skull. I still had Hilton in my sights and didn't know what to do. Hilton turned his head towards me and shouted.

"Drop that gun – not that I suppose you know how to use it." Well that got right on a nerve – sexist pig, and I held onto the gun. But I forgot that any anger I showed set the birds off. Mistral flew straight at Hilton, who, in one swift movement grabbed Kaisun around the throat and aimed the gun rapidly at Mistral. Two shots rang out almost simultaneously. I looked on with horror, expecting to see Mistral tumble from the skies. Although her flight faltered, her momentum carried her on and she raked a groove down Hilton's head as she passed. Then the gun he had held a minute ago spun into the air and dropped at Kaisun's feet. Taking advantage of Hilton's momentary lapse of concentration Kaisun reached for it and backed away.

The other shot – that had disarmed Hilton – had come from behind the waterfall. Andrew emerged, holding the gun, I assumed, that I'd last seen being hurled out of the hand of Hilton's henchman who had kept Ella hostage. At least that was the only way I could account for it being in Andrew's hand. I had no idea he still had it, but was I thankful that he had! Mistral flew to me and I could see a furrow at the top of her leg where the shot had passed – it had been that close. It was hardly bleeding, so, until I could examine it closer, I left well alone.

Gabriel emerged by Andrew's side.

"There is nothing for you here, Long. You've come too late, as usual. This time you won't have a chance to steal what is not yours." He then turned to Kaisun. "They are on their way – they should be here within the hour."

"That is good. So, we will wait."

Ben had made his way down from the rock pinnacle to where we'd last seen Vigilant. I knew he was hurt, but he was not near to death. Mistral flew down immediately and guided Ben to the place we'd last seen Vigilant. He emerged a few minutes later to a cheer from Callum and Joe who were still above the waterfall and had a good view. On his fist was Vigilant. Even from here I could see the one wing was hanging, but he was alive. I could feel the anger in him when he saw the one who'd hidden in the trees.

Kaisun turned to the people in front of him. "You were told this is a Special Place. You have seen a little of those that guard it. Now we will show you how strong are the Spirits of these Guardians." He called me down to him.

I climbed down, holding the gun carefully – one of the things I did know was where the safety catch was. I handed the rifle to Kaisun and he handed Hilton's gun to Gabriel, who took it reluctantly, but held on to it.

Kaisun whispered to me. "Your Little Ones must fly as they never have before and Omen and Wraith. Tell the others. It is a warning to those that would destroy."

I walked through the waterfall and up the passageway to

the arena. I then followed the track to the top of the waterfall. I walked gingerly to stand by Joe and explain what Kaisun wanted. Together it was easier to control the birds and we told them what we wanted.

Mistral's leg did not affect her tremendous flying ability. She led the other Falcons in a dance that wove in and out of every crevice in the rock face and soared joyously up until they were almost out of sight high in the sky. I heard the gasps from those at the bottom of the waterfall as they plummeted down from the height at a speed that should break them apart, to skim the top of the waterfall. Mistral, Rift, Scrap and Omen in such exact formation it was staggering. They danced intricate dances above the heads of those at the bottom of the waterfall, so that they were torn between watching an aerial display they were never likely to see again, and ducking in fear that these Spirits of the Skies may fail in their accuracy.

Warning Mistral, I threw a feather into the air. She caught it as it fluttered down and turned upside down as she passed it to Rift who passed it to Scrap and then on to Omen, all in the blink of an eye and a matter of only twenty feet from the ground.

Then they spiralled upward, all four so close they seemed intertwined and, Mistral leading, charged down to earth in the shape of a perfect arrow, swooping low over their heads, so that I could see the hair lift on their heads.

I shouted down to them above the sound of the waterfall. "You, the one who shot Vigilant – place your hat on your head and keep still."

This was the most difficult thing I'd tackled. I visualised in my mind what I would like them to do and set them to it. Caught up in the excitement of the moment and the love we shared they responded. Mistral flew low over the heads below and whipped the hat off his head. She soared up with it and tossed it to Rift who tossed it to Scrap, who caught it, turned a somersault and dropping gently from the skies, placed it back on his head. It gave me great pleasure to see his face pale in fear of those huge long talons so close to his face.

I looked over at Callum. He nodded. I could see the concentration on his face. Then Wraith was airborne. He soared up to give himself the height he needed before gliding down with a control that was incredible to see. He headed down to the group below and, side slipping to the right at the last minute, grabbed the rifle from the water where it had fallen, and, labouring a little under the weight, flew back to Callum with it and dropped it carefully into his hands.

"Know you that we control these Spirits and all the Spirits in this area. They are ever Vigilant and will know if you return." Kaisun's words rang out.

Then there were sounds from behind the group in front of the waterfall. Several men came round the corner all with the high cheekbones and warlike stature that marked Kaisun. I saw the slight slackening of Kaisun's shoulders, as though the worst was over. Gabriel relinquished his gun with pleasure and headed back into the waterfall, closely followed by Andrew. The cavalry had definitely arrived, even if only on foot and we never saw Hilton and his followers again.

Joe took my hand and helped me from the plank that spanned the waterfall. Callum gave me a big hug as we all went down the path to the arena. Relief was coursing adrenaline through our veins and it was good to be alive. I was aware that I was very hungry.

We met Gabriel and Andrew coming up the passageway and I was literally swept off my feet by Gabriel, who grabbed me in his arms and spun me round.

"God, I was worried about you, but oh, so proud."

I returned his kiss with fervour, but we were interrupted by a pat on the shoulder from Joe and then Ben, who'd been waiting in the arena. Gabriel let me go straight away and went with Ben to where Vigilant stood, looking sorry for himself but still with head held high. He knew what he'd done today and I sent all my pride in him through my thoughts. For the second time I looked him straight in the eye and was staggered by the dignity he had, even when in pain. I still preferred the playfulness of my falcons, but had nothing but admiration for a creature so sure of its place.

Gabriel examined the wound to Vigilant's wing. It'd cracked the bone but not shattered it and had passed on without further damage, although, from the angle, it'd missed penetrating his body by millimetres. All the birds had come down into the arena and were sitting on the rock face or the Pole. I approached

Callum and asked if he would introduce me to Wraith, the only member of the team I hadn't so far met. Callum still had his glove on – so he handed it to me.

"Call him down, but be ready – he's a bit of a weight."

"Are you sure, Callum – you don't mind?"

"I've seen you in action, Sara – go on, call him down."

I closed my eyes and threw my mind open for Wraith and, for a moment sensed Callum 'talking' to him. When I opened my eyes it was to see Wraith flying to the top of the cedar tree, where he balanced precariously while pulling off one of the leaf laden twigs with his strong beak. He then flew down towards me with it and landed on the fist I had raised for him, making very sure that it was the one with the glove on – those feet were huge. He proffered me the branch and – very gently – I took it from his beak, all the time feeling him in my head, reassuring, loving. I couldn't believe the beauty of him close to, the amber of his eye set below the golden eyebrow that flowed into the burnished bronze of his head. I was in love – again.

He raised his head at the sound of the applause that welcomed his gesture and almost seemed to bow his head graciously at this deserved accolade. He then went and joined the other birds on the rocks.

Dazed, I returned Callum his glove but held tight to the branch. He saw the look in my eyes and laughed.

"Stunning, isn't he – bit of a show-off, though. That's from us both, by the way – you've been so – well – you know." He blushed – the quiet Callum once more taking over.

I reached up, quite a long way for my five feet four inches, and kissed him on the cheek, surprised at the softness of his beard. "I'll keep it forever."

Kaisun came forward with the body of the Ancient One and laid her gently on the wooden plank below the Pole. So this was to be her funeral bier.

It seemed tragic that the world should lose access to such a creature – yet for her it was the most dignified end and I understood Kaisun's desire to send her body to the skies where it could fly once more in peace. Behind the pole I saw the pale image of Ben's grandfather and his face was infinitely sad. I was only vaguely aware of the tears that ran down my cheeks, unchecked, as Kaisun placed the intricately patterned blanket he'd been wearing under her body and wrapped it around her. I felt the need to place a gift with the body of the Ancient One but had nothing. I went and laid my hand once more on the rounded head and left a smear of blood from my damaged hand where the Raven had pierced it the day before. The Raven called and Kaisun smiled.

"That is his gift to the Ancient One. He drew the blood which will protect her journey and will keep him ever your Guardian."

Kaisun went through the carved door in the cedar tree towards the house and I called Mistral down and had a better look at her leg. It was only a slight flesh wound and I thanked god for the agility that had saved her.

Andrew and Callum came up to find out how much damage had been done and Misty enjoyed the attention she was deservedly receiving. I smiled at Andrew.

"Thanks. If you hadn't kept that gun, we could all be in a bit of bother by now."

"Bother, you call it! Typical British understatement." But he looked pleased.

I looked up at Joe. "I've been thinking, now they know it's here there's no way that Long isn't going to come back, even if only to satisfy his curiosity. Do you think Kaisun is just going to abandon the place, or do you think he's going to destroy it?"

"I, too, have been thinking this, Sara."

It would be a tremendous loss if the carvings were destroyed. They were a unique record, not only of the diversity of bird life but the harm that can be done, sometimes unwittingly, when man interferes with the balances that Nature has decreed. This lesson, surely, could not be wasted. A thing of such beauty may well touch hearts that other means may not.

Gabriel had stopped the bleeding on Vigilant's wing and had strapped it to his side. Vigilant was busy examining the strap and it was evident he didn't think much of it. I felt Ben reassuring him, but he still wasn't very happy. No pain came through to me from him and I wondered if that was because of Gabriel and wondered what it must be like to have the skill to heal. I wasn't sure I would want the responsibility – I'd seen some of the demands made on Gabriel in the early days when he'd discovered he had the gift.

We went through to the front of the house and there seemed to be people everywhere. They came towards us and drew us into the house by the ornate, ceremonial door. There was bustle going on everywhere and we had glasses of some home brewed beer placed in our hands.

Kaisun approached beaming from ear to ear. "Welcome to the feast for the Ancient One."

"But why is Long here?" I asked, surprised at seeing him there.

"He, too, is a guest." He saw the look on my face and placed a hand on my arm. "All will be clear, my friends."

"I'm just going to have a word with Dr Long." Gabriel excused himself. "Perhaps he can shed some light on Paul's disappearance."

"Kaisun," Andrew began "what do you intend doing about the carvings?"

"Have faith and all will be revealed."

We had to be satisfied with that. I found something to eat as I was beginning to feel the potent effect of the home brew on an empty stomach and a blood system already jam packed full of adrenaline. No sooner had I begun to eat than Kaisun led us all outside again and to the arena. The birds were all there sitting on top of the overhang above the rock carvings, except Vigilant who sat on a lower rock that Ben had placed him on earlier. Vigilant called as Kaisun entered and a shadow flew down to the pole – the Raven was there – the Raven who had been there when we needed him – here now to say farewell to the last of a race he'd flown with.

I caught a glimpse of Long's face as we came into the arena with the midday sun showing the carvings at their most magnificent. The initial shock was followed by a softening in his face and the admiration shone through. Oddly it brought a lump to my throat. So much beauty could still move this man who had threatened us all for his own selfish ends. Was there hope yet for the world?

It appeared that Kaisun thought so or he wouldn't have given Long the privilege to be here – or were his motives otherwise? It was clear that the members of his family and friends had seen the carvings before, so they stood aside as Kaisun took Long from the beginning of time and the carving of the Ancient One round the circle to the end, each time making him touch the carvings in black as though to help bring home to this man who sought for his own glory, the glory of those beings that had paid with their lives for the greed of his kind. He made him watch as he took the pot of black paint and painted the outline of that first carving of the Ancient One.

Long followed Kaisun as though mesmerised and when they came to the end he followed Kaisun back to the centre of the arena with a look of wonder on his face. But Kaisun hadn't finished with him. He took him up to the bier that the Ancient One lay upon.

"Look well upon her, you who would be plunderer. Look well at the hole in her chest and her head. A man, like you, greedy to be the first, did the one and he has paid with his life. How will you pay for the other?"

I saw fear drain the blood from Long's face and replace the awe and longing that had been on it at the sight of the Ancient One. He swallowed but said nothing.

"Then I will tell you how you will pay. You will watch as the body of the Ancient One is returned to the skies so that her body may be at peace from such as you."

Long found his voice. "But she is unique. Surely – surely you don't mean to burn her?" His voice rose a pitch in disbelief. Here, indeed, would have been an opportunity for Dr Julian Long to outshine his colleagues – a bird unknown anywhere else in the world and, until recently, alive. He could have had it stuffed and lectured with her all over the world.

One of Kaisun's relatives came forward with a blazing torch and handed it to Kaisun. Long threw himself at Kaisun, trying to stop him, but he was grabbed by several strong hands. He could only watch as Kaisun walked round the bier twice, once clockwise, once anti-clockwise as he uttered a piercing, keening sound – not unlike the call of an injured bird. Then he lowered the torch to the branches beneath the body. I gripped Gabriel's hand hard as the flames caught and I felt the sadness in the birds.

Then as the branches blazed and reached the body I saw again the pale image of Ben's grandfather and I saw him reach out his hands into the blaze and take up the body of the Ancient

One. Then they both became as a twisting pall of smoke and were gone skyward. At that moment the birds all took to their wings and flew once round the arena before settling again on the rock face. The sadness was gone – acceptance replaced it.

We watched until the flames had died down and there was nothing but dust and a few bones. A kind of fatalism had settled on Dr Long. Kaisun turned to him.

"You have seen the power of the flames and you have seen the power of the Spirits which guard this Place. Now go – tell the world. Tell them of our ancestors who cared for this place and all the living things they carved with love into these rocks. And tell them that they live still and will guard this place against those that would destroy. Tell them that the time for killing is coming to an end – that respect for life is everything.

"Remember also that the Spirits will be watching over you wherever you go. They will remain silent about the taking of the life of one of the Brothers in Spirit so long as you and those with you speak only the truth."

One of the Haida then led Long away.

Kaisun called the rest of us to follow him to the house.

"We have only a little time until most of you will leave. It is important that you, Andrew, reach your newspaper before Dr Long can tell the news. We have arranged a delay for him and his party, but you must leave soon." He put a pile of papers in Andrew's hand. "Here we have the proof of the Ancient One and you will find photographs which will show her to the world. Also the Special Place.

"We have known for many months now that we must share the secret with the world that they may learn. While the Ancient One was alive this was difficult but now we want the world to see the Place of Carved Rock. You will be the first to tell them of it. Tell them also that it will always be guarded and only those with permission may enter." He held out his hand to Andrew who took it eagerly.

"Thank you, Kaisun, I'll do you proud, I promise."

"I know. Now you will say your farewells and go with my people."

Andrew shook hands all round, but Gabriel detained him.

"Thank you, Andrew, for bringing us here." Andrew nodded, still a little wary of Gabriel. "But I need one more favour. Long knew nothing of Paul except the first night he was in Vancouver. He doesn't deny trying to persuade him to give up the feather – but he heard no more of him after that. Could you see what you can find out your end – maybe check with the police."

"Of course I will. I'll contact Ella if I hear anything." Gabriel touched him briefly on the shoulder and Andrew smiled, the prickles gone.

Then he came to me.

"Thanks, Sara. You've certainly 'paid your pound of flesh' and given me the best story I could ever hope to have." He smiled. "You've given me a lot more too. Promise you'll look me up when you can." I nodded. "I hope you and Gabriel make it. He's better around birds than I am!"

"You'll not mention them in your story will you, Andrew, please?"

"No one would believe me anyway, so – no – your secret's safe with me. But I'll never forget the display you put on today – wow." He leant forward and kissed me full on the mouth. "Just the once -" he muttered and turned and walked away.

Gabriel came and put his arm lightly around my shoulders as we waved them off and I leant against him. I didn't realise until then how desperately tired I was.

CHAPTER TWENTY

We spent the rest of the afternoon talking. Kaisun told us much about his heritage and the people who had inhabited these islands for over 10,000 years. Of their beliefs in the supernatural spirits of the creatures who shared their domain – of the terrible decimation of his people when the white man came and brought measles and smallpox. He showed us photographs of the totem poles his ancestors had carved and talked with justified pride of the prowess of these carvers and how the tradition was being kept alive. He spoke of Ben's grandfather who had cared for the Special Place before he, Kaisun, had taken on the honour. I told him how important the image of that kindly face had been but I couldn't understand how he had come to me so far away in Wales.

"It is not for us to know, Toucher of Spirits, but for him the peregrine was always his favoured bird, though the Raven was his family bird and the first bird he cared for. Who can tell if the blood that is in your Little Ones does not sing to you of their father and his roots here."

He turned to Joe. "For you the journey from the heat to the cold was a difficult one yet the Spirit sang in you also."

He looked at Callum. "For you the Spirit sang twice – once in the heart of the Eagle and again in the soul of the carver of rock. We have need of help in mending some of the carving where the water has misted the lines. For this I believe you were called."

"I'll help you gladly," Callum responded immediately. I 'd seen the way his eyes had glowed when touching the rock. For him it would be a veritable labour of love.

"And I have with me a silver box," Joe added eagerly, "which I carry with me for the remains of Peal, should I find him. Will you accept the box instead for the ashes of the Ancient One? I would consider it to be the highest of honours."

Joe handed Kaisun a beautifully engraved box about nine inches long and inlaid with abalone shell and turquoise. Kaisun held it in his hands and traced the engraving lightly with his finger, then smiled his beautiful smile.

"It is a thing of great beauty and will do honour to the remains of the Ancient One. For her, I thank you for the gift. I also have a gift for you, brother in Spirit." He went to a chest in the corner of the room and returned with a long, dark primary feather in his hand. "It is a feather of your Brother, Peal. I kept it for your coming."

Joe took it and lovingly ran it through his fingers.

Watching him made me wonder what would happen with the birds now. The thought of them staying here and not coming home wrenched at me, but equally the thought of the long journey ahead of them to reach home filled me with foreboding. I hadn't known the extent of their journey out here, so I hadn't worried that much, but the thousands of miles back would be hazardous. It brought home to me the feat they had performed. They had proved they had the stamina but the weather could turn against them at any time.

Also would Scrap go with Omen or would Omen come to live with us? I had Misty and Rift, Joe would have no one if they came to live in Wales. That would be a great loss for Joe, but I didn't like the idea of Scrap living in that hot climate. I decided to have a word with Gabriel about it.

We walked down to sit at the foot of the waterfall, leaving the others happy to talk about the future of the carvings. It was amazingly peaceful down there and it was hard to think of the battle that had raged there only hours before. The water looked very tempting considering how dusty and sweaty the last few days had been, but despite the sun it looked cold. Gabriel was tougher than me, and, stripping down to his underpants, dived straight into the pool at the foot of the fall. Just the thought of it took my breath away, as did the sight of the lithe, browned glimpse of body I had seen.

He surfaced gasping for breath but laughing, apparently at the expression on my face.

"Coward!" he shouted and splashed water at me. I removed my boots to try my toes in the water and it didn't feel that bad. I was just thinking about going in when something caught my eye in the water. I'd have had to wade out to reach it so I asked Gabriel if he'd reach for it for me. It came up in his hand, an earring with a bedraggled feather and a black, carved bead hanging from it – Kaisun's lost earring.

I reached my hand for it but Gabriel was too quick for me. He snatched it back out of reach and thus catching me off balance, helped my descent into the water by a quick pull on one hand. It was freezing and I'd have given him a mouthful if I could have dragged enough air into my lungs. I made for the edge of the pool but Gabriel headed me off.

"Come on – you're in now – and you need a wash!"

By now I'd got used to the temperature of the water and it began to feel really good. I was hampered by my clothes, so I stood in the water, took off my jumper and threw it onto the bank, followed by my jeans. I remembered how refreshing it always was swimming in the river back in Wales, but to have Gabriel by my side in this strange, remote place was real joy. There was a wonderful languid yet erotic feeling of being so close to him half naked, so that the water caressed my bare skin and set it tingling.

I went and sat on a submerged shelf of rock so that only my head and shoulders were above the water. Gabriel came and sat by my side and put his hand around my waist and pulled me against him. I turned my face up to his and smiled happily into his eyes. He put his hand under my chin and tilted my head towards him, then bent and kissed me gently. He lifted his head and looked again into my eyes, one eyebrow raised in query, still holding my chin. In answer I snaked my arms around his neck and pulled him down to me again. All the old yearning, which I had no intention of denying, rose in me and I felt Gabriel respond.

He picked me up and, climbing carefully out of the pool, he laid me down in a patch of sunlight and put his dry jumper on me for warmth. It covered me decently but was, thankfully, baggy enough to allow easy access for his hands – his warm, healing hands – to caress every inch of my body. The desire I'd suppressed for him over the years sparked to life and we made love in that strange, tranquil place. It was as wonderful as I'd remembered and deepened my love for Gabriel to a degree I didn't think possible. I'd shown him with my body what I'd found so difficult to tell him all that time ago and I knew there'd be no going back now and rejoiced in the knowledge.

As we lay afterwards in each other's arms, I voiced my worry over the birds. He kissed me on the forehead.

"Will they always come first, Sara?" he asked.

I laughed at his use of phrase and he flicked my nose with a blade of grass. "You know what I mean."

"Yes, Gabriel, I know. But with the birds it's different. They're like special children. What I feel for you is – well – different. But I'd worry just as much about you."

"Well, thanks for that. But I just get a little jealous from time to time because they can get into your head easier than I can."

"You'll just have to be happy with my body then." I replied teasingly.

"Oh, don't get me wrong, I'm very happy with your body – in fact ..."

"Gabriel, take your hands off – the others will be wondering where we are."

"Not if they heard you screaming like a banshee."

I blushed. "Perhaps a little cry escaped my lips – but I was enjoying myself – you see."

"Oh, yes – I noticed alright!"

As we walked back Gabriel suggested I took time to ask the birds what they intended to do. I tried to explain that it wasn't as easy as that. I could visualise things for them but I couldn't always interpret their response.

"Try anyway. Go through to the arena – they're probably still there. I'll bring your dry clothes out to you."

I chose a patch of ground in sunlight near the still gently smoking bier to dry my hair and sat down. Immediately Mistral, Rift and Scrap came to the pole. I called Mistral down to me and she sat on my shoulder and tried to straighten the straggles of my wet hair. The thought of never seeing her again hung heavy on me but I cleared my mind and asked her the question. I visualised the rock at home and her, Rift and Scrap on it and I visualised the rocks around me. She threw an image into my mind of sea and land from a great height and then a feeling of lightness as she dropped several hundred feet as she crossed a shoreline. Then a feeling of achievement as she arrived at the house I recognised nestled in the Welsh hills.

I reached up and stroked her breast, relief light in me.

Turning my head to look at Rift, I asked Mistral the same question. In answer she showed me the same view, but beside her flew three shadows. So that meant that Omen was coming with Scrap. I had to speak to Joe.

Instructing them not to go until I came to speak to them again, I went towards the cedar tree door. I met Gabriel on the way with my dry clothes and it felt wonderful to change into them in front of him without feeling embarrassed, and the appreciation in his eyes lightened my heart. I told him what Mistral had shown me and how I worried about Joe.

"Come on, we'll have to tell him."

We met Ben and Callum coming out on their way to the rocks with Kaisun to see what repairs needed doing. There was a difference in Ben's step and, as I caught his eye, I saw that it was buoyancy put there by the knowledge of his new self-esteem. There was a sense of pride about him – no – more of dignity and it warmed my heart. I didn't know if Grandfather was gone forever, but I felt he would still be looking out for his grandson.

We found Joe packing his few things. He sensed the oneness between us and smiled broadly. Then he looked again at my face.

"Sara, you have news for me – I see it. My Omen goes with your Scrap, does she not?"

I sighed – I should have known he's have sensed it. "I think so, Joe, from what I understand of what Mistral told me."

"I have felt it too, Sara. But do not be sad. We will not be long parted." I looked at him questioningly. "For many years now, as I get no younger, I think often of my days in Oxford. I like your country and your people – they were always gracious to me. I also tire of the battle against the hunters that kill the tiny birds. How little is the weather to put against this?"

"You mean you'd like to come and live in Britain?" I asked incredulously, thinking of all that lovely sun in Malta.

"For part of the year – yes, Sara, all the more since I have made such great friends this last week."

"But that would be wonderful, Joe. Then you'd be near Omen and Scrap and all the little ones they are sure to have."

Joe laughed. "You run away with your head, Sara. They have a journey before them. Does this not make you fear?"

"Greatly, Joe. But we have to leave it to them. The only other way is to put them under the stress of transporting them home by boat or plane and I don't fancy that."

"They are creatures of freedom, not cages. I agree with you, Sara. If it would not be ungracious, I would like to make my preparations to return to my country as soon as possible, so that arrangements can be made."

"I must admit, I feel drained and – beautiful though it is here, I too would like to go home. How about you Gabriel?" As I asked the question, I felt a contraction in my stomach. I'd been so wrapped up in the joy of at last being so close to him that I had not thought of the difficulties that lay ahead with me in Wales and him in Australia.

"I'd like to come back with you, Sara, for a while. I'm officially on leave for another ten days." So I wouldn't be parted from him straight away.

Kaisun came up to us, his face grave. He placed a hand on Gabriel's shoulder. "I have news, Healer, from your Guide. It is not good news about your friend."

"Paul? What's happened?" Gabriel asked.

"It appears that his car fell from the road into a ravine a week back, amongst the deep forest. He was only found yesterday – I am very sorry."

"Is he dead?" I asked, quietly, as Gabriel didn't.

"Yes, Sara." It was Gabriel who replied. "I have felt it for a while now. Where was he found Kaisun?"

"On the road beyond Hope – some miles north east of Vancouver."

What a fitting name, I thought, 'beyond hope' indeed. "What was he doing there?" I asked.

"Who knows, Sara?" Gabriel replied, shrugging his shoulders. "Maybe he thought it would be less conspicuous if he travelled by road– if he felt Long wasn't going to give up. Long was certainly shifty about it all when I asked. I think they put the fear of god in him."

"The police wish to speak to Dr Long, your Andrew says" Kaisun commented. "Perhaps the car did not 'fall' off the road."

"Poor Paul." Joe remarked, sorrow in his voice. "If he had only waited for us to arrive."

"Poor Kate," Gabriel muttered. "Oh god, does she know yet, Kaisun?"

"I'm afraid I did not ask."

"I must get back to her as soon as possible." Gabriel looked about him distractedly. "I'm sorry, Kaisun, but can I make plans to leave straight away?"

"Of course, Healer. I have already arranged it. There is space for you in the seaplane which awaits." He went off in the direction of the cabin.

Gabriel turned to me, rushed now. "Sara, I'm sorry – I have to go to her she's due any time – god knows what this'll do to her. If there's anything I can do for her, I must. You understand – don't you?"

My humanity understood, but my heart didn't. Yet I couldn't stop him from doing what he considered right. I felt a block of ice develop in my stomach. I would be going back to Wales alone. Gabriel was going to Australia to Kate, whom he'd 'known' before she married Paul – how well I couldn't bring myself to ask. I couldn't even be sure when or if I'd see him again – Australia was such a long way away. It was as though what had happened between us had been a dream. Perhaps, after all, it hadn't meant as much to Gabriel as it had to me. I was suddenly too tired to fight. Misty flew down onto my shoulder, but it just seemed to add to the problems as I worried about her journey as well as my own.

Ben and Callum returned from surveying the carvings.

"You're not going so soon, are you, Gabriel?" Ben asked, seeing the packed rucksack.

"Paul's dead, Ben, and I need to get back to Kate."

"Sure – sure – hey – I'm sorry."

"Thanks, Ben. Joe – could I have a word, please." They walked a little way away together. Kaisun joined them and I saw him introduce one of the rescue party to Gabriel. Gabriel then picked up his rucksack and strode towards me.

"It's time for me to go now, Sara. Joe will take care of you and see you home safely. I'm really sorry I can't. I'll be in touch soon. Take care." He drew me to him and the old desire rose in me at his touch. I cursed myself for being so weak. A brief kiss on the mouth and he was striding off, down towards the waterfall.

Kaisun turned to Joe and me "You wish to leave also, I think?"

Joe answered for me, as I was speechless with misery. "Not without regret, Kaisun. We are greatly honoured to be here. But we are worried about the journey the Brothers in Spirit need to make. When we go they too will go."

"That I know and may the Great Winds be with them. But stay one more night, then I will make the arrangements."

I didn't relish a night without Gabriel, but had little choice in the matter. I was still in the hands of fate it seemed.

After we'd eaten I went and sat in the arena, my jacket pulled tight around me against the chill in the air. Callum came and joined me and we sat for a time in silence.

Then I could keep silent no longer. "Callum – how long have you known Gabriel?"

"I don't know – ten years or more – we were at Uni together."

"So you knew him when he and I first got together?"

"Yes."

"So do you know why he left, Callum? Was it because of me?"

"It was all very complicated, Sara. Why don't you ask him?"

"In case you hadn't noticed – he isn't here – he's dashed off to a – a – damsel in distress, a mistress – I don't know."

Callum was shocked. "But Kate's his half-sister."

"His half-sister?" I asked, my voice sharp. "But he never told me."

"I'm sorry, Sara – I thought you knew. That's one of the reasons he went to Australia in the first place. His grandmother was an Aborigine. He thought that out there he'd maybe find an explanation for his healing. Didn't he tell you?"

I felt overwhelmed. "No – it seems he told me very little. One minute he'd gone to Scotland to visit a friend with cancer who then died and the next minute he was gone to Australia."

"That friend was Anna, Sara – my wife."

My stomach lurched. "Oh, god, Callum – I'm so sorry – I had absolutely no idea."

"It affected Gabriel badly, you see – that he could heal the birds but he couldn't help Anna."

"It must have been awful."

"It was – she had the whole of her life ahead of her – god – what a waste." He shook his head at the memory. "But Gabriel took it so hard – he sort of went into crisis – like he was to blame. He swore he wouldn't use the healing again."

"Why didn't he tell me any of this – we were lovers, Callum?"

Callum looked embarrassed. "I don't know, Sara."

I thought back to that time – when Gabriel had told me about going to Australia. I remembered the row we'd had just before, because he wouldn't help me feed a young Goshawk who died a day later – wouldn't help me heal it, because it was too close to death – he said. I'd taken it as a personal insult – as if I'd done something wrong and he no longer cared. This feeling wasn't helped when he told me he was going. I was too hurt to think straight – to see his needs – only my great need of him.

I sighed. "Perhaps I wasn't always there for him – too wrapped up in the birds. But I thought we had something really good, really strong."

"He thought so too, Sara. He'd been offered the job before he met you, but turned it down when he got together with you. He was lucky it was still available when he needed to go later."

"Not so lucky for me, though."

"Maybe not, Sara – but it wasn't your fault either. It was just something he had to deal with alone."

"I'm sorry – where I come from you deal with problems together. It felt more like he was running out on me."

Callum was looking embarrassed again. "Is now too late to discuss all this with him – after all you seem to be – close – now?"

"So I thought, Callum – but where is he – I don't see him to talk to – and, quite honestly, I have no idea when I'll see him again."

Joe came out and joined us and must have caught the last bit of the conversation. "Come, Sara – there is hope everywhere. Love will find a way – no?"

"I can only hope so, Joe." I replied doubtfully.

"Good. Meanwhile – Gabriel has asked me to accompany you home – to see you safe – yes?"

"I'll be fine on my own, thanks Joe." I replied resentfully.

"But I have made a promise so I will make arrangements." Joe was quite firm about it and I knew he'd look after me well, so I didn't protest again. "We have an early start in the morning – so to bed early – no?"

"Yes, Joe." I got up obediently. I was so tired and unhappy I could have slept on a log let alone like one. I'd be able to think clearer in the morning.

We were woken early by Kaisun and we watched the glory of the dawn heralding a beautiful sunny day in this place apart from the world. It gave us a chance to relax with the birds before we all began our journeys, none of us knowing how it would end. It was painful saying goodbye to the three falcons, but I reassured them the best I could, being fully aware it was really myself I was reassuring. Their loss would leave a huge hole in my life that nothing else would quite fill.

Joe put his arm around my shoulders as we left them. There was no need for words between us. We said our goodbyes to Callum and then Ben.

"Ella says you're welcome to stay with her if you don't want to go straight back." Ben offered.

"Thank her most kindly for us but I think we'll start our journey at once. Sara?" Joe turned to me.

"Yes, Joe – but thanks, Ben, all the same." I gave him a hug, feeling temporarily comforted by the strength of him. I heard Vigilant in my head and I knew that there'd always be this contact between us – I only had to reach out. "I'll never forget you or this place – and may your grandfather always guide you."

"Thanks, Sara – for everything." His voice was gruff.

Then it was time to take our leave of Kaisun.

"Your going will leave the Special Place sad for me, Toucher of Spirits. Yet always will I remember you and your falcons and the battle we won yesterday. That will bring back to me the love you have left here." He looked me deep in the eyes. "And the love you will carry always with you."

I wasn't sure if he was referring to my love of the birds or my love and need of Gabriel. I felt tears well in my eyes – tears of pain and gladness – pain on maybe losing Gabriel, but gladness that I'd met this noble and caring man in this unique place. I longed to hug him – to show him I would never forget him. I heard Vigilant call in my head and the softness of the call led me to throw caution to the winds. I held out the earring we had found in the pool and placed it in his right hand. Then I reached up and kissed him on both cheeks. With a quick hug I stepped back. A smile lit the strong face. He lifted the earring so that it swung, dry now, in the light – then he handed it back to me.

"I have the little Peal's feather – this one is that of Peal's father. May his courage go ever with you, my Toucher of Spirits." Gently he reached out and touched me on the cheek. I could feel the imprint of his hand for many days afterwards. It warmed my heart and his words gave me courage on my journey home. "Remember the Raven."

CHAPTER TWENTY-ONE

Joe was a good travelling companion – considerate and kind. During the nine-hour journey back to Manchester, we either slept fitfully or chatted companionably. It felt like I'd known him for years instead of days and I was glad he'd been able to get a seat on the same flight. I was mentally exhausted after the last few days and wouldn't have relished the journey home alone. I told him more about my time with Gabriel and what it had meant to me, and how unsure I now felt.

"You are perhaps not listening to your heart, Sara," he said kindly. "Perhaps your brain is muddled by all the signals from the birds and you cannot hear the ones from your heart. Have you tried reaching for Gabriel as you do the birds?"

"I don't really know how – and – I don't know – it would seem like intruding."

"It is your love of the falcons that lets you hear them. Is your love for Gabriel not as great?"

"Yes, of course – but, I suppose my need of him is greater and that interferes."

"And, at the moment you are cross with him for leaving?"

I sighed. "Am I being unreasonable, Joe?"

"No, Sara, you are not. But also you see his desire to go always where he is most needed and this makes you uncertain – obviously." He smiled teasingly. "After all, he has left you for another woman – no?"

"Okay, I know now she's his half sister and she must be going through hell right now. But I've had such little time with him and we've not had a chance to discuss the future. What if he never comes back?"

"Then it was not meant to be, Sara for his love would not be strong enough," he must have seen my face because he added, " – but I believe it is, that he knows your need of him, Sara – I have seen you two together and you are right together. Do you not feel this?"

"It's certainly what I want – for us to be together. But what if that involves going to live in Australia?"

"Then you would have to leave the falcons to do as they pleased – as you have done at all times. There is always some sacrifice asked of us in life – but for what gain!"

I knew he was right. I couldn't let Gabriel go a second time. This time I'd fight – I just wasn't sure how – a trip to Australia was way out of my pocket after this last trip.

We stayed the night in a hotel near Manchester, as Joe was to fly on to Malta the next day. It took me a while to fall asleep, messed around by jetlag, but for the first time in a long time I wasn't aware of any dreams. It was as though the emergency was over and it was now time to recuperate and perhaps get back to normal. I wasn't sure that was exactly what I wanted. I would never forget the last few days and all the wonderful people – and birds – I'd met, but there's something to be said for coming home.

When it came time for me to say goodbye to Joe – he handed me an envelope.

"Please, Sara – I would like you to accept this."

"What is it, Joe?"

He looked embarrassed. "It is a cheque Sara – now ..." he held up his hand as I began to protest, "it is for emergencies only – keep it till you need it. It is expensive flying round the world is it not?"

The kindness of it brought tears to my eyes. "For emergencies only." I repeated. "I can't thank you enough, Joe." I hugged him tightly, not really wanting to see him go.

"No – it is I who should thank you, Sara, our Toucher of Spirits. I have learnt much about love and courage from you – and you will be looking after my Omen, don't forget, and it was you who helped solve the mystery of Peal's death. I also believe it is best that your love for Gabriel should be allowed to grow for both your sakes – and the birds."

I watched till I could see him no longer – lost in the crowds. I then retrieved my suitcase and headed for home, aware of a feeling of anticlimax that I now knew the answer to the compunction that had taken me so far away – only a week ago.

I told John and Margaret just the bare outlines of the trip when I went to pick up Bran. They were curious to know why I'd come back early but I just told them I was home sick which they didn't believe for a minute. Bran didn't ask for any explanation, just smothered me with love and wouldn't leave my side. It was good to be back with him.

Margaret took me to one side. "How are things with you and Gabriel?"

"Pretty good, I'd say," crossing my fingers behind my back.

"Well don't let him go this time – okay?"

"That could be difficult with him living in Australia and me in Wales. So not a lot different from last time really, I suppose."

"God, if I had the chance to live in Australia I'd take it with both hands."

"What and move the children to a new school and take them away from their friends? I'm not sure you would, Margaret, and it's not that dissimilar for me with the birds."

"But they're only birds, Sara," she cried exasperated.

I just smiled. Maybe one day I'd tell her.

Bran and I arrived back at the cottage in glorious sunshine that lit up the valley and made me really glad to be home. As I got out of the car I heard a buzzard mewing as it soared on gentle thermals above the wood and I thought of the falcons. Hopefully they'd be on their way but it would be many days before I could hope to see them again.

When I got into the cottage I saw that Mum had been and left me some food for my return, which helped make the place seem less empty. Coming back to an empty house had always been the down side of living alone for me – as well as the fact that the person I wanted to be there with me was in Australia.

A letter had come from the local police while I was away, to say that Nigel had informed them of the shooting of Scrap and Rift's brother. They'd found the person responsible – would I be willing to give evidence? I contacted Nigel and he told me that he'd reported it after he'd had to deal with another nest that had been attacked. They'd only tracked this bloke down because he was boasting about it in the local pub. To me it all seemed a long time ago but I knew I would do what I could to make sure he paid for his misguided actions – perhaps he too could learn a lesson from the birds. I doubted if he would ever be able to come anywhere near Misty again without risking attack.

Joe rang to let me know he was back safely and had made arrangements for his nephew to take over the stone dealing. From now onward Joe intended to go back to the silversmithing at which he was so proficient. I could picture in my mind the exquisite detail on the box that now held the remains of the Ancient One and I reckoned he'd have no difficulty making a living in this country if he still intended to come. He was planning a visit soon and I promised to let him know the minute Omen arrived with Scrap. I knew he was as worried as I was.

It was four days before Gabriel contacted me. I was outside repairing the aviaries, taking advantage of having no birds in the hospital, when he rang. I refused to sit by the phone waiting for his call – which was as well as I'd have wasted a lot of time. I was out of breath when I picked up the phone.

"Is that you, Sara?"

The familiar rush of adrenaline hit my stomach at the sound of his voice. "Yes, Gabriel – sorry – I was outside."

"Sara – I'm an uncle – well a half-uncle!" I could hear the pride in his voice despite the crackle. He must have been on a mobile.

"Kate's okay, then?"

"Well, she had a bit of a rough time – the shock sent her into premature labour – but the baby's fine – only three weeks early."

"Boy or girl?"

"Girl – she's beautiful."

"How is she coping with the news on Paul?" I asked trying

not to be jealous.

"She cried a lot at first, but since the baby she's had other things on her mind. Not really knowing what happened to Paul doesn't help, though."

"You haven't heard anything more then?"

"Nothing came from the police interview with Long. But he didn't take kindly to being interviewed."

"Not good for his reputation?" I asked. "Maybe he should choose his friends a bit more carefully, then."

"He's stirred up a lot of trouble this end. Paul shouldn't have been using the University to do his personal research and..." I heard my doorbell ring and cursed at the bad timing. "Are you still there, Sara?"

"Yes – there's someone at the door – hang on while I find out who it is." I carried the phone to the door. On the doorstep was our local policeman, Bob. I'd forgotten that I was going to give them a statement. "Hang on." I said to Bob and gestured him in. "Gabriel, I'm sorry I'll have to go – it's the police – about the bloke who killed Misty's youngster – you remember?"

"Okay, Sara, I understand."

"Will you phone later – please?" After all we hadn't talked about anything important like our feelings.

"I'll try. I just thought I'd catch you before I went to bed – to say ..." Bob chose that moment to trip over Bran who was greeting him enthusiastically.

"Gabriel – I'll have to go." I took my courage in my hands and added. "Love you." I couldn't hear his reply for the crackle.

"Sorry. Bad timing?" Bob asked nursing a damaged shin.

I sighed. "No – it can wait." Although I knew it couldn't. Hearing Gabriel's voice had deepened the longing and I still had no idea when I'd see him. I could go nowhere until the falcons returned.

It was necessary to concentrate whilst giving the statement to Bob as I had little concrete evidence of the event – only what I'd seen in the dream, and I wasn't about to tell him about that. Fortunately I knew him quite well from birds I'd had in the past whose origins were rather suspect, but it all reminded me of those early, carefree days with the falcons. I began to worry again.

Worrying didn't help me calm down enough to contact them

and I still had no sense of when – or if – they'd be back. They'd dropped out of my dreams – instead I dreamt often of Gabriel, dreams mixed with joy and anxiety.

Gabriel didn't ring the next day as I'd hoped. I looked up the number that I'd contacted him on all those weeks ago and resolved to ring that night. I just needed to hear the gentle tone of his voice and to know he still cared. But there was no reply.

That night I did dream of the falcons again – dreamt of flying with them over the cliff where the two youngsters had been born. But then I fell, tumbling from the sky, completely out of control, so like the dreams I had before Misty had entered them – only this time, instead of waking with a jolt just before hitting the hard earth, I felt myself caught in gentle arms and laid softly on the ground. I knew the arms were Gabriel's although I couldn't actually see him. I woke with a feeling of being cherished and the certainty that the falcons would be back.

So I set off to the cliff at first light, taking food with me for the birds, Bran and myself in my rucksack. I determined to be there when they came back to show them my love and admiration for their courage.

As I neared the cliff where the trees thinned out, my eye was caught by a dark shadow high in the sky. Momentarily distracted, I tripped over a tree root and tumbled over the edge of the narrow path. My fall was broken some twenty-foot down by a rock cannoning into my left shoulder. A stab of agony shot through my body and I couldn't prevent a scream of pain erupting from my mouth. I heard Bran whimper in response as he rushed down the steep slope towards me.

"No, Bran!" I yelled. I knew he was sure-footed enough but I was fearful of him knocking into me in his enthusiasm.

Very gingerly I felt my shoulder with my good hand and it didn't feel quite as it should. No way could I use it to drag myself back up the long, vertical and slippery slope to the path, the only thing to grip being patches of bracken. I tried standing up – very carefully – but a wave of dizziness and nausea engulfed me so that I sat back down quickly and retched the pain up. I lay back against the rock and wondered what to do next. I couldn't risk climbing up the steep slope feeling as dizzy as I did and the chances of anyone using the path, particularly as it was a working day, were remote. So I'd just have to wait a while for the light-headedness to pass then try and make my way, bit by bit, to the path. But then I'd got the two-mile walk back to the house. I groaned. I hadn't bothered bringing my mobile as I knew there was little chance of a signal, but even the chance would have been a comfort now.

No one knew where I'd gone. If I had a call out to a bird I always made sure someone knew where I'd gone. I'd been in the odd sticky situation before which made this worthwhile – but I was only going for a walk this time so had taken no precautions. Perhaps I could persuade Bran to go for help. He was only too willing to please, but how was I to communicate to him what I'd like him to do? My love for him should allow me to talk with him as I did the birds, but I'd never tried it – yet.

It was hard to concentrate and relaxing was beyond me – the two things I needed. I just couldn't slow the beating of my heart enough, as the pain interrupted and I couldn't ignore it. I eased the rucksack carefully off my back and reached into it for the painkillers I always carried there, along with the plasters, the scissors, Swiss army knife and other emergency gear. There was a length of cord in there too, but with nothing to tie it to, I didn't see how it would help, but I got it out anyway. I was too nauseous still to be interested in the emergency bar of chocolate I also carried everywhere. Who knew when I might get stuck in a snowdrift – or fall down a hillside in the middle of nowhere!

I lay back with the rucksack as a pillow, which held my shoulder off the ground. I noticed my arm was at a funny angle – sort of turned in on itself, but looking at it didn't help my state of mind. I breathed deeply, willing the painkillers to work. Eventually, I felt calm enough to try and reach Bran. Throwing my love into my heart I pictured the house where Ted lived and asked him to go there and get help, but Gabriel's face kept getting in the way and I longed for him to be there. Thankfully, though, Bran looked at me with his head on one side and then ran up to the path. He looked down at me once, then stood on the path looking towards the way he needed to go and sniffed the wind. Then he ran off – fortunately in the right direction.

I breathed a sigh of relief and closed my eyes. At any other time I'd have relished the chance to gaze down the valley and watch the river meander through the rocks after its plunge from the waterfall at Misty's nest site – but this was not the time.

I lost all sense of time as I drifted in and out of a light-headed sleep. Then I heard Bran bark from the path. I opened my eyes but couldn't turn to look back up without jarring my shoulder. I just hoped he'd managed to bring someone with him. I called in case he had and then closed my eyes for a moment as the pain hit again. I could hear the sound of someone slithering down the slope and sighed with relief.

Then I opened my eyes and stared straight into those of Gabriel. For a moment I thought I must be hallucinating or maybe I was still asleep. I blinked, but when I looked again – he was still there.

"Gabriel – oh, Gabriel – why aren't you in Australia – or are you – and I'm hallucinating?" My voice sounded slurred, as if I was drunk. It must have been the pain.

"No – I really am here, Sara. Bran found me and just in time it seems. Can't leave you alone for a minute, can I?" There was more affection behind the tone than exasperation.

"A week it's been not a minute."

"I know, Sara, but now's not the time for recriminations is it?" He sat down beside me. "Now what have you done?"

"Given my shoulder a bit of a bash, I'm afraid."

"Is it alright if I take a look?" I nodded through gritted teeth. I knew this was going to hurt. "Before I do, though, Sara, there's something I must do."

"What?"

"This." He leant forward, not touching me, and with the utmost gentleness he kissed me full on the mouth, not asking anything of me but giving me the reassurance of his love. My spirit flared with a mixture of desire and tenderness that overlaid the pain and sent it into the background of my consciousness. He pulled back and looked me in the eyes searchingly. "Good – that seemed to work. Now let's take a look."

Gently he helped me off with my jacket. "Mmm – doesn't look quite right does it?" I had no particular interest in looking. "Don't worry, Sara, I think it's just dislocated, so I should be able to get it back into place for you." I looked at him doubtfully. "Don't worry – I've done it before. My time in Australia wasn't wasted – I learnt a lot about healing. But first I'm going to ease the pain. Trust me, Sara?"

I nodded, knowing that he could do what he liked – I'd longed for him to come and he'd come. What more could I ask. Okay – freedom from pain would be good, but I could still feel the fizz in my blood from his kiss, which was helping to hold it at bay.

"Right let's get your shirt off – then I'll have a better view," he smiled at me mischievously, "of your shoulder, of course."

Despite the predicament I was aware of a sharp sensual pleasure when he eased the shirt from me and pulled me gently against his chest, but all was soon forgotten as he laid his hand on my forehead and I felt it's great warmth and my body relaxed against his. I felt as though my spirit was floating high in the sky with the falcons ... and then he eased my arm back into its socket and I felt myself tumbling from the heavens. I opened my eyes in panic and found myself on the ground in Gabriel's reassuring arms.

"Okay?" Gabriel asked.

"Very." I replied, surprised, but so glad to be in the sanctuary of his arms.

"It might ache a bit – and you'd better get it checked as the ligaments will have been stretched, but at least we'll be able to get you home."

"But I'm waiting for the falcons, Gabriel. That's why I came."

He sighed. "Can you still hear them, then Sara?"

"Only faintly – but I dreamt about them last night – and you."

He ran his fingers lightly down the bare skin of my arm. "A happy dream – I hope?"

"I dreamt that you caught me as I fell – just as you have." I shivered from his touch but I felt far from cold.

All the same Gabriel reached for my shirt and helped me on with it. "I can't think straight with you sitting there like that – and we've still got to get you back home." I was warmed, though, by the look of desire in his eyes. "And you really think the falcons will be here today, Sara?"

"Yes – I feel sure that they're nearly home." As I said this I realised they'd been trying to get through to me for some time. "The Great Winds must surely have been good to them." I saw the face of Kaisun in my mind and realised that there was a look about Gabriel that reminded me of Kaisun. It filled me with a sense of strength and well being which flooded through me. At that moment I concentrated all my love in my mind and focused it on Gabriel, willing him to feel it as the birds did.

He'd been looking into the sky above the cliff, but suddenly he turned his head towards me and quietly said. "I love you too, Sara." I knew then that he'd been aware of far more than I'd given him credit for and I wondered when he'd begun to listen again. It filled me with great happiness because it meant we would never be far from each other however many miles were between.

"Sara, I tried to ring to let you know I was coming, but I've been travelling for nearly two days, although it feels like forever."

"You must be exhausted."

"Yes, but I had something special to look forward to at the other end." He touched me lightly on my good shoulder. "Not quite how I expected to find you, though – but then life around you was never boring, Sara."

"Is that a compliment?"

"Yes, yes it is." I noticed he was rubbing the bump on his nose, so I knew he was concerned about something. "Sara – I need to ask you something and this is as good a time as any, before I get you back up to the path. After all," he teased, "if I don't like your answer then I can just leave you here."

"My knight in shining armour!" I muttered.

"Actually – I'd like to be, Sara but I've made a pretty poor hash so far, haven't I?" He didn't wait for an answer. "I know I shouldn't have just walked out last time, but I was really thrown by Anna's death and I couldn't see a way forward. The only hope I felt I had was to return to my roots – seek an answer to this healing thing. I wasn't any good to you the way I was. I couldn't even help with the birds and I knew how much they meant to you – they still do, I know – even more so now."

I began to worry about what this was leading to, what the question might be. Was he asking me to go and live in Australia and leave the birds?

He went on. "But leaving you left a huge gap in my life which I tried to deny, concentrating on believing that I knew what was best for us both. Now I know what is best for me – to be with you – but I don't know what you feel is best for you."

"What are you asking, Gabriel? If I love you – well, you know I do. Would I leave everything I have here to come with you to Australia rather than lose you," I swallowed the lump the thought brought to my throat, "yes, Gabriel, I would."

"You'd leave the birds?" I heard the wonder in his voice and when I glanced at him I also saw the tears in his eyes. "After everything – you'd do that." He shook his head, unable to go on.

"I want to be with you, Gabriel, not just in spirit, but physically – every day. I want your body alongside me every night. I want to go to sleep knowing I'm safe because you're there. And if that bed happens to be in Australia – then so be it." He was still silent. I laid my hand on his arm. "Please – just let me see the birds back safely, then I'll start packing."

"Don't, Sara – please – don't." His voice was thick.

"Don't what?"

"I love you, Sara, more than I can say, but – please don't start packing."

I felt my stomach lurch. He didn't want me to come back with him to Australia. "Oh," was all I managed.

"Because, Sara – I've already packed."

"I don't understand."

"I won't be going back to Australia – I've given up my job – before I was pushed after the problems with Paul – so I just wondered – could I stay with you for a while?"

"That's what you wanted to ask?"

"Yes, but you told me so much more – so much more than I deserved – and I'll never forget that, Sara – whatever happens – I'll never forget." He hugged me to him. "Now, we'd better get you home."

"But what about Kate?" I asked.

"She'll be fine – she's got her doting mother and aunts – and uncles. Now she's got Polly, she'll be fine. . I've wanted to leave for a bit – she knows that. And, seeing the start of a new life like that – well it made me think that now might be a good time for me, too." He reached down a hand for me. "Come on"

There was no pain left in my shoulder, but I was glad of Gabriel's help as we scrambled our way up to the path, Bran bounding ahead encouragingly. We stood for a moment getting our breath. Suddenly Gabriel turned me by the shoulders and pointed out over the cliff pulling me to rest against him as he did so.

"Look!" Gabriel pointed with his free hand.

What I saw filled me with such joy I thought I'd explode.

Four falcon shapes erupted over the top of the cliff. They called triumphantly with the small strength they had left, and the sound reverberated – magnified by the rocks. Mistral, Rift, Scrap and Omen were back home, happy, proud and exhausted.

Through the tears of relief that coursed down my cheeks I saw another dark shadow cross the sky – and I heard the call of the Raven.

If you would like to find out more about the Bird Hospital,
please go to www.naturegallery.co.uk

ISBN 141209950-1

9 781412 099509